A brand- _____ *set in Regency London!*

In return for their heroism, the Crown awards spies Caine, Kieran and Lucien Parkhurst aristocratic titles...which will only become hereditary if they wed within the year! Failure means the titles die with them, which, given their tendency toward wildness, might be sooner rather than later...

But after their brother was killed on a mission, the remaining Parkhursts are looking for revenge, not brides! Can they find room in their hearts for more than vengeance?

Find out in

Book 1, *How to Court a Rake*

Caine receives the title of marquess and proposes a fake courtship to Lady Mary, the *ton*'s most well-bred debutante...but she's not all she seems. Could she hold the key to his revenge as well as his heart?

Book 2, *How to Tempt an Earl*

Kieran is tasked with protecting Celeste, a traitor's ward, whose testimony incriminates his brother's killer. They journey from the crowded ballrooms of London to the isolation of the countryside, where they soon find their intoxicating attraction impossible to resist...

Available now

And look out for Book 3, Lucien's story, coming soon!

Author Note

Kieran and Celeste's story is about a journey. Literally, because a large part of their story takes place on the road. But in other ways, as well. They are both on a journey of self-discovery. They share the dangerous similarity of having little trust in fellow humankind, and when that similarity meets itself, it has the potential to become combustible. All they can control is the outcome of the explosion. Can they find it within themselves to overcome their past experiences in order to reach for happiness? Their journey poses many questions: Can things be different this time, and what will make them different? How do we escape repeating the past?

I think their journey parallels the journeys we all make from past to future. If we do what we've always done, we'll get what we've always got. But in order to have what we've never had, we have to do what we've never done. Celeste and Kieran discover that is how cycles break and how things become different for them. I hope you enjoy their story and perhaps take a moment to reflect on how you are your own engineer of change. What works for you?

HOW TO TEMPT AN EARL

BRONWYN SCOTT

Harlequin

HISTORICAL

Harlequin®
HISTORICAL

ISBN-13: 978-1-335-54013-3

How to Tempt an Earl

Recycling programs for this product may not exist in your area.

Harlequin Enterprises ULC
22 Adelaide St. West, 41st Floor
Toronto, Ontario M5H 4E3, Canada
www.Harlequin.com

Printed in U.S.A.

Bronwyn Scott is a communications instructor at Pierce College and the proud mother of three wonderful children—one boy and two girls. When she's not teaching or writing, she enjoys playing the piano, traveling—especially to Florence, Italy—and studying history and foreign languages. Readers can stay in touch via Facebook at Facebook.com/bronwyn.scott.399. She loves to hear from readers.

Books by Bronwyn Scott

Harlequin Historical

The Captain Who Saved Christmas
Cinderella at the Duke's Ball
The Viscount's Christmas Bride

Wed Within a Year

How to Court a Rake

Enterprising Widows

Liaison with the Champagne Count
Alliance with the Notorious Lord
A Deal with the Rebellious Marquess

Daring Rogues

Miss Claiborne's Illicit Attraction
His Inherited Duchess

Visit the Author Profile page
at Harlequin.com for more titles.

For my agent, Scott Eagan, at Greyhaus. This is book 75. None of this would be possible without you from the first step to this one and to the next. Here's to another 75.

Chapter One

Late August, London, 1826

Kieran Parkhurst had set a personal attendance record: two churches in less than two days. Usually, he was lucky to set foot in a church once a year for Christmas, and that was only to please his mother. Sentiments of faith and hope had no place in the world he inhabited. Kieran swung off his horse in front of St Luke's—*Old* St Luke's, to be precise, and he was always precise. Details saved lives.

He patted the sweat-soaked shoulder of his horse. They'd ridden hard and fast, straight from his brother's wedding in West Sussex. Now, Tambor was as lathered as he. Kieran wiped a hand across his brow. He wouldn't mind a bit of Christmas at the moment, given the state of the London weather, which was so hot and humid that one's clothes stuck to one's back after the slightest physical exertion, and his exertions had not been slight. He wondered if he smelled as bad as he looked— probably—but there was nothing to do about it now.

He squinted up at the stone church with its tower and ordinal chapels, wondering if his contact had already arrived. Given the choice, he preferred to take possession of the ground first in his encounters, but there was no question of dashing in and claiming his ground just yet; his horse took priority. Grandfather's urgent business for the Crown would have to wait a few minutes more; he wouldn't leave Tambor outside, sweating in the heat without care. His horse needed water. There must be some nearby... Ah yes, there was, next to the church.

He led Tambor to an elevated water trough and flipped a coin to the desperate-looking urchin who stood beside it. The boy's eyes, too big for his thin face, lit up. That coin would mean bread for a week. Kieran had lived too long in London not to be aware of the plight of the city's poor.

'Business looks slow today.'

Kieran took in the boy's ragged breeks and tatty vest. Business would be slow until November, when society came back to town from the cool northern grouse moors. Boys such as this one depended on the spontaneous trade of gentlemen—to hold their horses, sweep street crossings, hail carriages, run impromptu errands and deliver messages; anything to earn a coin. When Parliament recessed, so did the London economy.

The boy's gaze was sharp with wariness—a consequence of living on the streets. He answered noncommittally, offering no more than the required words. 'Yes, sir.'

Kieran ought to correct the boy. He should be addressed as 'my lord'. He was the Earl of Wrexham but he'd only held the title for six weeks. It hardly seemed fair to make someone else 'my lord' him when he could barely remember to do it himself. In fact, he'd prefer not to remember it at all. The title was a reward for bravery, having averted sabotage regarding a shipment of money and arms to aid the Greek War of Independence. But it was also a reminder of loss: his brother, Stepan, had not survived that night. The Four Horsemen—England's elite, covert band of dark diplomats—had been cut down to three.

'What's your name?' he asked the boy, keeping his eye on Tambor to make sure the horse didn't gulp the water. He didn't need a colicky horse on his hands.

'Samuel. What's yours?' This was asked in cheeky challenge, as if the boy didn't expect the courtesy to be reciprocated.

'Kieran.' He nodded to the church. 'You have a good view of the building. Has anyone gone inside?'

The boy shook his head. 'Most people nowadays go to the new St Luke's.'

Which would also be bad for the business of water tending when one's trough was at Old St Luke's.

'Is there a trough over at the new church you could mind?' Kieran made the casual suggestion.

'There's other boys that work that spot,' Samuel answered sullenly and Kieran's heart went out to him. The boy was too young to know a life of quiet desperation. At his age, Kieran and his brothers had whiled away summers at their home, Willow Park, swinging on ropes over a shady swimming hole to cool off.

'Are you certain no one has gone in recently?' If the boy was right, there was still time for him to claim the ground.

'No one, just a widow in a veil.' The boy gave a shrug. Samuel clearly didn't count the widow as a person of notice any more than he counted himself of any import. Only grown men were of note in London. They were the ones with the money, the power. 'She went into the south chapel just before you came.'

Kieran was instantly alert. Women and children, socially and legally, were designed to be invisible. Which was why, in his experience, they were such excellent… spies. He'd learned early not to discount anyone and he had the scar an inch to the right of his liver to remind himself in case he ever forgot. Invisibility was a gift; being a male who sported a height of six foot two inches, it was not a gift that came naturally to him. He had to cultivate his own invisibility in other ways.

Hmm. So, Grandfather's informant was possibly a woman. Unease prickled at the back of his neck. Women were often more dangerous in this game than the men.

Kieran took out another coin. 'Can you watch my horse? Make sure he doesn't guzzle the water; it will make him sick. I have business inside the church. I shouldn't be long.' Just long enough to meet Grandfather's contact and determine if the person in question and their information were legitimate. He gave his limp cravat a cursory tug in a futile attempt at improving his appearance and set out for the church and whatever lay beyond its doors.

Inside, the church was dim, a blessed respite from the sticky heat outside. Kieran let the coolness of the interior wash over him. If churches were good for one thing, it was providing sanctuary from torpid summers. He gave his eyes a moment to adjust before he approached the south chapel. He could not count on stealth here. He must be ready from the first step he took. Stone floors and boots made poor partners in silence. He'd be expected and he would be heard, which was of no real importance as long as the informant had come alone.

Out of an abundance of caution, Kieran loosened the pistol beneath his jacket and checked the knife in his boot. Just because one *said* they were an informant didn't mean they were. Assumptions were death wishes in disguise, especially if a woman was involved. Frankly, if this *was* a trap, it wouldn't surprise him. The intelligence the informant purportedly possessed was almost too juicy to be true. It was exactly the kind of information that would tempt his grandfather and lure the Four Horsemen into the open—information they couldn't afford to overlook; information that could lead them to the man responsible for Stepan's death. For that, much would be risked.

Pillars flanked the entrance to the south chapel, calling rather stark attention to the reality that there was only one way in and out. A veiled woman knelt at the rail, her back to him: Samuel's widow. If it was a trap, he'd be in tight quarters for fighting. Kieran did not relish that. On the other hand, churches had more weapons available than one might expect. Candles meant fire. Long, slim, iron-wrought candle stands could be converted to cudgels and spears in a pinch. He'd fought in churches before. He'd fought with women before.

Kieran quartered the space with his eyes before approaching, his gaze seeking lurkers in the chancel pews, or someone pretending to piousness across the way in the north chapel. But his visual sweep revealed no one. The boy at the water trough had been right: only the woman had entered. Perhaps the informant *had* come alone and was indeed what they claimed to be. How novel, for now…such truthfulness wouldn't last. Already supposition was taking root in his mind. Was she truly a widow, or was the veil a convenient disguise? In his line of work, no one was ever wholly what they seemed. Everyone had secrets. It was his job to uncover them. Lives, his included, depended on it.

His boots clicked on the stone floor, the sound echoing in the chancel. The woman did not turn but her shoulders straightened and her posture tightened. Her body's awareness of him was confirmation: he was expected. It was her, then; she was his contact. With a final glance at his surroundings, he approached the rail and knelt beside her.

'*Pax tibi,*' he murmured quietly: *peace be with you.*

'*Et cum te.*' *And also with you*, came the required reply in low, throaty tones more suited for a bedroom than a chapel. If Latin had sounded like that at Oxford, he might have attended class more often. Contact had been established but her face remained fixed on the altarpiece.

'I believe you have something for me.' He, too, kept his gaze fixed straight ahead but his eyes dropped surreptitiously to her bare hands where they gripped the rail tightly. She was tense; nervous, even. Whoever she was, passing information was not her usual mode of conduct. Those hands prompted speculation. Was she nervous because of him? That implied she'd been sent by someone to draw him out. Or was she nervous because of someone else? Did she fear she was being watched or followed, because she was acting independently? He glanced again at her hands. She wasn't a widow. He didn't need to see beneath her veil to safely deduce that.

'Do you think it's just that easy? That I will tell what I know to a stranger in a church simply because he asks?' Nervous or not, the woman had the ability to keep her wits about her. Kieran gave her credit for that, especially if this was not her usual game. But the question chased itself around his mind—*why was she nervous?* Followed by another question: if she was nervous because she worried she'd been followed, why not tell him and go? She'd want to expedite the meeting, not draw it out.

'Your knuckles indicated you were eager to depart,' Kieran murmured. 'Lingering makes you nervous. Should I be expecting company?' That company would come in one of two forms: those who also wanted her information for themselves or those who didn't want her information to get out. He did not want to play host to either form.

'I do not think I was followed.' There was defiance in her tone as if what she really wanted to say was, *I was not naïve enough to be followed.*

'Forgive me if I don't trust the assessment of a novice.' Kieran growled impatiently. 'Remember, *you* summoned *me*. How do you recommend we resolve this slight impasse?'

Her long, slender fingers curled around the prayer rail. 'How do I know *I* can trust *you*?'

Yes, clearly a novice if she thought trust was on the table, that its presence mattered as a means of guiding discussion. Trust, like faith and hope, did not exist in his world—not after Sofia had nearly gutted him in a bed chamber for the contents of his diplomatic pouch.

'You can't, no more than I can trust you.' Kieran gave a dry laugh. 'Did you think you were the only one with something to risk? Did you stop to think what *I* risked in coming here? This might be a trap and your supposed information the lure. But, still, I am here. Perhaps that is proof enough that I am who I say I am.' He edged closer to her and she reflexively brought a hand to her nose.

He gave a quiet laugh. 'You cannot doubt I am a Horseman now. Forgive me for the fragrance. I rode hard and there was no time to change. Your message indicated a certain urgency.'

Kieran covered her hand with his. People confessed to all nature of fears and feelings when they were touched. Touch inspired confidence. Perhaps she needed a dose of that now in order to open up. 'We've established who I am. Now, my lady, who are you?'

Who *was* she? Such a complex question; Celeste hardly knew any longer. Once, she would have said she was a wealthy man's ward, a boarding-school-educated young woman who'd spent her youth on the Continent. Up until two weeks ago she'd been that same man's pawn, a tool he used now that school was behind her. It wasn't a very flattering picture of who she'd been, but it was accurate.

Now, kneeling here in the church, she was a fugitive, a woman on the run with nowhere to run *to*...all because she'd eavesdropped on the wrong conversation, which had been the final straw.

'It doesn't matter who I am. It matters what I know.'

His hand was warm on hers and, despite the fact that he smelled of sweaty horse and worn leather, his touch felt...*good*...like reassurance. And for a moment it felt as if she wasn't alone, that she was *safe* at last. It was an illusion only. Men betrayed; she knew it empirically. If he knew she was the ward of the Continent's most notorious arms dealer—the man responsible for his brother's death, the man *he* was hunting—it would go poorly for her.

Still, for a few brief moments she would allow herself the luxury of the illusion, a chance to refresh herself after two weeks of looking over her shoulder, of doubting everyone she came into contact with; two weeks of being scared twenty-four hours a day. Even when she managed to sleep, her sleep was filled with nightmares of being caught, of being returned to her guardian and the unpalatable fate that would await her.

She lived in a zero-sum world now. There was no margin for error, and she was in over her head. There was no other choice. She simply could not live in her guardian's world any longer. She wanted out. Every day she stayed was a day closer to becoming like him, to being dragged irrevocably down a path of violence and corruption from which there would be no escape. The Horsemen were her ticket to freedom.

'What do you know?' The Horseman's voice was quiet, encouraging, his thumb running a slow caress across her knuckles.

Celeste swallowed. After hoarding her secret for so long, it was hard to let it out, to give someone else knowledge of it.

Just tell him, her mind cried. *Then you can lay down the burden.*

This was what she'd come for. She was so close to the finish line. 'Cabot Roan has left his munitions factory in Brussels. He is coming to England for revenge. He is hunting you.' She'd surprised him. She felt his thumb stop for an infinitesimal moment.

'Why?' His thumb started its caress again but she had all his attention now. She'd become an expert at reading men. Her survival had depended on it.

'He is personally hunting the Horsemen in retaliation for the killing of Amesbury and foiling his chance at an arms deal to Greece.' She was glad his chance had been ruined. Roan was already supplying the Ottoman forces arrayed against the Greeks. He took perverse delight in selling firearms to both sides, prolonging the war as long as it pleased him and thinking he could control the outcome of that war.

The man beside her slid her a considering look with eyes like sharp agate, his tone quiet. 'Have you come to warn me or simply to deliver Roan's message on his behalf?'

Are you his tool or his enemy?

Celeste jerked her hand away as if his touch suddenly scorched instead of comforted. Her temper flared, its fuse shortened by exhaustion and hunger. 'How *dare* you insinuate I am that despicable man's puppet?' That very fate was among the many reasons she'd fled. To be accused of it was the height of insult, if only he knew it. 'If you understood what I have endured these past weeks, you would know I would not lower myself to be his messenger.'

'You are not the only one who has suffered recently.'

There was grit in his growl. He was thinking of his brother, no doubt, the one who'd been lost. His gaze swung towards her, giving her a glimpse of his face in full for the first time since he'd knelt beside her. His eyes flashed with dark fire and his jaw was lined with dark stubble, perhaps evidence of his claim that he'd ridden hard.

She was suddenly and keenly aware of his size: the breadth of his shoulders; the strength in his hands. It was difficult to reconcile the earlier offer of comfort with the sheer ruggedness of him. He could overpower her with little effort if he chose. Her previous sense of safety evaporated. A shudder rippled through her. She knew big men and how they used their strength. Roan surrounded himself with them and had no compunction about turning them loose on those less powerful in order to get what he wanted. She'd been on the receiving end of that once. But not ever again—not from Roan or from any man.

It was time to leave before she lost control of the interaction. Celeste rose somewhat awkwardly, her joints stiff from kneeling so long.

The Horseman rose with her. 'Where do you think you're going?'

'It's of no consequence to you. Our business together is finished.' Her task here was done. She could get on with claiming her freedom. Roan would be too busy with the Horsemen to care about her. At least, that was what she hoped.

His hand was on her arm and she flinched before she realised his touch was stalling her, not grabbing her. 'I have questions. Who are you? How did you know to contact us?'

'Those answers are not relevant. I've delivered the news I set out to impart.'

She could not control whether the Horseman with

dark eyes and dark unruly waves chose to believe her or not. She met his eyes with a steely gaze of her own.

'I rather thought you'd be more interested in my news. You've already lost one brother. Roan is coming, not his minions. *He* is coming. His need for stealth will slow him.'

By law, Roan was not allowed to set foot on English soil on penalty of arrest. 'You have a little time to lay your plans and protections for those you care for: your brother's new bride, that bride's father, your sister and her husband. I believe they're expecting a child. Your parents...'

She felt his grip tighten on her arm at the mention of family. She could see his next question ripple behind his eyes and she answered before he could ask it. 'It doesn't matter how I know.'

'Oh, I think it does. Are you just going to walk out of here?' the Horseman challenged as their eyes held. 'Do you think Roan is going to stop coming for you because he's coming for me and mine instead?'

She gave too much away in those moments. Yes, that was exactly what she thought. If the secret was out, he would have no urgency to find her. Stopping her would solve nothing.

'You see the flaw in your reasoning, surely?' The Horseman gave a long-suffering sigh that said, *Lord, save me from fools.* 'He'll come for revenge. Whoever you are, Roan won't let you go unpunished even if he can't stop you from spreading his secret.'

Secret*s*, plural... She knew more than one secret about Roan. What she held against him went beyond this vengeful episode.

'Then it is more important than ever that I leave here as soon as possible.'

She was proud to get the words out without a tremble in her voice. Inside, she was collapsing. She'd convinced herself she'd be safe if she could get this far. That she could become a person of no consequence, that she could slide away and disappear once her message was delivered. But the chase was not over. It might never be over. She'd made a serious miscalculation.

She stepped away from the Horseman and fled, even as he called to her.

'Wait!' The single word echoed in the emptiness of the chancel. But she could not wait. She had to hide. She had to run. After Roan had come for the Four Horsemen, he'd come for her. She needed whatever head start she could manage.

Chapter Two

Kieran gave her the briefest of head starts. Enemy or ally—although he was leaning towards ally; she was too naïve—he could not let her leave. It was absurd that she thought he would. How far did she think he'd let her get? Or how far would Roan let her get, for that matter? Whoever she was, she was clearly untutored in the rules of espionage. The most basic rule of them all was that, once begun, the game was never done. One could not simply step aside and choose not to play. One did not win the game; one merely survived it.

He caught up to her before she reached the heavy doors leading out into the street. 'Wait, please. I want to help you.' He kept his tone calm and even. Beneath her aplomb, he recognised the presence of fright, although not the source. Was she afraid of him? Of Roan? Of circumstances that had led her to deliver the warning? Maybe all three factored into her fear. Perhaps she recognised in full for the first time what it meant to summon a Horseman and that she was in well over her head.

He put a gentle but firm hand on the door, holding it shut. The fewer who saw her or who saw him with her, the better, until he had things straight. A picture was starting to emerge, but it was not yet fully formed and he needed to be right before he went further.

She turned to face him. He caught a glimpse of eyes flashing beneath her veil. 'Do you mean to trap me here?' she challenged.

Kieran did not rise to the bait. Sparring in the chapel had got them nowhere. 'I mean to determine who you are and how best I can help you. You are in danger, perhaps more danger than you planned, regardless of your role. But I think you've realised that.'

'You still don't believe me. You still think I might be in league with Roan.' Beneath the veil, her chin went up in defiance.

'I think there is still much we should discuss before decisions are made—yours or mine.' And they could not discuss those things here. He'd already lingered in the church longer than he'd have liked. He was exposed here, and she was too. 'Where were you going?'

'Back to my rooms.' She offered no address. It was time to do something to earn her trust, at least for the short term; trust enough to get her talking so he could determine how best to deal with her information and with her. For that, he needed her to doubt herself, to be more wary of Roan than she was of him.

He nodded. 'I am sure Roan will expect that.'

'He's not here, not yet,' she countered.

'No, but if you're escaping him, if you are truly here to warn me out of the altruism of your heart, then that means Roan's men are chasing you. What you know is not something he wants to get out. It steals his element of surprise. He'll know you'll head to London because that's where the Horsemen are. Your trail is not a mystery to him.'

He watched her body tense at the mention of Roan's henchmen. That told him she was close enough to Roan to know how he operated, how his men operated, and that she knew they were cruel. Kieran ran the options in his mind. Was she Roan's wife? His daughter? A niece or female relation? Roan was obsessively private. They knew nothing of his family, or even if he had one. If he did, his roots were hidden deep. In Roan's line of work, family connections were a weakness to be exploited.

'So, you *do* believe me,' she pressed again. 'If I'm not your ally, keeping me here doesn't make sense.'

'Keeping you here keeps you alive,' Kieran replied patiently. 'If you're my ally, it will make it easier for me to keep you alive. If you're Roan's messenger, you'll be dead the moment you go back to your rooms, perhaps even the moment you step out into the street.'

Lucifer's balls, he wished he could see her face. He wanted to rip that damned veil off and see her reaction. Had his words shocked her? Had they frightened her as they would anyone who didn't realise how perilous it was to discharge one's assigned duty and serve no more purpose for their overlord?

'He'll have no use for you if you've done your job. He certainly won't want you running about in possession of his plans, free to tell anyone you meet.' Kieran gave a nonchalant shrug. 'Either way, you're dead. It's just a matter of how soon.' He let her have a few long seconds to take that in before offering her a lifeline. 'Unless you want to come with me.'

'My protection at what price?' she countered

shrewdly, showing off again that intriguing mix he couldn't quite sort out—the naïve peppered with the sharp. Which was real? Which was ruse? His very life could depend upon it.

'Information is the currency the Horsemen deal in. You know that much because you're here. *I* want to know who you are and what has brought you to this point. In exchange, I pledge you my protection and I will see to it that you are free from Roan.' If she was Roan's messenger, she would have to turn traitor. He hoped he'd given her reason enough to consider it if that was the case.

She did not answer immediately, her gaze shrouded behind her veil as she thought. At last, her words came. 'All right. I'll go with you.'

Kieran slowly released a breath. He'd not wanted it to come down to throwing her over his shoulder and manhandling her home. It would be far better this way, where she thought she had a choice in the matter.

'When we step outside, I am going to put my arm around you and pull you close, as if I am supporting you. Perhaps it is the anniversary of your husband's death and you are overcome with grief. The closer I can keep you to me, the more difficult it will be for any potential snipers to get an accurate shot off. My horse is at the watering trough outside; we will take him to my townhouse.'

And, in the meantime, all Kieran could do was hope no one took a shot at him. Some might argue it would be better to put her in a closed carriage, but carriages had no manoeuvrability in traffic or flexibility in a chase. Racing a bulky hired cab on London streets was not nearly as reliable as Tambor in a tight spot. Between his horse or a carriage, he'd always choose his horse.

Outside, they met with no resistance other than the late-afternoon heat. He helped her mount, paid Samuel a few more coins and encouraged him to keep his eyes open for anyone out of the ordinary. The boy had proven himself observant. Such skill wouldn't go amiss over the next few days. He checked Tambor and swung up behind his nominal widow. He settled in the saddle, his arms about her in order to hold the reins.

'Comfortable?' Tambor was an intimidating horse. One could see the world from atop his height. One didn't want to fall off, though; it was a long way down.

'I'm fine, thank you.' But her body told a different story. She remained tense, alert, although Tambor might not be the source of that tension. She was not gripping the saddle with white knuckles. It wasn't the horse that unnerved her, it was the circumstance.

'Do you ride?' She seemed at home aboard his horse. If they ran into trouble, it would help to know if she could.

'Yes, some.' Her response was curt. He could forgive her for her shortness. She had a lot to think about at the moment and she'd just consented to ride off with a man she didn't know to a place she'd never been. 'Might we stop at my boarding house to collect my things? It won't take more than a few minutes.'

Ah, so her lodgings *were* close by. 'No, I'm afraid we cannot. Did it occur to you that you might not have been followed to the church because they knew where you'd be afterwards? They could be waiting in your rooms now.' They could be waiting for her or for him. If she was working for Roan, perhaps she'd been meant to lure him back there after their meeting.

'You're trying to scare me,' she argued.

'I'm trying to help you think about your situation more broadly.' He swept the street with a practised eye and turned Tambor into the meagre traffic.

'All I have in the world is in that room,' came the protest. Someone less seasoned than himself, someone who'd not nearly been stabbed in the liver, might have seen this plea as further proof she was Roan's messenger, sent to lure him. Kieran did not. He knew better. Her words confirmed it: messengers would not bring their worldly goods with them on a trip. A messenger expected to return to wherever they'd come from. They packed light. That she was travelling with everything she owned suggested she was on the run. Still, he had no intention of going there at the moment.

'Either way, the boarding house is too dangerous now. If you're his messenger, perhaps you are to lead me to them so they can take me unawares.' He clucked to Tambor. 'I will not be shot down like a dog in the street. If that's the plan, Roan will have to try harder. And, if you're running from them, you certainly don't want to find out the hard way they've caught up to you.'

'I resent the implication that I am an accessory to premeditated murder.' She seethed. He could practically feel the anger roll off her, mixed with the scent of a light summer floral toilet water—hyacinth tempered with orris root to turn it powdery. A fresh scent, too delicate, too youthful, for a widow who made church Latin sound like an invitation to sin. He filed the contradiction along with the others.

'I'll send someone to collect your bags later tonight.' The compromise would serve him. Sending Luce to retrieve her things would be a chance for reconnaissance. He'd pay the landlord to keep up the pretence that she was still in residence. If Roan's men hadn't arrived yet, the façade would alert him to their arrival when they tracked her to the room.

She wanted to be innocent; so be it. He'd give her a chance to prove it. Kieran withdrew his pistol. 'Can you shoot?'

'If I don't have to shoot too far.'

'We'll work on that.' He handed her the pistol. 'Truly, can you manage it if needed?' he asked in all seriousness.

'Yes,' she replied solemnly, settling the pistol across her lap. He felt her shoulders rise and fall with a deep breath. There was a stalwartness to her, a bravery, that he appreciated even if it also came with some naïvety. They'd work on that, too. The naïve didn't live long in his world and he'd like her to live long enough for him to know who she was.

So, *this* was where the Horsemen lived. Celeste shielded her eyes and looked up at a bright-white, pillared townhouse with black shuttered windows and three storeys soaring into the summer sky in the middle of Mayfair, as if the Horsemen were ordinary gentlemen of the ton. Why was she surprised? Of course they lived here, she scolded herself. They were grandsons of an earl. Where else would they live—in a dark cave where they only sallied forth when England was in need? Although, at present, it was difficult to imagine the man seated behind her on the horse as a society gentleman with his stubble, unruly dark waves and potent need of a bath. He wasn't alone in that last attribute. At this point, she needed a bath too.

The ride from Old Church Street in Chelsea had been hot, dusty and full of noxious street smells. There was no glamour to summer in a city. Those smells had helped take her mind off other things, such as the press of his granite-hard thighs and the rocking of his hips as he moved with the horse—all very natural movements but they offered intimate awareness, nonetheless.

He steered the horse around to the mews and swung off first, taking the pistol from her before he helped her down. 'We'll use the back entrance,' he directed after turning his horse over to a groom with strict instructions. 'There's always a full staff at Parkhurst House. You'll be well looked after.'

There was that duality again—the rugged gentleman, rough around the edges with his stubble and gruffness juxtaposed with the mannered gentleman within who offered comfort *and* discretion to a woman he wasn't convinced he could trust and gave too many coins to a street boy.

Inside, he led her through the kitchen, introducing her to his cook before leading her upstairs to the public rooms. Celeste peered inside a drawing room that seemed more St James gambling hall than Mayfair mansion. It was filled with card tables, a piano set against one wall. The room was empty except for two men idly playing a hand of something at one of the tables. She pictured the room full of people and laughter, different high-stakes games going on at each table. She slid a covert glance at her host, a realisation becoming clear: the Horsemen were hellions in public, heroes in private.

The Horseman gestured to a maid who stood nearby. 'This is Liana. She will take you upstairs and see to a bath. We installed running water a couple years ago. You'll enjoy that after weeks of travel. You must excuse me, now. I have arrangements to make, so I will see you at dinner.'

Was he leaving her alone in this big house? Celeste felt a sudden sense of being bereft, adrift in a strange world where she knew no one. 'Wait,' she called to him. 'Might I have your name first?' That she didn't know his name threw into sharp relief the risk she'd taken in coming here. This man *was* a stranger.

He turned with a smile, his agate eyes dancing. 'You most certainly may, just as soon as I have the pleasure of yours, m'lady.' He made a bow and was gone.

The bathing chamber was a pleasure for the senses with its dark-blue marbled floor veined with silver to resemble the ocean itself, and the sound of rushing water as it filled the white porcelain tub. Celeste shed her travel-worn garments with alacrity, looking forward to the bath. It felt like something out of a fairy tale to be here alone, one of those tales in which the castle beast left during the day only to return at night. Although, the Horseman was hardly a beast.

Celeste slid into the lavender-scented water and closed her eyes, letting the peace of the chamber and the susurration of the water against her skin soothe her body, even if her mind remained alive, moving from thought to thought. She wasn't really alone here. There were servants; he'd been quick to point that out. At the time, she'd thought it an act of comfort, letting her know her needs would be met. Now, she wondered if it had been a reminder he'd be aware of her every movement. If she roamed the house, he would know. Someone would tell him, if not the servants then perhaps the two men in the drawing room. Did that make her a guest or a captive?

One did not usually allow captives baths and thick towels. Then again, comfort and luxury had their own seductive properties. Had he decided, if he couldn't have her secrets outright, he'd seduce them from her with the comforts of home? Kindness was an effective ruse when employed on the unsuspecting.

Cabot Roan had used that trick aplenty. After her father had died, Roan had sent gifts on her birthday or at Christmas: a locket or set of barrettes. He'd seemed gracious and kind, a true best friend to her father and a devoted guardian to her. It was not until she'd finished school and Roan had sent for her that she'd realised he expected payment for that kindness; that he'd been grooming her to take her place and more in a world that was dark, dirty and dangerous. She'd been wary of gifts and kindnesses ever since.

And yet, she'd gone off with a man whose name she didn't know. She knew why: his reputation spoke for him. He was one of the Four Horsemen and the antithesis of all Cabot Roan stood for, and her father. She could not forget that, as much as she would like to. The two men she'd admired the most in her young life had not been what they'd seemed. It was hard to reconcile the idea that she'd loved her father but hated what he'd done. Not so with Roan. He was rotten clear through, and so she'd run to the only people she could think of who might possibly help her.

She slid deeper into the water and sighed. She ought to be celebrating. She'd done it—she'd found the Horsemen. That was no small thing. She was in their home. She'd delivered her warning. They could fight Roan and she would be free. After years of living under Roan's thumb, the concept of being free was both heady and unformed. Where would she go when this was over? She could go anywhere, assuming she might cajole some funds. What would she do? That was more complicated. A woman had few choices. She knew what she didn't want to do and that was answer to a man; to give up her freedom in service to another. But those were worries for another time, a later time, after Roan was defeated.

At last, her mind quieted and she imagined sending her thoughts away on lily-pads down the gentle stream of lavender-scented consciousness, drifting…drifting…

'Miss? Miss? Wake up, we can't have you drowning, now.' A gentle shake of her shoulder was enough to bring her back, as was the cooling water. Perhaps she really had drifted off. Celeste reluctantly opened her eyes and pushed herself up a little higher in the tub. Liana was holding a thick, white towel. Celeste wondered where her relaxed limbs would find the willpower to get out of the bath. At the moment, it seemed like a gargantuan effort.

'We've got to get you dressed for supper,' Liana coaxed.

Celeste groaned. 'I don't have anything to wear.' She did not relish the idea of putting on her dirty clothes again after getting clean. 'Perhaps a tray in my room…' she began, but Liana shook her head.

'You're not to worry, miss. There are clean things

laid out for you in your chamber. M'lord had Madame Dumont send clothes for you.'

'And Madame Dumont is who?' She hoped Madame Dumont wasn't the Horseman's mistress. She was in no position to be finicky, but the idea sat poorly with her. She'd been forced to dress the part of the whore before.

'Madame Dumont is a dressmaker near Bond Street— very respectable. All the fine ladies get their gowns there. She had some items that had not been claimed.'

Curiosity at the prospect of new, clean clothes propelled her out of the tub, as did the thought that the Horseman had sent for clothes for her, that he had done this especially. The nuance was not lost on her. This was not merely the culling of closets to see what might have been left behind by other visitors. He'd sent for clothes specifically for her. That was an extreme kindness and must be treated with extreme wariness, even as excitement fizzed through her.

Liana produced an ivory silk dressing robe—another item that must have been sent over by Madame Dumont— and helped her into it. 'Your chamber is through here.' Liana gestured to an open door that gave on to an airy room done in soft powdered blues: *her chamber.* Another type of gift—the gift of privacy, the gift of owning space. The maid said the words as if she was a welcome guest, someone who would be staying a while. It was a lovely thought but an unlikely one.

On the wide bed, with its carved mahogany posts, lay an array of garments: chemises, stockings and a gown of cool white muslin decorated with tiny green flowers. Not a single item had been overlooked.

'Hair first, I think.' Liana steered her towards a

lady's dressing table where more surprises awaited: a hairbrush and a small bottle of a light floral scent that nearly matched her own. By the time her hair had been put up, scent dabbed at her pulse points and the muslin gown with its green sash dropped over her head, one thought ran rampant through her mind: the Horseman wanted more than her name. She'd best be on her game tonight.

Chapter Three

The game was definitely on. Kieran's gaze locked on the woman poised at the top of the stairs in the white gown, glossy chestnut tresses artfully pinned to show off a slim and elegant neck a swan would envy. She began her descent, her gaze meeting his with temerity. Perhaps she had the same goal in mind—to make a study of him even as he made a study of her. His grandfather's informant cleaned up well, and she'd discarded the veil as he'd hoped. She began her progress down the stairs, the movement drawing his eyes to where the swish of skirts offered an occasional glimpse of well-turned ankles. A few more steps and he'd be able to see her face in detail.

Just three stairs to go before she reached him. He could truly see her now, unlike in the church. The green sash brought out the colour of her wide, beautiful eyes set beneath slim, dark, arched brows. A man could spin a million fantasies in that sea-glass gaze with its hint of mystery, its spark of intelligence and, he suspected, a host of other things. Perhaps she was not as innocent as he'd assumed at the church. There was a worldliness to her that was on better display without the veil, although he doubted she was more than three and twenty.

He wondered again who she might be to Roan—a paramour of some sort? He could certainly see the appeal. The fine bones of her face gave her an air of good breeding. The straight, narrow perfection of her nose, the defiant point of her chin, and the delicate curve of cheek and jaw complemented the steel that could exist in her gaze. And that mouth… One might argue that her mouth was the real treasure with its full lips that could just as easily offer a compelling pout as effectively as they offered an invitation to a kiss. If she was a mystery in muslin, she'd be pure seduction in satins and silks.

What an asset she'd have been to Roan, teasing men out of their secrets over supper.

She reached him at the bottom of the stairs and he offered his arm. 'I am glad the dress fits,' he said, then added with a charming wink, 'and that you've discarded the veil. The ruse does not suit you.' The ruse of young gentlewoman did, though. Or was it real? Dinner would tell. Eating often caught people out in subtle ways.

She cocked her head to glance up at him as they walked. 'What makes you so sure it is a ruse?'

Kieran chuckled. The minx would hold her ground until the last. 'Your hands gave you away.'

She made a pretty pout. He'd not been wrong about her mouth. 'Surely you can do better than that? A ring or lack of one does not tell all. There can be several reasons why I didn't have one on. Many widows take their rings off.'

'The ring is too easy.' Kieran reached for her hand and held it up between them. 'There is no ring mark, no telltale signs there's ever been a ring on your finger at any time.' He let his eyes linger on her, let the timbre of his voice lower and quieten, allowing the lecture on observation to turn into something more seductive. 'But then there is the issue of your skin. When I ran my thumb over your knuckles, your skin looked and felt smooth, supple—too youthful for a likely widow.'

'Some women lose husbands young. Perhaps I married an elderly man.' Her sea-glass eyes narrowed with the challenge and locked on his.

'And suddenly found the need to deliver a warning about Cabot Roan? That makes little sense. Given the circumstances, your veil was a disguise only.' They passed the dining room, dark and unlaid for supper. She arched a slim brow in question.

'I thought we'd eat outside on the veranda. We have a bit of a garden out the back and it's cooler than eating inside.' Kieran gave a smile meant to charm. 'Out of doors will also offer us privacy for all the things we have to talk about.'

'Are we alone?' she queried as he held open the French doors for her. 'What about the two men from the drawing room?'

'They're gone, but the servants are here. You needn't worry for your safety, if that is what you're asking.' But how telling that she might have reason to fear for it, to fear being alone with a man.

The servants had done well on short notice. A round wrought-iron garden table had been covered with a white cloth and a thick round candle had been set in the centre and lit, protected from any gentle breeze by a glass chimney. Champagne stood at the ready, cooled to perfection. He nodded to the footmen to bring up the meal and saw to the uncorking himself.

'I admit to enjoying chilled champagne in the summer,' he said, pouring two glasses with precision. 'A true connoisseur of the beverage might argue that I prefer it too cold, but I like the sharpness.' He handed her a glass and set his aside to pull out her chair.

'Is this to be interrogation by candlelight?' She arranged her skirts and fixed him with a pretty smile that belied the nature of their relationship. Kieran wondered for a moment what the odds were that they were both playing the same game—seduction for information. Not that he meant to seduce her fully, but he was not opposed to cajoling and flirting to put someone at ease. He did it every night, whether in Mayfair's ballrooms, or in the drawing room when gentlemen came to play cards.

Kieran took his own seat, flipping up the tails of his evening clothes. She was not the only one looking her best. Women responded to a well-groomed man. His first lover, an older woman in Venice, had explained it to him like this: if a man had the self-discipline to keep themselves up, perhaps it stood to reason that man also had the self-discipline to keep secrets. She'd not been wrong.

'"Interrogation" implies we are at odds, which you have insisted we are not. You suggest we are allies, and allies do not interrogate one another. But I am no fool and I have questions before I risk the Horsemen with your information.' He raised his flute. 'Here's to an evening of enlightenment. May we start the night as strangers and end as friends.' Although, 'friends' was probably asking for too much. One did not really have 'friends' in his business.

They drank his toast and Kieran waited until the footmen had laid the cold summer repast before he began.

They would serve themselves from now on to ensure privacy. 'Shall I make up a plate for you?' he offered, mentally wagering with himself that she would not want to be catered to, and he was right.

'I can manage, thank you.' They took a moment assembling their plates from the meat, cheese and bread on the tray set before them. Her plate was full, unlike most of the debutantes who ate on scale with the smallest of birds. She was hungry, then. The journey had taken a toll on her. Perhaps there'd not been finances enough to eat as often as she'd have liked. Kieran tucked the knowledge away.

'There's plenty in the kitchen. I can always call for more,' he said, holding back a chuckle when she hesitated to take another piece of ham. Hunger was no laughing matter, and she'd had cause to know.

A pretty pink stained her cheek. 'Travelling works up an appetite.' Kieran gave her a smile and assembled a sandwich. 'I trust you enjoyed the bath?'

'You know I did. And the clothes and the maid as well. I didn't tell her anything useful, though, if that's what you were hoping for.'

She took a sip of her champagne, the candlelight picking out the hints of red in her chestnut hair, and Kieran was struck with the sudden wish to sit with her in a Parisian café, perhaps in the Latin Quarter, debating something, anything; or to walk the Seine at twilight and stop in one of the many turnouts on the bridges to view the river; to steal a long kiss. He wondered if she was doing it on purpose, this subtle flirting through argument, or if it came to her naturally.

He offered a grin in the wake of her cynicism and

gave her a long study. 'I cannot decide about you,' he said at last. 'Some moments I think you are an innocent caught in a very dangerous game you don't know how to play.'

'I am not *naïve*.'

There was more chagrin than protest in her response. He'd insulted her. Kieran shook his head in disagreement. 'Yes, you are. The widow's ruse *was* naïve. It was flimsy and it was never going to hold up under closer scrutiny—an amateur move, as was wanting to go back to your rooms. But let me finish; I was about to say, or perhaps you're truly shrewd.'

He gave a cheeky grin meant to tease. 'You *do* have moments of brilliance, like thinking I'd use the maid to spy on you. And,' he drawled, flashing a boyish grin designed to charm, 'your suspicion of comfort suggests you have a high degree of cognitive complexity; that you are able to see things from a variety of angles.'

She smiled a little at that, her armour cracking ever so slightly. He was getting to her at last—good. He wasn't used to such resistance. Most women fell for his smile and trusted his eyes. For the most part, they could. He was no betrayer.

He leaned forward, elbows on the table. 'So, have I earned your name? After all, I've let you into my home and exposed myself, in good faith that you do not come to do me harm.'

She gave him a look of disbelief. 'You do not strike me as a man who is ever truly at a disadvantage. You would not have brought me here if it didn't also serve your purposes. *I* am the one who is exposed. *I* am in the belly of the whale here, adrift among strangers in a strange home.'

'It seems to me that you're in the belly of the whale wherever you go. Why so reticent? Surely you knew you'd have to give up a name at the very least? Understand this: whispers, rumours, the stuff of information, must be substantiated. The Horsemen cannot afford to follow every whiff of conspiracy and assassination that comes our way. It would make us nothing less than puppets to be jerked on the strings of others. Now, a name, if you please...'

He was not going to tolerate further refusal. Celeste could see it in the set of those broad shoulders beneath the dark evening jacket, the insistence that lingered unspoken in his gaze. He'd made his overtures and it was her turn to respond. She understood this dance. She understood, too, that she had an obligation to perform the steps. 'I think if you knew who I was it may shade your attitude towards me and towards the information I've brought.'

'Or perhaps towards my willingness to help you. Why don't you try me and find out?' Those dark eyes narrowed in contemplation and it was hard to look away. In fact, it had been hard to look away all night since the moment she'd descended the stairs. He cleaned up well—too well.

'Yes, that, too, when it comes down to it. Your willingness to help would not go amiss.' Why not admit it? He'd proven persuasive. His methods had been effective. The pull of his smiles and long, lingering gazes were more magnetic than she wanted him to realise.

She sighed and he refilled her glass. She'd only known this man for the span of an afternoon but she knew he was a protector. She wouldn't mind using his protection a while longer—or his bathing chamber—but being a protector didn't mean he wasn't also dangerous in, oh, so many ways...starting with her champagne-imbued sensibilities.

In the end, it wasn't the seductive niceties, the bath, the clothes, the food, the house or even those brown velvet eyes that made her decide. It was the simple words, 'You're safe here. More than safe, whoever you are. You don't need to go back to him.'

She'd not been safe for years. The idea that she might be, could be, safe was more intoxicating than champagne to a woman who was alone and tired. Intoxicating enough that the words were out before she knew it.

'My name is Celeste Sharpton. I'm the ward of Cabot Roan.' She worried her lip and waited, waited for his vaunted promise of safety to disappear, waited for him to explode, waited for him to say he felt betrayed and that he'd let the enemy into his home. But the eruption didn't come. There was only silence, punctuated by those dark eyes lingering on her while pieces fell into place behind them like a puzzle assembling itself.

When he did speak, it was not the rejection she'd expected. 'I'm Kieran Parkhurst.' A slow smile crossed his mouth. 'I promised you a name for a name, did I not? Now you know I am a man of my word. If I say you're safe here, you are.' He poured more champagne, the summer night deepening around them. 'Now we can have a real conversation. Bring your glass; let's take a walk about the garden.'

She knew what came next: a game of questions. She took her glass in one hand and his arm with the other. She understood the reason they were leaving the table. He wanted complete privacy for this discussion...privacy for him or for her? He waited until they were on a gravel path, lit by tiny lanterns posted on rods that came out of the ground ankle-high, before launching his first question. 'Why come forward now?'

'Because I'd had enough, because I could and because I had to.' She was honest enough to admit that if she hadn't been suspected of eavesdropping the night she'd fled—an act of which she was absolutely guilty—she might not have found the courage to run, regardless of how much she'd wanted to. It had been the hardest decision she'd ever made to date. But it was perhaps also the most right.

'Had to?' he queried.

'I'd been on my way to the music room for a shawl I'd left behind and Roan's office door was ajar. I overheard him talking with our guests after supper. The temptation was too much to resist. They were discussing the Horsemen.'

The Horsemen were mentioned often in the Roan household. It was no secret Roan found them to be the bane of his existence, regular spoilers of his plans. She'd come to romanticise the idea of knowing there were four horsemen out in the world riding for good against evil. By the time she was nineteen, she'd turned them into something idealistic, born from the mind of a lonely young girl surrounded by corruption in which she was an unwilling part. How many nights had she gone to bed wishing the Horsemen would rescue her, before she'd realised she would have to make her own rescue?

She chose her next words carefully. 'They were toasting the hopeful demise of one of the Horsemen.' She watched his strong jaw tighten; a tic jumped in his cheek. 'Then they vowed to bring down the rest of you because of Amesbury's death.' She'd met the blond Duke once. She was not sorry he was dead. 'Then Roan said he was going himself, that he wanted to be the one to pull the trigger.' That was when a servant had come round the corner and seen her in the hallway. She'd moved on quickly but the servants were all loyal to Roan— frightened into it, but loyal, nonetheless. Her presence would be noted.

'So, you just left, to warn us? Three men you don't know?' He knew how to probe, how to hunt motives.

'Would you do less?' she challenged. 'They were laughing over the death of a Horseman, over the death of a human being. Death is not laughable. Deliberately taking a life is not laughable. It angered me. It reminded me that I was, in my own way, complicit in such behaviour if I stayed, if I did nothing.'

It had galvanised her into action along with the need to see to her own safety. Roan took punishment seriously and she knew its power for maintaining conformity among his ranks empirically.

'I left for myself as well. I'd been wanting to leave for a while. I simply hadn't been brave enough.' She'd been paralysed by fear of failure and what would await her should her escape not be successful. Escapes were a sign of disloyalty. She'd failed a loyalty test to Roan before. She'd not been brave enough to face the consequences again. Fear had kept her rooted in place until that night when the need to protect herself had collided with the need to protect others.

Celeste let her fingers trail over leaves, a sweet fragrance releasing into the summer night. 'Sometimes we can do for others what we can't do for ourselves.'

'And now here you are.' Kieran was studying her intently, no doubt turning over each word in his sharp mind, mining each of them for more, reading between the lines in his search for understanding. 'Is that the only secret you've come this far to impart?'

She'd not expected that. 'Why do you think there's more?' But it was a weak defence to answer a question with a question.

He finished his glass. 'Because you were his ward. You lived in his house at least part of the time. And because Roan coming after us is not entirely a surprise.'

'But *when*, and that he is coming in person, most certainly is,' she countered. She did not like him dismissing her warning as inconsequential.

'Still, it's a long way to come to tell us something we could guess. We already knew he was behind the bargain for arms,' Kieran countered gently. 'But, as you say, you also came for yourself.'

She faced him in the moonlight, letting him have full view of her seriousness. 'Yes, I also came for myself. And I would go even further still to ensure my safety. If you've never been unsafe, you cannot possibly know how integral it is to one's well-being, one's ability to function, to live.' She'd not even been safe with her lover, David, whom she'd thought would protect her unto death. She'd not known how to read men in those days. She was more cautious and more astute now. She understood what motivated them, that for them love was not a prized emotion to feel but a tool to wield.

He gave a nod of contrition. 'My apologies. I did not mean to imply otherwise.'

No, but he'd certainly sensed there was more to tell, and his instincts had been right. But those things veered into the personal and she was not going to go down that path tonight.

'I think there have been enough questions for one night,' she said quickly when she saw he might ask another. 'If you don't mind, I would like to retire.' She wondered if the card tables in the drawing room were full of men with secrets waiting to be revealed along with their hands.

He smiled as if he'd read her thoughts. 'I'll see you up.' It was guardianship disguised as gallantry. He didn't want her roaming the house on the way to her chambers. Fine; she would have other chances to have a look around, to work out Kieran Parkhurst. Tonight, she would allow herself the simple joys of a clean white nightgown and slipping between fresh sheets with a summer breeze ruffling the curtains. For tonight, she would be safe, and that would be enough.

Chapter Four

A name had been enough, for now. Kieran sat across from Luce in front of the cold fire in the study at the back of the house, sipping brandies and mulling over the events of the day. Or, more precisely, the events of the last thirty-six hours, which had been hectic and, in their own way, life-changing. His glance strayed to the big desk that dominated the room—the desk from which Caine had spent years presiding over the Horsemen. But Caine was married now, and happily so, even as that marriage fulfilled one of the requirements that went with the new titles: that the Horsemen marry within the year or the titles would revert to the Crown upon their deaths. Proof that nothing in this life was guaranteed.

'You miss him.' Luce nodded towards the empty desk.

'I know he's not gone. I know he's a letter away. It's the immediacy I miss, and his sureness. As annoying as it was at times, Caine was always right. Caine never doubted his instincts.' Not the way he did. He had the ghost of Sofia to thank for that. Doubt was a different sort of scar from the one he carried near his liver.

'He *was* annoying, and I am sure he will be again— only from Newmarket instead.' Luce laughed and then sobered. 'But I understand. It's just us now.' He fingered the short stem of his glass in a gesture that indicated he had something difficult to say. 'It is *us* now, Kieran. You *and* me. I am here for you. You *can* count on me.'

'I know,' Kieran assured him. Luce was referring to his recent physical absence from the Horsemen. After Stepan's accident, Luce had retreated to his newly inherited estate and buried himself in beginning to restore the estate's library, while Kieran and Caine had bravely forged into the investigation, rooting out those who were responsible for the sabotage and for their brother's... death...disappearance? These days, neither word felt quite right. It had been two months and there was no body or word to indicate Stepan's fate that night in Wapping. The uncertainty haunted him, the doubt mocking. Should he do more to find Stepan? Where else should he look? Was it wrong for life to go on while there was no resolution?

'I shouldn't have left the Horsemen blind like that. You needed my services and I was absent. It was a lot for two to handle; a third person would have helped.'

Kieran offered a rueful grin. He might torture himself with 'what ifs' but he would not allow his little brother to do the same. 'Don't scold yourself over it. Once a Horseman, always a Horseman. You didn't really leave us. I wasn't exactly stalwart either. I went through the motions of going to the clubs and listening for rumours, but mostly I went out to the clubs and hells for me, to drown my sorrows, to numb my pain. It didn't work. But Caine was patient with me. We all miss Stepan.'

They might miss him for ever; or, even worse, they

might start to forget—forget to search, forget to scan the post each day in hope of some word.

It felt good to talk with Luce like this. It was a kind of remembering, a kind of grieving. They were brothers but they were also partners. Whenever the Horsemen had split into twos, it had been he and Luce who'd paired up. It always had been. Caine and he had arranged it that way even from childhood: the two oldest brothers each taking a protégé from the two youngest. It had created a unique, unified fraternity between the four brothers instead of age-based factions—the two oldest set against the two youngest.

There was more he'd like to talk with Luce about. The titles: did he intend to meet the marriage deadline? Stepan: did Luce think Stepan was dead? If not, where did he think Stepan was? But those items would have to wait. There was a more pressing matter to discuss and it was sleeping upstairs.

Kieran took a long, slow swallow of brandy and changed the topic. 'What did you find at the boarding house?' He'd sent Luce on some reconnaissance and, if possible, some retrieval—Luce's specialty.

Luce crossed a long leg over his knee and took the change of conversation in stride. Luce was flexible that way, his nimble mind able to anticipate what someone was thinking, or what they would say next. As a result, he was seldom caught off guard. 'I was able to get her valise and, before you ask, I did not look through it. Anything that was lying about the room, I threw in and I left.'

Kieran nodded. To have nosed around would have raised the landlord's suspicion and Celeste's. If she thought anything she'd been hiding had been disturbed it would undermine the careful truce he'd established tonight. 'How was the landlord?'

Luce shrugged. 'Bribeable, which is both good and bad. For a price, he and his wife were happy to let us know if anyone turned up asking for her, and more than happy to accept that I was her brother come to fetch her home. I think they'd also be happy to tell that story to anyone who asked, for the right amount of coin.' Luce finished his drink and rose, heading for the sideboard to refill their glasses. 'What do you make of her? Is she for us or is she a decoy working for him?'

Kieran accepted a glass. 'That's the real question, isn't it? What to do with her and what more does she know? The last will likely affect the answer to the first.'

'Hmm.' Luce looked into his glass, studying the amber liquid. '*Do* you think there's more to know? She's not a one-trick pony?' Luce was dubious.

'Of a certainty, she knows more. Her "warning" is merely a wetted finger testing the direction of the winds. In and of itself, what she shared with me is not information worth the journey she's made and the risk she's taken. She wants to be sure of us first.'

Sure that they'd protect her. After all, she had run for her own safety as much as theirs. Whatever information she possessed, she meant to use it the way an émigré might dole out precious gems to live on, one at a time. Information was her currency, her jewels. He played back in his mind every word, every facial expression, intonation and gesture that had accompanied the story she'd told him in the garden.

'She is running, and scared. A canny hare among the foxes to be sure, but still a hare.' And a beautiful one at that. Despite the logic of knowing his interactions with her were for business, there'd been no denying his reaction to her beauty tonight, even if that reaction had been far from practical. 'She says her name is Celeste Sharpton and she's Roan's ward. She's close to him in terms of physical proximity. She lived in his house until the time she left.' That proximity had made her complicit in Roan's plots and strategies. Those had been her words tonight; she was not wrong.

Both he and Luce knew how living among a particular milieu offered the advantages—or, in her case, disadvantages—of natural absorption of the climate. Summer trips to his grandfather's estate had put him and his brothers in close contact with their grandfather's world of spies and diplomats. It had been innocuous at first and, as they'd grown and shown certain aptitudes, more deliberate. By the time he'd been fifteen, Kieran had been running messages to his grandfather's agents. By the time he'd been nineteen, he'd been in Venice delivering messages and taking lovers. He could only imagine how living in Roan's household, in close proximity to the corruption Roan meted out, would affect a person.

Luce looked up from his brandy. 'Do you think she was privy to Roan's inner thoughts and plans? From what we know of him, he is highly secretive and closed. But perhaps they had a relationship that offered an outlet for those secrets.'

For Celeste's sake, Kieran hoped Roan had remained closed. Secrets often became burdens. 'Are you suggesting she was more than his ward?' A sudden defensiveness for Celeste rose at the suggestion, and protectiveness too. Roan had no code of ethics. He would not flinch at developing a less than appropriate guardian-ward relationship if it served his purpose.

'As distasteful as it might be to ask the question, we must consider who she is to Roan. Will he want her back because of what she knows or because of what *she* means to him?' Luce fixed him with a look. 'I did not see beneath her veil, but if she's lovely she isn't the first woman who has relied on wits and looks for survival.'

Luce grinned and Kieran knew he'd given himself away in some infinitesimal manner. 'So, she *is* pretty. Hmm…'

'Pretty, young, brave, mysterious…' Kieran said.

'You believe she is escaping Roan instead of working as bait for him,' Luce said matter-of-factly.

'Yes. Her luggage, or lack of it, matches what she told me in the garden—that she had to flee on a moment's notice. And Falcon believes her.' Falcon was their grand-father's agent on the Continent, the one who'd brought word to Caine's wedding about an informant who had intelligence about the arms sabotage—not a warning about Roan, although the two weren't necessarily sepa-rate issues.

Luce thought it over. 'Miss Sharpton has said nothing about the arms and she hasn't told us much more than what we would readily deduce ourselves.'

It was the same concern Kieran had put to her in the garden. 'Not *yet*,' he qualified. 'But, yes, I have noted the discrepancy between what Falcon told us to expect and what Miss Sharpton has given up to date.'

Kieran rubbed the bridge of his nose. 'This is what

I propose: you should ride to Sussex and confer with Grandfather. Tell him we have made contact with Miss Sharpton. Tell him who she claims to be and that, with all evidence considered, I am inclined to believe her. Tell him that the information we thought would be disclosed has not yet materialised but that other information has—that Roan is headed for English shores in person and is targeting the Horsemen for revenge. The family will need to know so that precautions can be taken.'

With luck, most of the family would still be at Sandmore enjoying some post-wedding relaxation before travelling home. It would make getting the word out easier if the family was all in one place. The only ones not there would be Caine and Mary, who would be on their way to their new home outside Newmarket.

Luce gave a grim nod. 'I'll do it, but I don't like leaving you alone in London, knowing that there is the potential Roan will soon be here.'

Kieran chuckled. 'I don't like that idea either, but hopefully I'll see Roan before he sees me. If it gets too risky, I will decamp. I am more concerned about Roan's minions arriving in search of her than I am about Roan. We have a little time there but Celeste—Miss Sharpton—does not. It's been two weeks since she left Brussels. They know she's gone and they know her destination. They cannot be far behind.' Indeed, he was surprised they hadn't caught up with her.

Luce stood up and stretched as the clock chimed the late hour. 'I'll set off at first light. While I am gone, be careful. Don't let gallantry get the better of you.'

'I won't. I've learned my lesson there,' Kieran promised, a hand reflexively going to his side. He rose and embraced his brother. 'You be safe too. If I'm not here when you get back, you'll know Roan's people are among us. I'll find a way to let you know where we are. Sweet dreams, brother.'

Oh, sweet saints be praised, her valise! It was here in her room, waiting for her. A special kind of relief swept Celeste as she knelt beside it and undid the fastenings. When she'd gone with the Horseman, the possibility of seeing these items again had greatly diminished. There was little chance he'd let her out of his sight long enough for her to get back to the boarding house, even if it was safe to go back. He'd made compelling arguments today about the threats to her safety, threats that seemed more real to her than she'd let on at the time. Roan's men could not be far behind. They might already be here and temporarily stymied by the vastness of the city in locating her.

The uncertainty of not knowing gnawed at her. She didn't like being so blind, to be left guessing, worrying. But she would have to get used to it. She could very well spend the rest of her days with that uncertainty, wondering if they were still looking for her. Uncertainty was the price for her freedom.

Celeste dug through the top layer of clothes, which amounted to nothing more than a shift and a spare dress, to the treasures below: her mother's pearls and the most precious item of all—the miniature of all three of them together when she'd been young. When they'd been a family. The items might have worldly worth but to her the value was in sentiment; they were all she had of a happier time when she'd had a family; a time before her mother had died and before her father had been entirely in Roan's thrall. Before she'd been sent away to various boarding schools. She'd been safe in those days, loved and cherished.

Carefully, she rewrapped the miniature and tucked it away. The valise had not been rifled through. The miniature had still been wrapped as she'd wrapped it, the pearls still as she'd packed them. Kieran Parkhurst had been kind to send for it, and kind not to have invaded her privacy.

She sat back on her heels. No; she could not start thinking like that. Everything in that sentence was dangerous to her, starting with his name. Everything he'd done or said tonight had been an invitation to encourage a sense of intimacy between them and intimacy inspired confidences. Each effort he'd made had been a pearl added on a string that led towards confession, the baring of her soul, the emptying of the dark reaches of her being.

Kieran Parkhurst was working her in the ways men and women always worked one another: with favours, false kindnesses and score-keeping. He was subtle, too. Some gifts could be refused, but the gifts he offered her could not be. She could not refuse her own valise. She could not refuse a clean dress or shelter, especially the last. Her coin was running low and the Chelsea boarding house would not be safe much longer. Only a fool would say no to what he offered.

So far, he'd wanted very little in return, but he *did* suspect she was holding back. The way their conversation in the garden had ended indicated as much. She thought of the list sewn in the hem of her gown along with her remaining coin. She did have more information to offer, but she was not about to blurt out all of her secrets at once. Her value to him would be sorely diminished. In her experience, she would not be worth protecting once she had no further information to offer him. That was how it had been with David and Roan. They'd discarded people the way rich women discarded gowns after only one donning.

This time it might be different.

The refrain ran through her head as she refastened the valise and slid it beneath the bed. The idea stayed firmly lodged there when Liana came to help her change into the clean white nightgown of Irish linen and brush out her hair. It was not mere whimsy behind the thought. There was some logic to it. She'd run to the Horsemen not only for their protection but for hers as well, because they *were* different from Roan. They were protectors; they had a reputation for selflessness, for good. Things *could* end differently for her this time. 'Could' was not the same as a guarantee, though. She'd made a disastrous decision in the past about what a man could offer her instead of considering what a man *would* offer her. And yet brown velvet eyes tempted her to think beyond the past, to consider the future with a clean slate.

Still, she thought as she said goodnight to Liana and slid beneath lavender-scented sheets, she would not be foolish enough to cast aside her sense of caution, no matter how much a man's eyes reminded her of melted chocolate, or how much comfort she found in the strength of his arms, or in the courteous kindnesses he showered her with. Never mind that he'd guessed her measurements to near perfection, or that with a simple touch he'd made her feel safer than she'd felt in months in what had essentially been her own home.

She turned down her lamp and fluffed her pillows with determined firmness. Kieran Parkhurst must have women falling at his feet. She could not let herself be one of them.

Chapter Five

Kieran was waiting for her in the morning room the next day, dressed for the day in polished tall boots, snug chamois breeches and a dark-brown jacket that matched his eyes. His presence was decidedly masculine amid the more feminine décor of indigo and yellow. Vases of Blue Star irises bracketed the trays filled with morning breads lining the sideboard, and another vase sat in the centre of the round table, calling attention to the contrast between the room and the man who sat in it. He'd been reading a newspaper but he looked up as she entered and flashed her a smile. The morning had not dimmed his attractiveness, nor had the night exaggerated it.

He rose and set aside his paper. 'Good morning, Celeste. I trust you slept well? Did you have everything you needed when you woke?' The morning had also not dimmed his informality. He made free with her first name.

'Yes, and yes!' She laughed. 'Liana is more than capable as a lady's maid, and I thank you for my valise.' She'd have said he'd been too kind to fetch it but they both knew kindness had nothing to do with it. Retrieving her bag had suited them both. She wandered to the sideboard and began to fill her plate.

'Thank you also for the clothes. I do not think I mentioned it last night.' She glanced over her shoulder with a smile. He was watching her, learning her—did she prefer the brioche or the plum cake? Rolls or toast? 'I'm rather amazed you guessed my measurements so well on such short acquaintance.' It was a bit of a lie. She was not that amazed, really. He'd seen through her disguise yesterday simply by paying attention to her hands. Kieran Parkhurst was a man to whom details mattered. It seemed he noticed everything and he used those details to influence his decisions.

Kieran dismissed the effort as being of no consequence. 'It was necessary. When I realised how little you were travelling with, I knew we had to do something about your wardrobe.' He smiled again and her stomach fluttered involuntarily. *Shame on it.*

'Rest assured, I did not go through your things. I merely judged your need on the amount of luggage you had, or in this case didn't have. I don't know a woman in England who could travel with so little—certainly not my sister.' There was affection in the laugh that followed.

She sat down with her plate and a footman stepped forward to pour a cup of coffee. 'You're fond of your sister; I hear it in your voice. Did she decorate this room?'

'Should I not be fond of her?' He smiled and his eyes crinkled at the corners. 'And, yes, she designed this room for us. She said even bachelor homes needed a woman's touch otherwise nothing sets them apart from rooms at the Albany.'

How right his sister was. 'Your sister sounds like a

wise woman.' Celeste sipped the coffee, inhaling the comforting aroma, the smell of morning and home. 'I think it's wonderful when siblings are close. I also think it is rather unusual, at least in my experience.'

'What experience would that be?' Kieran helped himself to a piece of toast from the rack on the table and slathered it with butter followed by a healthy dollop of strawberry jam. 'I find myself intrigued by your background. I assume you have no siblings?'

His tone was genial, his gaze friendly, but he *was* interrogating her. There was no harm in answering these questions as long as she didn't forget what was really happening here—and it would be easy to forget, easy to be flattered by this man's singular attention and to think that he was asking because he was charmed by her.

'You guess correctly. I am an only child.'

He took a large bite. 'I cannot imagine being an only child. My father's home, Willow Park, is not large. My brothers and I shared two rooms between us. My sister had her own room simply on account of being female. She's the youngest of the five of us.'

He waved his toast and laughed. 'We all thought it was highly unfair. How does the baby of the household reckon a private room? But looking back, I wouldn't have wanted it any other way. My brothers and I were always on top of each other, inseparable. We still are— inseparable, I mean—although we're seldom living on top of one another these days.'

There was ruefulness mixed with nostalgia in that comment, she noted with a hint of smugness. He was not the only one who marked details. She found herself smiling. 'Your childhood sounds idyllic.'

'Chaotic. We were always up to something; always tearing around the countryside on our ponies, swimming, fishing, climbing. Falling: off horses, out of trees, down hills. You name it, we probably fell from it.'

He grinned and, caught up in the images of his memories, she was careless with her next words. 'It's a wonder you all survived.' She clapped a hand over her mouth, her eyes wide with the horror of what she'd said.

The joy faded from Kieran's gaze. 'We didn't all survive, though.' He shook his dark head. 'Stepan was good at a lot of things. He was good with horses, good with knives, but he excelled at swimming—which is why the irony is not lost on me, and why it is so hard to accept that he drowned.'

'I'm sorry.' She could barely meet his gaze. 'I was thoughtless.' There was pain in those eyes where joy— real joy—had so recently resided when he'd talked about his sister and his brothers. She hurt too, on his behalf, that something so beautiful had been lost. She didn't know much about that night in Wapping, only that its outcome had made Roan extremely mad. He might have celebrated in company over the success of bringing down a Horseman, but she'd gleaned from private rants that had echoed throughout the house that, while a Horseman was down, there was no body and the weaponry he'd wished to stop from shipping had still gone to Greece.

'Are you certain he *is* dead?' she asked quietly. She asked the difficult question now out of hope, out of wanting to stanch the pain she'd unwittingly set loose amid the comforts of fresh, roasted coffee and jam-slathered toast. She'd not meant to cause him suffering.

'I do not know what else we can think at this point.'

Grief edged Kieran's voice. 'It's been two months. There's been no word from him, and no body from the Thames. The Horsemen have a code: we have sworn to let the others know where we are if we're ever separated. He would not have violated that. What other conclusions can be drawn?' He made the argument with hopeless vehemence.

She felt that vehemence to her core, a sharp stab of grief. She'd known it when her own father had died— the hopelessness, the helplessness, the emptiness. 'When my father passed, it felt as if I'd lost part of myself,' she said quietly. 'That I would never be the same again.'

She'd not been old enough when her mother had died for her to remember what it felt like, only that she felt immense sadness. But she remembered vividly the feelings that had accompanied losing her father. He'd been her last anchor to the world of her childhood. She'd had to grow up fast. 'Not that it's the same to lose a brother as it is to lose a parent,' she added hastily.

'It is different, I suspect.' Kieran set aside his plate, his toast unfinished. 'In some ways, we expect to face the death of our parents. We don't expect to outlive younger siblings. Without Stepan, I feel like the three-legged dog that lived on a farm not far from us—I am minus a limb but I must limp on as best as I can.'

She sipped her cooling coffee to cover the emotion swelling in her throat. Up until now, she'd conveniently set aside the fact that Kieran Parkhurst was a human being, endowed with emotions and feelings, someone who could grieve, who could be hurt by another's actions. She'd come to warn the Horsemen because they were heroes. She'd not thought of them beyond that. The fallen Horseman had, in her mind, been more akin to a fallen comrade in arms. She'd not personalised him, thought of him as a fallen brother or as a fallen family member.

Her quest had become enormously humanised this morning. The man across from her was no longer just a hero with a mission, or a handsome rake who manipulated charm for his own benefit without meaning a word of it. It had been easy to understand Kieran Parkhurst within the confines of that box. To add the extra facet— brother, family member, mourner—created depths she wasn't prepared to navigate. It not only reminded her that he was human, but it also reminded her she was human too. And both realisations made her squirm. Being human was painful. Hurting, loving and losing was painful. Being vulnerable was painful.

Kieran slapped a hand down on the table, making her jump, along with the coffee cups. 'Enough of this, or we'll spend the day feeling sorry for ourselves,' he decreed, that charming smile of his starting to play on his mouth. 'I only began my line of questioning originally to determine if you've ever been to London before.' He wagged a finger at her. 'And you are a sly-boots to derail the conversation.' He fixed her with his gaze. 'So, *have* you been to London before?'

'No.' She offered a smile as an olive branch. 'Although I am quite a connoisseur of boarding schools. I attended the Smolny Institute in St Petersburg for a time, and then, after my father's death, I finished my education in Austria at the school for officers' daughters.' Not because Roan or her father had been officers but because certain people in the Austrian military had courted Roan's favour.

He raised an appreciative brow. She'd managed to impress him and found she couldn't resist impressing a little more. 'I acquired Russian, French and German languages at an early age, all of those being important tools for negotiating life in St Petersburg and Austria and the other places we lived.'

'Duly noted.' He grinned. 'And don't forget Latin. It seems there is a polyglot among us. It can be useful for navigating London as well. London is one of the most diverse cities in the world, full of people from all over the globe.' A spark lit behind his eyes. 'Did you enjoy your time in Russia?'

'Yes, as much as a girl confined to a boarding school can, I suppose. We had cultural outings, and I enjoyed my friends there. One friend, Nadya, would invite me home with her for the summer holidays.' He was fishing for something but what, she could not tell.

'Would you like to have Russian food today? There's a place in Soho we can go to, but only after I show you the rest of London,' he added with mock sternness. 'We must see how London compares to other great cities. Run up and get your hat and gloves; I recall that particular gown came with such things. I'll have the curricle brought round.'

A day out laughing and talking with this man, having this man's undivided attention. The prospect filled her with an unlooked-for sense of pleasure at doing something normal. And yet that same sense of pleasure had her hesitating.

'Do you think it's safe?' She'd thought to spend the

day wandering the garden, reading a book… In short, pent up in the house under the watchful eyes of the servants, half guest, half prisoner, as had been her existence at Roan's.

'I think we'll be moving around enough that, if anyone is following us, it will be noticeable. We're just as safe enjoying the sights as we are sitting in this house waiting for someone to fire a shot through the window or break in through the back door.'

She shuddered at the images. 'Don't say that.' But she saw the logic. 'I'll be back down with my things.'

Celeste's hands shook as she gathered her gloves and hat. She didn't like the last suggestion he'd voiced: that safety was an illusion, even in this elegant house, even with a Horseman beside her. How easy it was to believe one was safe when there were clothes in the wardrobe, a roof overhead and food on the table. In truth, Kieran was right: she was no safer here than she'd been at the boarding house. The only difference was that now she wasn't alone.

Her hand halted on the banister as she headed back down. That was the real danger—thinking that she and Kieran were in this together as a team. When had that transition happened? She'd certainly not thought that way when she'd gone to bed. Last night, she'd been full of wariness and admonitions, vowing to keep her distance, which meant it had happened over breakfast. Coffee, toast and confidences had built a tenuous connection between them, humanised them to one another, for better or worse.

On the one hand, she wanted to be more than an informant to him; it gave her value beyond her information. But the trade for that was allowing him becoming human to her as well and, drat it all, she *liked* the humanity she glimpsed in him. She liked the boy who'd run wild with his brothers in the summer, the man who'd pressed too many coins into the water-trough boy's hand yesterday and the gentleman whose first question was always about her comfort.

He showed his humanity in other ways too. It was there in his touch—a tool he used liberally. She'd lost track of how often he'd touched her yesterday but she remembered how it had felt each and every time. It felt natural, as if he *should* touch her. It felt comforting and powerful all at once, even arousing, the way she'd always thought a man's touch ought to feel but had since come to realise often fell short of the mark.

The comparison drew a shudder from her and she pushed the reminder away. Today was to be full of sunlight and opportunity. There was no room for darkness. She'd need her wits about her if she was going to spend the day with Kieran Parkhurst: Horseman, hero, human. He'd clearly planned to propose seeing the sights of London all along—he was dressed for it—which meant today would be conducted on his terms. What did he think to learn? If she was watchful, what could she learn? So far, Kieran always offered something in return.

Celeste pulled on her gloves with a thoughtful grimace, reminding herself of the rules. He wasn't the first attractive man she'd ever met, although he might be the first she'd actually liked, and a little liking could be allowed—up to a point. She could even flirt with him, also up to a point—that point being when the liking and flirting began to cloud her judgement. At which time, she needed to draw back and restore her objectivity. Well, forewarned was forearmed. At least she'd see the danger now before it was too late.

It was a delight to see London through Celeste's eyes—this woman who'd been educated in St Petersburg and Vienna. Her remarks were intelligent and insightful as he toured her first through the British Museum and then the smaller venue of Somerset House, where the summer show would still remain on the walls for another week.

They stopped in front of Constable's *The Cornfield* and he thought to test her opinions. Mainly he wanted to know if those opinions were her own or if they were merely a parroting of those of the general populace. The painting had been poorly received by the crowds earlier this spring and as a result it had not sold yet, which was unusual for Constable's work. As for himself, Kieran rather liked it because of its details, many of which would go unnoticed or unappreciated by the casual viewer. What would she think?

She shook her head when he asked his question. 'You have me at a disadvantage, I fear. This is not a picture on which someone can pass immediate judgement. If so, it will be found wanting, plain, but it's not.' She went silent, her gaze fixed on the painting. 'Would you allow me a moment?'

Kieran removed himself, taking up a seat on a wide, square ottoman a few paces away to give her space for contemplation. He leaned back on his elbows, taking full advantage of the empty gallery to lounge casually, to study her intimately. He'd like to untie the bow of her hat and remove it—as fetching as it was—so he could see her face. She did like to hide it: the veil yesterday, the wide-brimmed hat today. Perhaps she was aware of how much a face gave away, or perhaps it was her beauty she preferred to conceal. Was her beauty also her bane, something used against her? He would not put it past Roan.

After a while she came to sit beside him, her blue skirts brushing his leg. Her light floral scent—her own scent, the one Luce had retrieved from her room at the boarding house—wafted on the still air of the deserted gallery.

'I like it. I think a botanist would like it even better, but I don't know how the general public would possess the skill to evaluate it.' She began her impromptu dissertation and something roused inside Kieran— anticipation, perhaps? An eagerness to hear what came next? The thrill of knowing that he was about to be treated to something interesting? Or was it the thrill of new attraction, of discovering someone?

She started to build her case and he found himself thirsting for each word. 'It's a summer painting, set at summer's hottest. Water is at a premium. It is the dry season, something that is indicated by the dead tree and the shepherd boy stopping to drink from a roadside pond. He is thirsty, the land is thirsty, as summer reaches its climax.'

Kieran shifted on the ottoman, acutely aware of her choice of word. Did she mean it to be provocative? Not for the first time he wondered if her flirting was intentional. Or maybe it came naturally, like those low, sultry tones that marked so much of her conversation. 'Also, the botanist will appreciate that all the right flowers are in full bloom; the grasses are at their summer zenith.'

Dear God, he'd never found a discussion of art as arousing as he found this. 'Are you seducing me?' It was teasingly asked but seriously meant. Perhaps she was playing a game of her own, trying to equal the scales he'd tilted his direction with a hundred little comforts. He did not want to play that game—a game where she used sex as a bartering tool or currency. Nor did he want it to be a game that she played often. Not that he thought she was a virgin—she definitely wasn't—or that he even wanted her to be one. Virgins and their timid rules held little appeal for him.

She denied seduction most coyly, her denial all but proving the opposite. 'Might I not have my own interrogation? I am trying to work you out as much as you are studying me.'

Kieran laughed. 'I have *not* interrogated you. I merely asked a few harmless questions at dinner and at breakfast.'

'There are *no* harmless questions.' She slid him a smile and a sideways glance from beneath the brim of her hat and laughed with him.

'Not even about Constable?' Kieran could not help but make the argument.

'Especially about Constable. You were testing me. You wanted to see how deeply my education runs. Do I parrot opinions I've been given or have I used my education to critically form my own?' She gave him a smug look. 'I trust I've passed.'

'Refreshingly so.' The education that had been lavished on her had not been wasted even if it had been marked by disruption. Her story at the breakfast table had revealed a girl who had perhaps craved stability but had instead been moved around Europe from school to school and left alone to navigate new languages, new cultures and new people. He and his brothers had gone off to school too, but they'd gone together—he and Caine, and later Stepan and Luce. They'd come home together between terms. He'd not faced school, had not faced leaving home, alone. Family had been with him every step of the way. She'd had only herself. It spoke of enormous courage, perseverance and loneliness.

He rose and offered his arm. 'Enough of museums for today.' If they stayed any longer, he'd be tempted to put the walls to other uses than hanging art. 'How do we compare to the Hermitage?'

She took his arm, the sound of their heels clicking on the hard wood. She flashed him another of her beneath-the-brim glances.

'*Is* there any comparison? The Hermitage is an empress's private collection. The British Museum is free to anyone with a curious mind. One museum makes learning available to all while another argues that education and learning is not for the masses. I saw a small part of the Hermitage because I attended Smolny—Catherine the Great's school for girls. But otherwise, unless one is invited to the Hermitage, one will never see the art within its walls.'

He could tell that angered her. 'Are you a Decembrist, Celeste?' he whispered, a chuckle rumbling in his chest at the discovery. What a multifaceted delight this woman was. In other circumstances, this would make for a most pleasant affair.

'There is some irony in that, isn't there? A Smolny

education is meant for aristocrats and yet it fostered in me the preference for a society that promotes the opposite, a society that protects its people instead of raising up the wealthy on the backs of the poor. I am sure Catherine the Great would not be pleased with the results.' She gave him a wry smile, her eyes challenging him, perhaps seducing him—a thought he found quite palatable. 'Do I surprise you, Kieran Parkhurst?'

'Only in the best of ways.' She was intelligent, beautiful, politically aware…passionate. Did she know how passionate? It was there in her words, in her voice, in her gaze. Was that passion tried or untapped? It was hard to tell with her, and perhaps that was part of her charm, part of her intrigue. What a change she offered from the empty-headed debutantes he'd been dancing about.

'There are people in London you'd enjoy meeting. Prince Nikolay Baklanov and his wife, Klara. He is from Kuban in the Russian south. He feels much as you do. He owns a riding school in Leicester Square. Klara's father is the Russian ambassador, and almost a Decembrist himself, although he did not participate in last year's uprising.' He made a note of the connection. Klara would be good, discreet company for Celeste.

'Do you want me to meet people?' Celeste made a questioning knit of her brows.

'Do you not want to make friends?' Kieran held the door for her as they exited into bright sunlight. It was past noon and the day was promising to be as hot as yesterday.

'Friends imply permanence.' She opened her parasol and twirled it overhead. 'I do not know how long I'll be here.' Ah, spoken like the boarding school miss who'd been uprooted too many times and who was now wary of investing in such friendships for fear of their inevitable loss. He could lay the blame for that at Roan's feet.

He helped her up onto the curricle seat. 'Where will you go?' She did not answer, which was perhaps for the best. He wanted her to rethink that decision when this was done. To be alone was always to be at a disadvantage. He could help her build a life here. There could be more Constable, more sparring, more discussion. He jumped up beside her on the seat as his tiger ran to the back bench. 'Hyde Park is next. I think we should cool off with a row on the Serpentine. There's nothing like being on the water on a hot day.'

He needed to cool down his thoughts as well as his body. Celeste Sharpton was an intriguing novelty in a London devoid of company at present, and a striking contrast to the girls he'd spent the Season with. That was all, he assured himself.

He supposed there was also the residual collateral of his brother's marriage, which had him more seriously considering the quality of his female companionship. If Caine could find the courage to wed, perhaps Kieran could too. There was no denying that his brother's marriage had stirred old dreams he'd given up on. But that didn't mean he should mix business with pleasure. This woman held the keys to finding the man who'd been responsible for Stepan's death. Celeste Sharpton was business only and that was all she could be.

He dropped a hand to his right side. He hoped the exertions of a row on the Serpentine would help him remember that.

Chapter Six

The Serpentine sparkled beneath the sun and a light breeze blew on the water. Oaring the boat gave Kieran an excuse to rid himself of his coat and roll up his shirt-sleeves while Celeste sat in the bow, prettily arranged and wielding her parasol for shade. The sight of her provoked a thousand thoughts, many of them prompted by manly insights. What had life been like for her with Roan? That man did nothing unless it gained him something. What had she done for him that had warranted him allowing her to live under his roof, to gown her, to financially support her? *Had* he used her beauty? Was that why, now, she was careful to conceal it?

She was no innocent miss. The way she'd so subtly flirted with him today at Somerset House suggested more of that worldliness he'd glimpsed yesterday in the church. She seemed to be inured to the world of men. He did not hold it against her. Often a woman's survival depended on that expertise. But these were questions he could not ask her…yet. If he rushed his fences, she would become skittish and the wariness he'd worked so hard to minimise would return. She might flirt with men but she didn't trust them. That was a part of her personal past he'd not yet unwrapped.

As they rowed near another boat, a feminine hand waggled in greeting as a male voice called out, 'Lord Wrexham, a beautiful day is it not?'

Kieran managed a tight smile. 'Lord Hadley, well met. Lady Elizabeth, good day.' He gave an especially hard pull on the oars and ensured his boat passed theirs quickly.

Celeste twirled her parasol, a smile teasing her mouth. 'Not friends of yours, *Lord Wrexham*?' She invited explanation.

'Hadley's a pompous, self-righteous fellow who thinks too much of his own consequence, and I spent a few weeks this Season squiring the lady around for work purposes only. I needed access to her father.'

Her father had been a potential player in Roan's arms sabotage, along with Caine's father-in-law, but that didn't need to be said. He wanted nothing to remind them of their business just yet. Today was for peeling the onion, as his grandfather called it. Onions and people had layers, both of which were delicate and must be revealed subtly, which meant slowly. He was starting with personal details of seemingly little consequence to their business. He told stories so that she'd reciprocate. The exchange would be the beginning of a bond, of comfort between them. From there, he would move on to the more strategically important questions. That they were also enjoyable discussions was a bonus.

'And the "Lord Wrexham"? I was unaware you had a title.' She was doing a little onion-peeling of her own but that was how it worked. To peel another's onion, one had to peel their own as well. Otherwise, it would indeed look more like the interrogation she'd accused him of and less like the conversation he wanted.

'My brothers and I were awarded titles for our efforts at Wapping.' He leaned on the oars, letting the boat slow and drift. 'It's a Welsh earldom, on the border with Cheshire. It's nothing grand. From all reports, the estate is in disrepair, although it has untapped resources of coal beneath the ground.'

'Have you not been to visit?' she queried and he heard the want in her voice—the want for a home, for a place that one never had to move from, a place where a girl who'd lived in boarding schools could put down roots and know that those roots were not grappling for purchase in rocky soil.

'The title is blood money for Stepan.' Kieran picked up the oars again and steered them a little further out, away from the other boaters. 'As if a price could be put on my brother's life, on his sacrifice.' That still galled him. 'To rub salt in the wound, those titles are only on loan unless we meet certain conditions within the year.' That galled even more.

Celeste leaned forward, her slim brows knitting. 'That sounds intriguing. What might those conditions be?'

'Marriage. The Crown has decided it is time for the notorious Parkhurst boys to wed. The ton's mamas are tired of we rakes flirting with their daughters. The public at large is in the dark about the details from Wapping. All they know is that the titles are for patriotic service and an inducement to wed. Matchmaking mamas have been throwing their daughters at us all Season, quite a change from the usual.'

'Your brother wed.' She trailed an elegant hand in the cool water.

'Yes, but not one of *them*. His marriage was a bit of a scandal. Mary's father wanted a duke for her, not an upstart marquess with an inconsequential title and a not-so-inconsequential reputation.' There was more to it than that and likely she knew what that was without him trotting it out. Mary's father had been deeply implicated in the arms sabotage at Wapping through his own ignorance of with whom he'd been doing business—Roan himself, although Roan had used an intermediary. 'You'd like Mary. She's practical and kind and honest.'

'Commodities that are not always available in our world,' Celeste offered with a hint of sharpness. 'I suppose I should be pleased you think I would like her, that I also value those things.' She gave her parasol a twirl. 'Does the ton know you and your brothers are the Horsemen?'

'No. It's an interesting duality. It's not a secret, per se. Grandfather's world knows who we are, but the ton is more facile. They see only what is right in front of them—four, I mean *three*, men in need of wives to bring them to heel. Marriage is everything for the ton, there is nothing else.' His gaze drifted to the shore, fixing on a lone rider ambling along the path to the pace of their little boat. The paths were not crowded today. The rider could have chosen his pace and yet he seemed to let their boat dictate it. He'd have to keep an eye on that. It might be nothing but, then again, given the circumstances, it might be something.

He let them float a while longer, letting her conversation wash over him as she regaled him with stories of boarding at the Smolny Institute and he indulged in pretending he'd found someone like her to court; that he, too, could make a match as Caine had. All the while he kept one eye on the shore until the rider disappeared. Good riddance. Perhaps it had been nothing after all. There was only one way to find out.

'Time to go ashore. I was thinking ices at Gunter's and perusing some shops.' If the rider was following them, he would reappear. Kieran discreetly loosened the knife in his boot. He would be ready for him.

The rider did not appear again as they continued their day, but Kieran still couldn't shake the sense of being followed. He turned a few times only to discover no one of note behind him or across a street. He was starting to think he was his own worst enemy. Having fabricated a foe at the Serpentine, he'd let that fabrication take over his senses. He thought about cancelling the visit to Soho and the Russian eatery but then thought better of it. He didn't want to worry Celeste over nothing he could prove and, if they were being followed, the fellow would turn up there.

The question was what was the intention? Were they being followed by someone with the intention to do them harm or with the intention to report back to someone else? If it was the latter, it would explain why the rider had disappeared. His job was done. But Kieran's was just beginning.

Something had been bothering Kieran since Gunter's. Despite the relaxed atmosphere and cool ices, Kieran had been tense. As a consequence, it was also bothering Celeste. 'Are we being followed?' she asked as he swung her down from the curricle, his tiger running to hold the horses' heads.

His hands lingered at her waist, and his mouth was close to her ear in a most intimate fashion that sent ripples through her imagination. This close, she could breathe in the scent of him—cinnamon and cloves with a hint of something smoky undercut with vanilla. He smelled more like the autumn that would come than the summer that lingered relentlessly, but he also smelled like comfort. 'Possibly, but we may have lost him,' he murmured.

'Or he found what he needed to know and has sheared off,' she replied in low tones, unmoving. Anyone passing them on the street would think them lovers instead of co-conspirators. She held his gaze, willing him to see the message in her eyes. If there had been a follower, it meant Roan's men were here and they'd found her.

'That's a big if. Don't do that to yourself,' Kieran cautioned, tucking her arm through his and strolling down the bustling street. 'We're going to enjoy our evening until we have reason not to. This is one of my favourite places in the city because it has become so diverse. Some people complain because the property values have fallen, saying it's no longer a prime neighbourhood for the ton and their sort. But I think it teems with life. There's French émigrés, and Russians and Poles, and people from all over Europe looking to make a life.' He pulled her aside. 'Shut your eyes and just take a listen. How many languages do you hear as people pass by? How many different foods do you smell? You could eat yourself across the Continent here in a single evening.'

She did as she was told, letting her worries leech

away as she breathed in Soho and listened to its rhythms. She heard it—the Russian, the German, the Yiddish, the Slavic languages she couldn't quite distinguish from one another, and dinner-time smells from the cafés. Oh, they were delightful reminders of other times and other places.

She opened her eyes and smiled. 'I smell *piroshky*.' She was hungry, she realised. Her nerves had settled. If Kieran thought it was safe to be out, then it probably was. And, she reasoned, if Roan's men were here she wouldn't have many more nights of freedom left to her. She ought to seize the opportunity while she could.

The streets were crowded with clerks returning from work and merchants closing shops. Unlike Mayfair, which was empty, the denizens of Soho wouldn't be departing for country estates and cooler climes. Due to the heat, bistros had moved their tables outside to the pavements so that the streets took on a festive air as people sat down to dine.

The Russian eatery wasn't far and Kieran was welcomed as a regular customer by the owner—a largish man called Grigori who wore a huge white apron—and his son, also Grigori. 'There will be music tonight, and dancing. Will you stay?' Grigori said to Kieran. 'Show off for the lady a little? You need to bring Nikolay by. He doesn't come as often as he used to.'

Kieran laughed. 'We'll see. Our plans may not be our own tonight. We've come for your wife's *piroshky*, and don't tell me there aren't any left. We could smell them streets away.'

'And vodka,' Grigori suggested.

'No vodka tonight. I need a clear head.' The banter between the two men faded.

Grigori nodded solemnly. 'Horseman business tonight?'

'Possibly. But not before *piroshky*.' Kieran smiled and the big man bustled off, shouting orders.

'I like this place.' Celeste looked about her at the others seated on wooden benches at long wooden tables. 'Imagine the stories that must be dining with us. Everyone looks ordinary, but they're not. On the surface, the proprietor has a very simple goal: to feed his countrymen the food of the motherland while they're away from home. Yet, he is first-name friendly with a Kubanian prince, an ambassador's daughter and an English espionage agent. Who knows who else is on the list? Those are just the ones I know.'

'No one is what they seem. I learned that early.' Kieran gave a shrug.

'Not even you?' she challenged playfully.

'Not even me. Not even you.'

'You still think I'm working for Roan? That I am trying to infiltrate your home, your circle?' She grimaced, surprised, confused and even dismayed. 'I thought we'd made more progress than that today. If Roan wanted infiltration, he'd have sent an assassin.' How interesting to note that she cared about his opinion.

'*Are* you an assassin?' he asked, and she thought she detected some teasing. He was playing with her now, which meant he did indeed believe she was ally and not enemy. It was an adequate sop to her pride and she made her own tentative attempt at teasing in return.

'Now you're being ridiculous. If I was, you'd already

be dead. I wouldn't be spending the day telling you stories about boarding school!' She huffed. 'I would have quietly slipped a knife between your ribs at the church and been done with it. This is far too much work and I'm not that good of an actress.'

The *piroshky* arrived, hot and fresh. Kieran held her gaze until the waiter left. 'To clarify, I meant my remark earlier more personally. None of us are what we seem on the outside. Everyone hides something: scars, doubts, the past…' He smiled. 'Now, eat.'

He bit into his *piroshky* and she would not forget the expression on his face. Gone was the Horseman, gone were the strategies and games he so carefully employed. In their place was the look of someone who was fully enjoying the moment. She yearned for that, craved what was in his face and in his being at that very point in time. 'Oh, this is heaven—absolute heaven,' he murmured. 'Try yours.'

She bit into it, the savoury spiced meat and the sweet crust flooding her mouth while memories flooded her mind. It was as good as he'd said, and all thoughts of testing one another's trust fled. There was only this moment, this meal, this man. Grigori came to the table and regaled them with stories that had them laughing. She'd not enjoyed an evening as much as this one, perhaps ever. The sun went down, gaslights were lit and this part of Soho came alive. Musicians tuned up and Grigori clapped Kieran on the shoulder as he prepared to leave the table. 'I expect to see you dancing.'

Couples moved into the dancing space and Celeste was filled with the urge to join them. It was irrational: she didn't know the steps; she didn't belong with these people; she was a stranger to them. She certainly didn't have any business encouraging further intimacies with Kieran.

Watching him oar the boat in his shirtsleeves, arm muscles flexing, had been temptation in the extreme. She'd not wanted to get out of the boat. She could have watched him row all day. It didn't help that he flirted naturally with his words, with his dark eyes that lingered just long enough on her mouth to make her wonder what it would feel like to kiss him or to be kissed by him. Such thoughts were proof she needed to exercise some restraint. But those reasons fled when Kieran held out his hand. 'Shall we? We can't disappoint Grigori.'

'You're not serious?' Celeste protested with a half-laugh. 'I don't know these dances.' Her protest was valiant but not-surprisingly short-lived. She wanted to dance with him; wanted to look up into that wide, laughing smile he flashed so easily; to fall into those dark eyes; to lose herself in the dance; to lose herself in him, if only for a moment. Surely she could afford that small luxury for a few minutes?

He laughed her protest away or perhaps he read her thoughts and knew the resistance was pro forma. He tugged her after him before she could launch another protest she didn't mean. 'You can do it; it's just a polka-style dance and no one cares if you know all the steps. Just keep moving and follow my lead.' Oh, he *was* good fun. Under different circumstances he would be quite intoxicating. He'd overwhelm a girl until she forgot why she was wasting time resisting.

His hand was at her waist, her hand at his shoulder as he grinned down at her, those eyes skimming her mouth for the briefest of moments. 'Ready?' He breathed as the music began and he swung them into the fray. Really, there was no other way to describe it—just a glorious fray of turns, trot steps and whirling. It was the most fun she'd ever had on a dance floor. Her dances were usually careful, structured steps full of protocol, nothing like this.

She was breathless with laughter when Kieran pulled her up hard against him, his mouth at her ear, his expression grim. 'Follow my lead.'

'I have been...' Her laughter trailed off mid-sentence. This wasn't about the dance anymore. Her gaze darted about the crowded room. What had he seen? She looked past his shoulder towards the entrance and froze. Ammon Vincent was here. Dear God: Roan had sent his bulldog after her. Her heart raced. She stumbled, paralysed with fear.

'Eyes on me,' he coached, righting her. 'Keep smiling, keep laughing; give nothing away.' He danced them through the crowd towards the back of the small restaurant. With a final spin, he twirled them into the kitchen and grabbed her hand with single word, 'Run.'

In that moment she knew *this* was why he'd danced with abandon, and why he'd eaten the *piroshky* as if it had been his best meal. Because, for a Horseman, it might be—a last meal, a last moment, particularly when he was accompanied by Cabot Roan's missing ward.

Chapter Seven

They dashed through the kitchen, zigzagging through the maze of tables and workers chopping vegetables. She cursed as her hip caught on a table edge. Kieran tugged her forward, pushing her past a hot stove as they pelted towards Grigori, who held open the back door, shouting *'Idti! Idti!'* Go, go. And they went, racing out into the narrow alley with its brick walls and rubbish piles, Kieran's hand gripping hers. She held on tight. To let go would be to be lost, to be caught by Ammon Vincent, her worst fears come to life.

She risked a glance backwards, knowing she would see Vincent pounding behind them, brandishing his ever-present knife. Instead, the threat came from ahead of them: two hulking men blocked the exit. She stifled a scream and would have stopped running, which was no doubt what the men expected—to stop would allow them to close in—but the men had shown themselves too early.

Kieran had time to adjust. He kept moving, bending low to his boot top, coming up with a blade and throwing it in a single motion that was too quick to anticipate. The first man gave a grunt and went down. Stunned, his partner was slow to react and Kieran took advantage, using his momentum to charge, ramming his head into the man's stomach. The force pushed him up against a wall and Kieran was on top of him with a fist to his gut… No, not a fist—another blade from somewhere. The man's eyes went wide and then he sagged. Kieran let him fall, the light in his own eyes feral when he turned to her.

He grabbed both blades and returned them to their hidden sheaths. 'Come on.' He grabbed her hand and led her past the bodies with a single command. 'Don't look.'

But she'd already looked, already seen the blood. How long had that taken? He'd dispatched those men in seconds. Gone was the laughing man who'd led her onto the dance floor. He was all Horseman now and the Horseman had saved her without a second thought. The transformation was overwhelming, a powerful reminder of what was real and what was not. This pursuit through a dim alley was real. Those beautiful moments at Grigori's had been an aberration.

They turned a sharp, dark corner and he drew her up against a wall, his eyes full of onyx fire as his body pressed into hers, protecting and shielding even as he offered rough counsel. 'Get yourself together. There's no time to fall apart. Forget what you saw. My curricle is across the street, over my shoulder. My tiger can drive like a fiend. I'll be right behind you, but if something happens, if I'm waylaid…'

She knew what that meant. If there were more men, if they were attacked when they broke cover—or, worse, if he went down and couldn't follow—she was to go on without him. Celeste started to protest. He gave a silencing shake of his head and she shut her mouth.

'Just keep going, head for the townhouse. Tell my people to harness the travelling coach. It will take them fifteen minutes; they're fast. Grab what you need but do not delay. Fifteen minutes, no more—do you understand?' His eyes were ablaze with the light of battle. She nodded, fighting back shock. To disobey him, to fail him, would make his efforts meaningless. He'd killed for her. She would succeed for him.

'Good. On my signal, run like hell.' He gave a final look over his shoulder, unpinned her from the wall and gave her a shove towards the street. 'Go, now!' he barked, and she went, dodging between unsuspecting passersby, skirts in one hand as she ran. The tiger saw her coming and leapt to the driver's box.

She clambered inelegantly up beside him, breathing hard. 'Is there a pistol?' Kieran had thought to cover her escape, but she could damn well cover his, as long as she didn't have to shoot too far.

'Yes, miss, it's beneath the seat.'

Celeste reached for it, her eyes on the alley. Her heart quickened, if such a thing was possible given it was already beating fast. There was Kieran! He moved through the crowd, his height making him an obvious target. If someone was looking for him, they'd find him. She watched, breath held, expecting Ammon Vincent to emerge, but luck was with them. No one followed. Kieran jumped on the back bench and gave the signal to go. He nodded towards the pistol. 'What were you planning to do with that?'

'Shoot anyone who came after you,' Celeste replied

coolly, settling the pistol across her lap as the tiger put the team in motion. She wouldn't put it away just yet. Who knew who they might meet in the dark? They were safe for the moment but the fact remained that they'd be found. It was only a matter of when and where.

Kieran's tiger was every bit as good as Kieran had claimed and they reached the townhouse in record time, Kieran barking out the orders for the coach and team. 'Upstairs with you—be fast, Celeste.'

She was. She grabbed her valise from under the bed, her travelling gown with its secrets and a hairbrush from the dressing table. She heard Kieran's heavy boots in his own chambers and then the sound of raised voices downstairs.

Kieran pounded down the corridor. 'Hurry, Celeste, we've got to go.' He raised his voice for all to hear. 'Everyone—out, out. Leave now, except for the footmen,' he shouted. 'Cooks, maids, boot boys, out—all of you. Scramble!'

The order was given not a moment too soon. She was behind him in the hall when the brick shattered the decorative window set high above the door. He pivoted instantly, throwing his body over her once more, glass raining down on them in sharp shards. Her fear spiked. This brick meant Roan's men were *here*! Ammon Vincent was here at this house where just last night she'd felt safe. He might even be outside this very moment, waiting to take her, to claim her.

She froze for a moment, overwhelmed with the realisation that violent men were after *her*—this was all happening because of her, because she'd chosen to run. In theory, she'd known she'd be followed. But the reality was something different entirely. Twice tonight, she'd seen proof that they would not hesitate to use violence on her. Roan had punished her before, so she ought not to be surprised, but this was a different type of violence, a bloodier type than the sort Roan meted out, and it was frightening.

Kieran's hand closed about her wrist with a tug. 'Don't think on it. Come on, out the back, to the mews. They can't hurt you if they can't catch you.'

Or him, she thought. They would hurt her but they would *kill* him.

The rest of the house was deserted as they raced through, except for grim-looking footmen turned soldiers who now stood armed at the windows and doors. The staff had indeed scrambled with alacrity and efficiency. Kieran ushered her out to the mews where the coach waited, along with four outriders and Tambor. 'We should be clear,' one of them said. 'We took out the fellow watching the alley.'

Kieran gave a curt nod. 'Eric, sit the bench with Bert. I'll ride Tambor with the outriders for a while. It will give us an extra gun if we need it. Later, you and I can switch. Celeste, let's get you in the coach.'

Kieran helped her inside with instructions. 'If there are shots, get on the floor and stay there. There are pistols beneath the seats but don't be a heroine.' He shut the door firmly behind her and was gone. She was alone and the realities of the evening had her shaking. His comfort would have helped. What she would give to be wrapped in his arms, to be held against the strength of his chest and to feel the warmth of him against her fear.

What a silly thing she'd become in such a short time!

She reached for a hand grip as the carriage picked up speed. She'd been on her own for two weeks, journeying to England. She'd been on her own since well before then, too. Goodness knew she had no allies in Roan's household. Perhaps it wasn't so much a testament to her weakness but to Kieran's charm that she found herself wanting him with her. He'd put himself forward as capable and reliable, among other things, all of which she hungered for, all of which she craved deep down.

The carriage lurched and she stifled a surprised scream. Outside, she could hear Kieran raise his voice and fear reignited. She told herself pursuit was expected, inevitable. Ammon Vincent and his men had made it to the house, and they were *close*—close enough to have thrown bricks through windows. Now, men were outside risking themselves—Kieran was risking himself—for her. She did not want to be responsible for the death of another Horseman, not when her intention in coming here had been to save them.

There was the sound of galloping hooves and the sharp report of one pistol then another. She hit the floor, groping madly for the gun box beneath the seat. Vincent would not take her without a fight. Outside, there were yells; the coach sped up erratically and she was thrown against the door, the gun box sliding away from her. Damn it, she hated this! Hated not knowing what was happening outside. Was Vincent even now taking aim at Kieran or had Kieran got a shot off first? She hated not being in charge of her fate. She was entirely dependent on the men out there. There was no more helpless feeling than knowing that things were happening to her that she could not control. It was the height of unfairness. Once again, men were deciding her fate.

There was another yell. Was it Kieran? At least that meant he hadn't been shot. She'd have loved to look out of the window and assure herself of his safety. But she might get herself shot in the process and if not that, she'd most certainly encounter his wrath. All she could do was lie on the floor and keep herself safe.

It seemed she lay there for an eternity, listening for clues outside, feeling for them in the rhythm of the coach. Their speed was consistent now, London likely far behind them. They would be in the countryside with the summer dark falling full around them. There were no voices, no yelling; surely, all was safe now? The coach began to slow. They were going to stop. She picked herself up off the floor and climbed back into her seat just in time.

The door opened and Kieran thrust his head inside. 'Are you all right?' She nodded and then he climbed in, shutting the door and giving the signal to go. So much for a longer stop, but at least she wasn't alone.

He looked windblown, the battle light in his eyes temporarily banked in exchange for alertness and it was... appealing. He had been her champion tonight. She'd not had one before, and it was a rather intoxicating sensation despite the fact that it didn't mean anything. This was his job. As long as she held information of value, *she* was his job.

He looked about the carriage, his gaze noting the pistol case half-out from under the seat. 'I thought I said no heroics?' He arched a brow, scolding.

'I had to do something, anything, to not feel helpless!' she shot back. 'It was horrible to be in here and not to know...' She could not restrain the questions any longer. 'What happened? Was anyone hurt?'

'We are unscathed.' Kieran gave her the most important fact first. 'They caught up with us on the outskirts of the city but we were ready for them.' He stretched his long legs. 'I've sent two outriders to confuse the trail and lay a decoy. With luck, Roan's men won't know where we've gone, and by the time they realise it they will have followed the wrong track.'

'Where *are* we going?' she asked, another sign of how helpless she was, how dependent she was. Nothing about this plan was her own.

'We're going to Wrexham.'

To the home he'd never seen—to Wales. To a place where she might be safe from Roan. She thought of the home they'd left behind. 'Will the townhouse be all right?' She hated thinking his house might be destroyed because of her.

'There's a fair chance it might be all right.' His broad shoulders shrugged. 'There's no one there to hurt so the house serves no purpose for Roan. Why waste energy on it? The house is just bricks and mortar. It holds no secrets, no people of interest that can be held against the Horsemen for leverage. It's just a place. Any message he wants to send through violent actions has already been sent tonight. He is hunting us, even as he knows the Horsemen are hunting him. What he isn't sure of is whether or not he is running us to ground or if we're luring him out.'

'He won't find us in Wales.' She would cling to that idea as long as she could. At present, she cared less about the Horsemen finding Roan than she did about Roan *not* finding her. 'And the decoy you've laid ensures he won't find us on the road.' To her dismay, Kieran offered no assurances.

'How many men do you think Roan has sent?' He was all seriousness now.

'I thought perhaps two or three,' she began, uncertain. That no longer seemed a likely number. It didn't matter so much to her if there was one or seven—as long as a particular man was among them, it would be dangerous for her. Ammon Vincent was known as 'the Bulldog' for good reason. He would stop at nothing to find her for purposes she did not allow herself to contemplate.

'We've seen more than that tonight. I am guessing at least seven, three of which are temporarily out of play now while they lick their wounds.'

Kieran fixed her with a hard stare. 'I think you've greatly under-estimated your worth to Roan. A notorious dealer in weapons has sent seven of his henchmen after a single young woman. He would not go to all of this effort simply to stop a warning. It makes me wonder what else you know. What else is he afraid you will tell us? Given that tonight I have been chased through the alleys of Soho, shot at, had a brick thrown through my window and been forced to abandon my townhome, I think it's time you and I had a talk. What's the rest of the story, Celeste?'

Chapter Eight

She'd known it would come to this—the request for more information. He'd protected her tonight and killed for her without hesitation. He would expect something in return, something that would make his efforts worthwhile. She'd hoped it wouldn't happen so soon. To give away too much would be to lose her leverage. And yet, to give away nothing might cause him to lose interest, to think she was leading him on. Her sense of fair play felt it only right that she told him. He had put himself at risk for her. He'd earned, if not her trust, then at least *something* from her. After all, protecting her *had* been in his best interest. If anything happened to her, it would also happen to her information. She had to give him a piece, but not everything: just enough to keep him with her, to ensure she remained of interest to him.

She drew a breath. 'I have a list. I will give you half of that list when we reach Wrexham and the other half once I am free of Roan.'

'Is this list important to me?' Kieran folded his arms behind his head and gave every impression of a man settling in for the long haul.

'Of utmost importance, I would think. It contains the

names of the men who were involved in the sabotage attempt at Wapping, and on that list is the name of the explosives expert who was to be rowed out to the ship that night.' She held her face impassive, her gaze steady, willing herself not to give away an iota of her desperation. She had nothing else to bargain with.

'My God, you should have said so at once.' A hungry dark flame leapt in his eyes.

'You know I could not. To give everything to you all at once exposes me. As you pointed out yesterday, I would no longer have any use, no longer be worth protecting, if I had nothing left to give.'

'I would give you my *word*,' he growled defensively, clearly insulted by her suggestion.

She shook her head. 'A word? Am I to stake my life on the word of a man I barely know? Tsk, tsk, now who is the naïve one?'

He fumed, clearly not liking having had his honour called into question, but she had no room for principle at the moment. This was about the practicality of staying alive. She needed insurance he would keep her alive, that he wouldn't leave her to fend off Ammon Vincent on her own.

His fuming subsided. 'I see your point. I do not like it, but I understand it.' He crossed his arms over his chest. 'How did you come by the list?'

'The same way I came by a lot of pieces in Roan's household. It was lying around.' She let that bit of information drop in the hope it might provoke curiosity. Instead, it prompted scepticism.

'You may have overplayed your hand there.' Kieran

grimaced. 'Roan's too careful. He wouldn't leave sensitive information out in the open for just anyone to see.'

'I wasn't "anyone". I was his ward, and I was never expected or allowed to leave.' She leaned forward in earnest to make him understand. 'When he sent for me after my schooling finished, he didn't just bring me into his home, he brought me into his world, whether I wanted to be there or not. There was no choice for me. It was made clear that I would not leave the grounds of his estate. On the rare occasion that I did, it would be under heavy escort. I was to serve as his hostess and, if the time came when a marriage could be advantageous, it would be a match made in his world, to a person of his choosing, and then I would act as his worm in another man's house.'

She shook her head. 'He could leave about whatever material he wanted. I was going nowhere. I was no threat to him. I was less than his prisoner. A prisoner might have hope of escape, of freedom in the future. I was his slave. He owned me in every way possible and the law allowed it.' Her throat clogged a little at saying the words out loud. That last had been her father's betrayal. She would never know what had possessed her father to make Roan her guardian.

'Dear Lord, what a nightmare that must have been.' He breathed deeply. She watched his eyes, waiting for pity to move in those velvety depths, and steeled herself for the inevitable. Pity would be a natural response from a man like him. He was a warrior. He was strong. He'd never be another's captive.

'Yes, it *was* awful, but I don't want your pity,' she said quickly, as if she could ward it off. She didn't want him to feel sorry for her. Pity was an emotion reserved for the weak, the pathetic.

'Is that what you see in my eyes? If so, look again.' Kieran pierced her with a dark stare that unleashed a complicated warmth—not only the warmth of comfort, of knowing she was safe with him, but the warmth of want, the precursor to a heat that could burn with something hotter—desire, something she could not allow. She was on the run and the running didn't stop here, didn't stop with him. It couldn't stop with him.

'I'm not in the habit of pitying survivors.' Kieran's voice was low, seductively inviting in the privacy of the coach. 'I admire survivors. I admire strong women. You are both, to have made it this far on your own. You got out, and you've lived to tell about it, if you want. It's your story, but it's a long way to Wrexham. Would you tell me?'

'Yes.' She breathed the single word. She would tell him. He would understand. Not because he'd experienced something similar but because he'd lived the opposite—the absolute freedom of summers at Willow Park with his brothers, embraced by the security and support of a family.

Kieran was used to hearing horror stories—stories of loss, of desperation and of revenge. These were the things that motivated informants to come forward, to sell information in dark rooms across Europe and to meet clandestinely with strangers. There were certainly all of those elements in Celeste's tale but the true darkness of her story came from what it lacked. Kieran recognised the absent elements within minutes: any mention of family, the security of routine, or the comfort and anchor of home. What security she had came from her own wits; what home she had came with the price of pleasing Roan and adhering to his wishes.

'School was a shield, a buffer of sorts for me; it kept me from understanding what Roan did and what my father did for him. I didn't realise it at the time,' she began. 'Instead, I resented my schooling. I moved establishments every few years based on where my father was working. To a young girl, it seemed that I was being pulled away just when I was getting settled, just making friends. Every time I moved, it took longer to settle, longer to believe that this time I would get to stay, although I would convince myself in the end—all to no avail.'

She looked up and met his eyes. 'I think now that Roan may have planned it that way. Not for me, especially, but for my father. I've come to think that Roan didn't want my father to get too comfortable somewhere. If he did, he might have friends, or allies, who would have been able and willing to help him get out.'

'Did he want out?' Kieran asked carefully. She'd trusted him enough to tell him her story. That was no small thing, but he didn't want to ask for too much too soon and scare her off, even as the questions mounted in his mind.

'I like to think he did.' Her gaze returned to her lap, fixed on her hands. 'The truth is, I didn't really understand what my father did until I was out of school and Roan had sent for me. I thought my father was a banker, a financier—and he was, just for a corrupt dealer in firearms. There was so much I didn't understand until later.'

She let out a sigh. 'When my father and I were together, just the two of us, we had this story we would tell each other—how we would stop travelling and get a house in the Alps. It would have a balcony we could sit on wrapped in blankets and watch the snow fall. It would be quiet. No one would come to bother us. We would play chess and cards all winter. In the spring, we'd walk the paths to the village; in the summer, we'd swim the mountain lakes, grow a garden and put up food for the winter.'

When she looked up, the wistfulness in her gaze stole his breath and something deep within him wanted to give that vision to her. 'Father and I dreamed of a simple life. No more chandeliered ballrooms, ten-course meals and all the fuss that goes with that.'

'But it never happened?' Kieran prompted gently.

'It almost did. My father had written to me that he had a place for us. When I finished the spring term, we'd go. He died in April, just three weeks before we were to leave. I was away at school. Roan sent a letter to the headmistress, telling her the news, and the instruction that I should spend the summer with a friend. I never got to go back to my father's home to collect anything of his. It was just one of many places that my father had lived but it was where I'd been with him last. Roan had everything packed. I didn't even go the funeral. It was too far to come, Roan said.'

She'd been sent away with no chance to say goodbye to her remaining parent. The inhumanity of it cleaved his heart. 'You were still a child.' Not that Roan would have cared—men, women, children, he used them all when it suited his purpose. 'How old were you?'

'Sixteen. I had two years of schooling left. Roan paid

for them, saying it was what my father had wanted. He told the headmistress he felt obligated to give me a home, to bring me out and to provide for me, and of course he'd been named my guardian. There was no reason for the school not to pack me up and send me to him when my education was complete. The generous donation he made didn't hurt either. I didn't protest much. I had no idea what I was getting into. I knew him only as my father's colleague and friend.

'He was very good at cultivating my services. He was liberal with his flattery and he started small— asking me to help with a menu for this or that dinner, and complimenting my choices. I was happy to help. I was living in a beautiful house, wearing fine clothes, and there was no hint of anything being off. He was busy. There were people coming and going from his office all the time. After I'd been there a year, he asked me to attend one of the dinners, to be his hostess. I was thrilled. He ordered me a beautiful gown of aquamarine French silk with a very sophisticated cut. Too sophisticated for a nineteen-year-old, but I didn't make the connection at the time. I was too busy being excited by the prospect.'

She hated herself for it; that much was evident. She blamed herself for being gullible. No wonder she'd resented it when he'd said she was naïve. She was trying so hard not to be, trying so hard to ensure that she wasn't taken in again, as she'd been taken in by Roan.

'You can't blame yourself. You had no idea.' Kieran offered the meagre absolution. No doubt, she'd told herself that a thousand times.

'That's not good enough. There were so many signs

and I missed them—all of them. Once I started to hear things and put things together, it was too late.'

He wanted to ask what those things were, along with a hundred other questions racing through his mind. Did she think Roan had had a hand in her father's death? Who did Roan entertain? But not tonight. Tonight was for her to tell her story, to tell him about her hurt. Tonight was for him, too. The more he knew, the more he could help her.

Whoa, careful there! came the warning from the small part of his mind not caught up in her story.

The goal was shifting. What had begun as a fact-finding mission to obtain information about Wapping had become a mission of protection. Keeping her safe meant keeping the information safe and now, here in the confines of the coach, it had become something far more personal. Wapping, Ottomans, Greek independence and the Four Horsemen aside, *he* wanted to help *her*. Hearing Roan had co-opted a young girl to sit at his table, to entertain other corrupt men, had deepened his understanding of why she'd run. He'd not been wrong earlier—she had run for herself as much as she'd run for the Horsemen—and it inflamed him that she should have been put in such a position.

She gave a dry laugh. 'So *now* the pity comes. You want to save me, like your water-trough boy the other day.' She gave a shrug and swept the length of her hair over one shoulder, a move that he found provocative and inflaming in an entirely different way.

Kieran chuckled. 'You saw.' She was observant, a skill that would keep her alive, and perhaps *had* kept her alive this long.

'Yes. I saw you stuff a fistful of coins in his hand.' She laughed and then softened her tone. 'Even when you were worried about our safety, it did not override your concern for him.'

'Am I not allowed to want to help you? You're in an untenable position, just as Samuel was. I will grant that the urge to help you is not unlike wanting to help the boy, but the motive is different. Perhaps I do want to help him out of pity for his circumstances, but that's not what motivates me to want to help you.'

'No, *I* have a list,' she said sharply, eyes sparking in challenge. 'That's what motivates *you*. Keeping me alive is also what keeps alive the chances of finding your brother's killer.'

'That's not all that motivates me,' he argued, offended by how mercenary she made it sound. But to suggest he was motivated out of concern for her would push too close to the pity she abhorred. 'I would protect you whether you had a list or not. I need you to believe that.'

He knew that she did not, despite his assurances, given both verbally and nonverbally. She still feared he would drop her when she had nothing else to offer. Now he knew the reason why. She'd been betrayed by men her entire life—her father and Roan, the two men who were supposed to have protected her, and who knew how many others? For all that she'd shared tonight, and as dark as that story had been, he suspected a darkness still remained untapped.

What had she done for Roan? What had he made her do?

'I don't know why you would do anything for me without the list. There'd be no reason. Helping me would make no sense. Without the list, I am just a stranger,' she countered. 'What would you want from me in exchange?'

'You are in danger. That is enough.' She was in danger from more than Roan. He'd seen her face at Grigori's tonight. It had been the expression of horrified recognition. 'You knew the man at the restaurant. Who is he?'

'Roan's vilest henchman, the one no one wants to come after them. His name is Ammon Vincent.' She shuddered as she said it, confirmation that his hunch had been right.

Kieran leaned forward and reached for her hand. It was cold. He rubbed it between his own. 'Let me ask that question in a different way. What is he to you?'

'Roan's men are all violent. I know how Roan exacts retribution from those who have crossed him.' She was being evasive. He wouldn't accept that—for her own safety he could *not* accept that. She was hiding personal history here...to protect herself in some way, perhaps?

He gripped her hand to give her strength. 'You are prevaricating. Now, tell me—what claim does he have on you to cause you to turn white, to stumble into paralysis, you who have braved two weeks on the road alone? You are not a woman who freezes, but you did tonight, twice.'

He could almost hear her swallow, and her heart beat in fear, as if saying the truth out loud would conjure the man himself. 'Roan has promised me to him.'

Chapter Nine

Good God… She'd not been offered in marriage but simply promised, like a prize of war. A reward to Vincent; a threat, a punishment, for her. Roan's barbarism knew no limits. Kieran felt the tic in his jaw jump at the implication of her news. He'd seen Vincent. He was a brute of a man, his body thick with muscle, his eyes full of meanness.

Kieran ran his thumb over her knuckles, soothing and stroking. 'I will not allow that to happen.'

He moved across the carriage to sit beside her and wrapped her in his arms. He understood better now the source of her fear tonight. It was fear that stemmed not just from the physical violence she'd witnessed but also from the long-seeded mental fear she carried with her. How awful this evening must have been for her, trapped inside here, knowing that her darkest enemy was outside, coming for her and what awaited her should her escape fail—should he fail, this man she barely knew.

'Are you all right? Do you want to talk about tonight? Any of it?' he murmured. They'd talked about the details of the subject: the men he'd killed in the alley; the brick through the townhouse window; and the almost instant conversion of benign, helpful footmen into a small militia.

'Those men in the alley…' she began haltingly.

'Would have taken you and killed me without hesitation,' he said sternly. 'This is a game with no rules, with no sense of fair play.'

'I know.' Her voice was quiet. 'But it is one thing to know it and another to have it directed at you in reality.' She gave a sigh, part resignation, part determination. 'I'll do better. I must do better. I froze, if you'd not been there…'

'I was there, so it doesn't matter. Tonight was frightening, and what lies ahead will be frightening too. It's all right to be scared, Celeste. We'll get through it. For now, there is nothing more to be done except to recover. Rest, lay your head on my shoulder and sleep. You are exhausted. We'll drive through the night and I'll keep watch. No one will harm you—Horseman's oath.'

She laughed a little at that and he was glad to hear it. The shock was passing. She stifled a yawn but she did as he'd instructed, her head finding its way to that indent between his shoulder and chest. 'Horseman's oath? What is that?' she asked drowsily.

'I'll tell you when you wake up.' He reached beneath the seat for a blanket and draped it across them both. 'Things will look better in the morning.'

At least, he hoped they would. The pursuers would be off their scent, and all they had to do was survive three days on the road to Wrexham—no problem. He'd done such things before and more. He'd swum a prize horse *and* its rider to safety in the Irish Sea after a royal ship had gone down in a storm. He and Tambor had navigated the desert wilds of Algeria to meet with Bedouin chiefs in an attempt to pre-empt what was sure to be French presence in the region in the next few years. Both had been far more difficult than evading detection on British coaching roads. He had inns to support him if he needed them, he had supplies in the coach and a guaranteed safe haven waiting for him at the end of the road.

Kieran looked down at the chestnut head nestled against him. But a woman changed everything. Women always did. A little snore escaped her and he smiled. She was truly exhausted if she was so deeply asleep already. Perhaps, too, it was a sign of her growing trust if she felt she could sleep in his presence. She was right to give it. He would see her protected, and he'd proven it tonight.

He shifted his position to accommodate them both more comfortably and began to think. He did his best planning at night. The first item to decide was shelter. They wouldn't use the inns: her protection outranked her comfort and he didn't think he could safely offer her both. Stopping at inns would mean they could be tracked, remarked upon. She was too beautiful to escape notice and trying to hide that beauty only called more attention—the wrong attention—to her. Camping it would be. He could send his coachman to town for food.

He ticked that item off in his mind. Food was no worry. The coach actually converted into a bed. She could sleep inside, unless she wanted to sleep outside under the stars with him. He wouldn't mind that. He liked sleeping beside a woman, falling asleep to her soft breathing and waking up to her soft warmth against him, although it was a luxury he didn't indulge as often as he'd like. A Horseman couldn't sleep beside a woman he didn't trust. Otherwise, he'd risk ending up with a knife in the gut. To prevent that, he left his lovers long before sleep could claim him.

He stretched his legs and yawned, careful not to bestir Celeste, and let his mind wander its checklist. Food and shelter were accounted for. Privacy would be a different matter. Camping was an inherently intimate activity. There were no doors or screens to protect a person while bathing or conducting other ablutions. He hoped she wouldn't mind the potential indignities.

He was encouraged by the story she'd told of her father's dream to live in the Alps. Maybe she'd actually enjoy a few days' camping. She was certainly hardy enough and brave enough to tackle the outdoors. She'd been brave tonight. It would be a long while before he forgot the sight of her at the curricle tonight, pistol in hand, determined to cover his own flight when he was the one who was supposed to protect her.

Yes, Celeste Sharpton was definitely brave. It was one of many things that made her so appealing and so dangerous to him personally. Mixing women and business had been disastrous for him. It was not hyperbolic to say even deadly. Common sense dictated he keep Celeste at a distance so that he did not repeat the errors of the past, primarily in assuming that trust was implied with intimacy, or to equate sex with intimacy. Intimacy was not a guarantee of one's safety, an axiom that was more easily affected from afar. The closer people got, the more blurred the lines became.

And she would *use* him. She'd already admitted she'd run from Roan to warn the Horsemen but also to protect herself. She was using him as her shield. When that protection was no longer needed, she'd leave. She might not have said the words outright, but she'd said it in other ways, demonstrated it in other ways. She believed he'd leave her if she had nothing to offer him because it was likely she'd do that in his place. It was why she kept asking for his motives. She couldn't conceive of someone simply doing something because it was right.

And yet, the lesson of keeping his distance was hard to learn with her. Despite his best counsel to himself, he didn't want to keep his distance, not entirely. He wanted to know her; his body answered to hers, roused to hers, craved her in an almost palpable way when they were together. His body made it clear it wanted to be more than her bodyguard or her short-term protector. His body would like to be her short-term lover, even though that would require breaking all the promises he'd made about mixing business and pleasure. Her body had made it clear it would not mind, which made resisting the temptation that much harder. They were both willing to explore whatever lay between them.

Maybe it was possible. His mind argued for compartmentalisation: perhaps they could separate the two as long as he knew where the lines were drawn? Which begged the question of whether compartmentalisation was even possible. Could someone truly just have part of a person and ignore the rest? Could someone just give part of themselves? Could he? Compartmentalisation was a convenient argument but perhaps not a realistic one. That was how trust was betrayed—in thinking that parts of a person's nature could be overlooked. In truth, reality was always still there, waiting to surface. Repressed reality was not an erasure of reality.

He yawned again, recognising the signs of a losing fight. He would not resolve this dilemma tonight. Sleep was coming for him despite his promise to keep watch and he let it take him. The world was safe enough for now.

She was safe. It was her first thought upon waking. Safe enough to wake up slowly, to gradually let her senses acclimatise to the world around her sense by sense. Was there anything better than knowing she was safe? She took in a deep breath. Yes, there was bacon and coffee. The delicious smells of morning. She must be dreaming.

Celeste sniffed again. It smelled enticingly real. There were sounds, too: men talking; was that a sizzle and a pop she'd heard? Surely, she was making that up? She sniffed again, savouring the smell. She opened her eyes, knowing that as soon as she did reality would come flooding back to her. And it did: the dancing in Soho; the flight from London; knowing Ammon Vincent was behind them somewhere, hunting her. But there was another man now, too.

The night of fear and flight had been tempered by Kieran's presence, his cool head in heated circumstances. The night had been marked by his grip on her hand, the strength of his gaze when he'd looked at her, the power of his words: *I admire survivors...* He'd kept her going when she would have frozen, when she would have had nowhere to run. That she was alive and whole this morning was due to him. To repay his efforts, she'd fallen asleep against his shoulder, with his arm wrapped around her. How long had she slept like that? When had he laid her down? She hoped she hadn't snored.

She wiped a hand across her mouth, another concern coming to her: she hoped she hadn't drooled. She ran her tongue across her teeth. Ugh; she wasn't...fresh. She needed to clean her mouth and teeth; she needed to wash.

Her conscience mocked her. *You are on the run for your life. These are silly considerations.*

Yet perhaps they were tokens of how safe she felt with Kieran—Kieran, who'd not shown pity when she'd told him her story. Kieran, who had instead insisted she was brave.

The smell of bacon beckoned. Her stomach growled, reminding her she hadn't eaten since the *piroshky* last night. She smoothed her hair as best she could and stepped down from the carriage, prepared to meet the morning.

And morning had never looked so good. Or so...shirtless. She nearly missed the bottom step of the coach at the sight of Kieran's broad shoulders and muscled back bent at a makeshift basin, washing. Her gaze drifted down his back to lean hips and to a masculine curve of buttocks encased in tight breeches. She'd not realised how tight those breeches were without a coat covering them. Without the coat, nothing was hidden and it created the wicked urge to want to see more, to see that exquisite derrière bared.

She might have spent the rest of the day staring at that exquisite backside if his arm hadn't moved, drawing her gaze up the muscled length of his back to watch him wash, an intimate act that had her blushing.

'Ahem, Miss Sharpton—breakfast?' One of the outriders approached with a plate loaded with bacon, toast and, miracle of miracles, eggs.

'Oh, thank you.' She tore her eyes away long enough to take the plate. The bacon smelled delicious, but Kieran *looked* delicious. Kieran reached for a towel and turned round, shaking water droplets from his dark hair. He dried himself and she had to remind herself not to gape. This was the body that had defended her last night; the body that had shielded her from shattering glass; the body she'd fallen asleep against. He was an atlas of muscled ridges and planes, all directing the eye downward to where his sculpted iliac girdle disappeared into the waistband of his breeches and...a scar. The jagged line disrupted the perfection of him but added to it. Perhaps a little imperfection enhanced the masculine beauty of him; it was a reminder of the life he led and the dangers he faced. They were real—knife-tip real.

'Good morning; I trust you slept well?' He tossed away his towel and reached for his shirt, unfazed by being caught bare-chested. Something secret and knowing flared in his dark eyes. He'd caught her looking and appreciating what she saw. He'd caught her wondering how it would feel to trace the lines of his torso to their terminus. 'I see Eric has offered you breakfast.' He nodded to the plate in her hand.

She'd forgotten it for a moment. 'Oh, yes. Eggs are a luxury on the road. Wherever did you find them?'

Kieran laughed and bent down to pour coffee from a blue speckled coffee-pot nestled in the fire, showing off the flex of his buttocks in the process. 'We had them with us as part of our supplies. But they cracked during the journey last night. We had to cook them this morning or lose them for good. Eggs never last but they make a good first-day-out breakfast.'

He came to stand beside her, smelling clean from his ablutions and making her keenly aware of her own less than fresh state. He was making it hard to think. He was telling her their plans, and she ought to listen, but all she wanted to do was look.

'We'll take time this morning to rest. The horses need to recover, even though the timing is not ideal. I'd rather not travel the horses in the heat of the afternoon, but they put in a long night, and so did my driver. Bert will sleep this morning in the coach while you and I stretch our legs and take some target practice. Eric and Matt will patrol our perimeter. They'll keep an eye out for any passersby, but we're far enough from the road that we shouldn't draw any attention.'

'Of course.' She nodded, her mind still trying to move past the sight of a shirtless Kieran while his mind had quite literally thought of everything for everyone. She eyed the wash basin covetously. 'Do you think I might be able to wash first?'

Kieran grinned and followed her to the basin. 'There's soap—it's mine—and a clean towel and washcloth. They'll dry before we have to leave.' He reached down and lifted a tin pitcher. 'And there's this. It should still be warm.'

Celeste gave a gasp of delight. 'Did you say *warm*?'

'Unless you'd prefer cold water? There's a stream not far from here; I could arrange it,' he teased.

She cut him off with a playful punch to the arm—a rock-solid arm. 'Don't you dare arrange anything. Warm water will be just fine. Give me a moment to get my valise.'

He snapped his fingers and Eric ran up with her bag. 'I've already thought of it.'

'You really do think of everything.' Although, she hoped he couldn't read her thoughts at the moment. They were quite decadent. She rummaged for her toothbrush and comb. 'You will spoil me.'

He took the bag from her when she found her items and set it aside. 'You may feel differently in a few days. Most women would not consider camping with four men along the roadside spoiling.'

She was aware of him behind her. She could feel the heat of his body as he bent to her ear. She slid him a sideways glance and a smile, his playful tone spurring a little daring of her own. 'Maybe I'm not most women.'

'You certainly are not.' His tone turned sober and his gaze lingered on her mouth, making her blood go hot with an attraction she was becoming unable to school. 'Be careful what you're asking for, Celeste. I might be inclined to give it.'

After last night, she'd be inclined to receive it. The blood, the violence, the fear had all served as reminders that life was short and possibly abrupt. There were no guarantees. Waiting carried its own danger of missing out.

Her body was all too ready to launch the argument that she didn't want to miss out on whatever Kieran Parkhurst offered. Her mind was all too ready to support the argument with the logic that it needn't mean anything beyond comfort, beyond simply celebrating life and what their bodies were made for. There would be no harm in that, only pleasure.

He took a step back from her, a rakish gleam in his eye. 'Maybe *you* deserve a little spoiling. Take your time. I'll clear the camp for you.' He turned and raised his voice, giving orders. 'Let's give Miss Sharpton some privacy while she freshens up. All except you, Bert. You get to sleep.' There was general laughter and rustling as his crew moved off. Another gift.

She'd not expected that; she had not asked for it. She wanted to fall into those kindnesses without fear, but to do so would be to enter the province of fools. She could not for a minute let herself forget that she'd bought these kindnesses with the promise of her list, or that safety was momentary. Ammon Vincent was out there and sooner or later he'd find her. For now, she had a few days on the road, a few moments out of time to enjoy a fleeting sense of freedom, and it was entirely up to her what she chose to do with it.

Chapter Ten

The place Kieran had chosen to camp was along a stream that managed to remain vigorous even after the efforts of a hot summer to deplete it. He'd set up make-shift targets along the bank and was waiting patiently for Celeste when she finished washing. The two pistols from the gun box beneath the carriage seat lay ready and gleaming.

'We'll start with loading,' Kieran instructed and she envied him the ability to switch roles so effortlessly: one moment the carefree flirt, the next moment the deadly Horseman, the protector, the bodyguard. Her own emotions were still running amok, her mind filled with images of him at the water basin.

'You need to concentrate,' he scolded, and she knew she'd missed something important. 'I want you to be entirely proficient with these firearms from start to finish.' Gone were the laughing eyes that had teased her—a reminder that freedom must always be fought for and that it came with a cost. She had to be prepared to defend hers. 'I hope you will not have to face Roan or Vincent alone, but one must plan for all contingencies.'

Celeste didn't like to think of those contingencies,

which necessitated that Kieran Parkhurst, Horseman extraordinaire, wouldn't be beside her at the crucial moment. But she did not argue. At some point, she would need to part from him and she would need the skill he was willing to teach her now.

In slow, deliberate movements, he showed her how to load the balls, how to add the powder and how to prime. 'Now, you try.' He handed her the other pistol and she followed his instructions as best she could, feeling herself glow when he praised her efforts.

'Excellent. Now, we shoot. Be sure your aim is good because, even if you're proficient at reloading, it will take twenty seconds at best to do it and we seldom have ideal conditions. Under pressure, nerves may get the best of you, which is understandable, but excuses won't keep you alive. No one is going to stop and wait. The enemy will keep coming. Only the most seasoned soldiers don't fumble under fire. In my opinion, the only shot you can count on is the one you have loaded. You may not get a chance to reload and try again,' Kieran said sternly. 'Make the shot count. Take your time. A hurried shot will not serve your cause. After you fire, you will be exposed. A lifetime can happen in the twenty seconds that follow.'

She swallowed hard against the image his words conjured: the dark alley and the men in pursuit. It was hard not to imagine a scene in which Ammon Vincent charged her while she struggled to reload. She shook off the fear. No; if Vincent came at her she would not miss. She would make sure of it.

'I don't mean to frighten you. I mean to be honest with you. Too many people feel empowered by a gun and they overplay their hand. Let's see you shoot. You've shot before but every gun is different.'

She was eager to show off and to make up for a lack of focus earlier. Maybe she even wanted to impress him with her passable skill. Celeste extended her arm, steady against the weight of the pistol, coolly sighted the target and fired, the gun jerking up at the last moment. The shot went slightly wide of her intended mark. *Drat.* She'd hoped for better.

'Good enough,' Kieran complimented her, striding forward with the other pistol. 'It would have hit your target somewhere, and that would have disabled him, giving you time to get away. The kick was more than you were expecting. You can always adjust your aim to compensate.'

He passed her the other pistol and took up a position behind her, aligning their bodies so that they stood in perfect profile together. His hand curled over hers as they aimed the pistol, the spicy smell of his soap catching her nostrils and his nearness making it hard to think of firing shots. 'Ready, on the count of three...' he murmured at her ear and together they made the shot, hitting the mark this time. 'Did you feel how we controlled the recoil?'

She'd felt more than that. She'd felt the power of his body behind her—the press of his hips against her buttocks, the muscles of his thighs and the semi-aroused state of his manhood. She could dismiss it on the grounds that such intimacy was required for the drill. It was no different from riding astride before him on Tambor. And yet, the echo of his words sent a delicious tremor through her: *be careful what you're asking for, Celeste. I might be inclined to give it.* It was proof he felt it too—this want, this curious hunger that sprang to life between them.

That they were *both* willing to explore it was a dangerous combination. There was no one to check them, nothing to stop them except her own good sense. But once that was gone then her own objectivity, her own ability to see actions for what they were, would be gone too. Caution reared its head. Was that what he wanted? Was he flirting with her, *seducing* her, in the hope of prising the list from her before she was ready to give it up?

She didn't *want* to think like that, about him especially. She wanted instead to think that last night had changed things between them; that facing Roan's men had brought them together in a common purpose. But she had to be careful with those thoughts. She'd been wrong before. She'd been wrong about David, to her great detriment. She knew now that intimacy was different for men and that sex could be merely physical, a source of short-term pleasure only. Whereas for her, sex was emotional, a source of intimacy and the foundations of trust. She could not make that assumption again.

Yet, even knowing that, the temptation continued to nag—that this time it could be different. That this time she would be smart enough to see betrayal coming. She could forestall it and protect herself against it. She could have the best of both worlds. Dear Lord: she was talking herself in circles, hoping that when her thoughts looped back round she'd have answers—or, more particularly, answers that she liked and that would allow her to do what she wanted. And what she wanted was Kieran Parkhurst as a lover. *Foolish, foolish girl.*

She turned and stepped away from the lure of his body. 'Why are you doing this? You already have access to the list. We've already negotiated for it. You don't *need* to do anything more.'

'I *want* to do more. You need more than my protection. You need to be able to provide your own.'

'Why do you care?' She kept coming back to that. Why would a stranger do so much for her? 'Horseman's oath?'

He put their pistols away. 'Come and walk with me.' He led them down to the stream and they strolled beneath shady oaks in silence before he spoke again. 'The Horsemen are sworn to the care and keeping of England and to the welfare of those who protect her. For that reason alone, you are entitled to whatever I can offer you. You are the key to bringing down one of Europe's most notorious and elusive dealers in firearms, a man who not only makes money from war but also proactively perpetuates war for personal profit. As such, he works against the hopes of the Vienna Congress and is responsible for the deaths of countless soldiers when peace might be made.'

She shuddered to hear Roan discussed—and by extension her father—in such bold and blunt terms, all of which were true. Roan dealt in war and thrived on it.

'And so did I, for a time. I lived on the proceeds of his ill-gotten gains,' she reminded him. She hated knowing it was something she could not undo.

'You didn't know any better,' Kieran assured her.

'Not at first. I knew, though, long before I ran. And, even when I knew, I did nothing.' That was, perhaps, her greatest sin. 'I stayed until I had to run for *me*. The threat of Ammon Vincent and being caught eavesdropping were what pushed me into it.'

Those words would give her the distance she needed from him. Once he understood she was not honourable, there would be no more lingering gazes on her mouth. He would despise her now. Any minute, he'd think what she'd been thinking since she'd eavesdropped on Roan's conversation—that if she'd run earlier, turned against Roan sooner, Wapping might not have happened and his brother might still be alive.

He stopped and faced her, taking a determined step towards her until she felt compelled to retreat, her back coming up against a tree trunk. Something fierce blazed in his eyes, desire sparking and naked. She'd not bargained on that for a response and more than she'd bargained on her own body thrilling dangerously at the knowledge that he wanted her.

'Why do you do this, Celeste? You seem compelled to drive a wedge between us. First with your scepticism, now with this idea that you are single-handedly responsible for what happened in Wapping. It would seem to me that you should be seeking the opposite—that you would want to draw us closer, to make us a team, not enemies. You did not like my scepticism when we first met and I do not appreciate yours now. You want me to trust you but you want to be allowed not to trust me. It can't work that way.'

He moved closer to her, eyes hot, voice low. 'I want this to work, Celeste. I want to keep you safe. I want to see Roan finished, not just because it's business but because I want it for you.'

Her breath caught. There was no hiding her reaction

from him. He was close enough now to see how his words affected her, how his nearness made the pulse at the base of her neck race, and embarrassingly so, as if she were a schoolgirl in the throes of infatuation. And yet, she could not look past him nor could she rally the resources required to step away.

He leaned against the tree trunk, an arm bracketing her. 'I want this for you because I find myself attracted to you. I've made no secret of it. You're beautiful, canny and brave. You intrigue me. Everything you tell me leaves me wanting to know more.'

He drew a finger along her lips and shock waves of desire crashed through her. 'This is not about Roan or Wapping or any of that. This is just about you and me. You intoxicate me, Celeste, and I think I intoxicate you too.'

He traced the column of her throat with a finger, letting his hand rest over the pulse note at its base. 'Don't deny it; your body doesn't lie.' His hand moved to cradle the nape of her neck, his mouth at her ear, uncovering her secrets one by one. 'Your pulse races, your sea-glass eyes are bright with desire, and if I were to touch you beneath your skirts you would be wet. There is no shame in it. You are not alone in this. I am hard for you. You know this is true—you felt me against you when we fired the pistol. Your desire is reciprocated. The question is, what shall we do about it in the short time our paths will cross in this world?'

She let out a shuddering breath. This must be what it felt like to slowly go insane, to feel oneself let go of reason's anchor. He had her mad with wanting when she knew this was not the time. With a few simple words he'd made the wanting seem logical. This passion between them was to be for a short time only, until their paths diverged once more. There need not be consequences, or a future. Such promises made a liaison safe from betrayal.

Her own wicked whisper added fuel to the fire of her want. *If not now, when? If not him, who? You deserve to be spoiled. Let him be the one.* And her body answered: *yes, yes...*

His mouth moved to claim hers and she raised her face to meet him. Mouth to mouth, tongue to tongue, their bodies pressed hard against one another until it was not clear who had started it. It didn't matter. They were in this together now. For a short while, she need not be alone.

She reached for him then, sliding her hand between them to the hard length of him, but he covered her hand firmly with his own, his mouth at her ear.

'Your pleasure first.'

Then his hands were beneath her skirts, pushing them back, the late summer breeze cool against her exposed skin, delicious and decadent as her desire ratcheted. She bent her knee, hitching it about his hip to help him, to hurry him. He kissed her, laughing against her mouth. 'Patience. It will be worth the wait, I promise.'

She nipped his lip in a lover's retaliation. 'That's an awfully arrogant presumption, sir.'

'We'll see, minx.' He laughed at her throat, his hand moving against her, his finger tracing the intimate folds of her which proved to be its own kind of tantalus.

She gave an accusatory moan. 'You are priming me

like your pistol.' Teasing her towards oblivion would be more accurate.

'Is it working?' His mouth was on hers in a series of slow kisses, his hand going at last to that hidden place secreted within her labia.

'Heavens, yes...' She breathed. Her nub was swollen and throbbing. She pressed against him, seeking release. She was greedy, hungry in her desire—perhaps because this was for her alone, perhaps because she'd chosen this for herself. The release came quickly, explosively, and hot. She closed her eyes and leaned her head back against the oak trunk, face turned upwards to the sky. Her mind traced the rivers of pleasure as they fanned out from her core, sending twin ripples of peace and repletion through her.

'Ahh...' she sighed in soft delight. 'If only this feeling could last.' She let her head loll against the tree and slowly opened her eyes to find him watching her, his own eyes dark with desire. *He* was enjoying this; he'd found a kind of pleasure for himself in helping her achieve hers. 'Do you think there's a name for this feeling?' she asked dreamily.

He pushed back a lock of her hair and gave a lover's smile. 'The French call it *"la résolution"*.'

She tugged at the waistband of his breeches and flashed him a coy smile. This fun, this play amid pleasure, was new territory for her and she was enjoying it immensely. 'Shall we find *la résolution* for you too?'

He stayed her hand, his eyes serious even as desire flickered there. 'Only if you want to. This does not have to be a trade. You don't owe me.' His voice was rough, edged with want, making it evident what those words cost him.

She *did* owe him, though. He'd saved her life, he'd given her shelter and so much more. But she wouldn't argue the point. She stretched up on tiptoe to reach his mouth with hers. 'I want to,' she whispered against his lips.

A woman in charge of her passion and his was heady indeed. When he added in the allure of the out of doors on a warm summer day, the seclusion of the stream and oak trees, there was no resisting. When she reached for him this time, he let her have him. She danced him about in a half-circle until they traded places. 'You may need that tree trunk before we're done,' she warned in a throaty whisper that held the promise of great delight.

He answered with an intimate laugh. 'That's awfully arrogant of you, minx.'

To which she replied with a twinkle in her sea-green gaze, 'We'll see, sir,' as she worked the fastenings of his breeches and took him in hand.

The first long stroke brought him to full attention. The first pass of her thumb across the surface of his cock-tip had him reaching overhead to grab the sturdy oak branches for purchase, and he held on for dear life. When had a woman's touch felt like this? It was like pleasure's agony and ecstasy's ache all at once, each stroke a wicked allegory of what it must be like to slide inside her.

She thumbed his tip again, playing with the moisture at its slit. 'You do not disappoint, sir.' Her voice was husky with desire; her eyes glittered like hot emeralds. 'Your cock is magnificent.'

What a delicious word that was coming from her mouth, and a bold word too: *cock*. There wasn't a well-born debutante in London who used that glorious word.

He pressed against her hand and she scolded, 'Patience. It will be worth it.' Her other hand reached for the tender sac behind his cock and gave a gentle squeeze that had him nearly breaking the branch he clung to.

'You are a mind-reader,' he rasped. It was hard to put two words together, let alone a whole concept. All he wanted in this moment was release. She knew it, too, the rhythm of her hand speeding up. He felt his body tighten and gather. She felt it, too. A satisfied smile took her face, and then she let him go, letting him claim the cliff that waited for him and jump off it into pleasure's free fall, while she held him in all his pulsing glory as he panted and spent until he was exhausted, purged and whole again for the moment.

He let go of the branches. 'You're right. These are the best moments.' His own breath still came short. He'd been entirely winded by her. He gathered her to him and she came, wrapping her arms about his waist and laying her head against his shoulder. Somewhere, a bird sang. In the stillness, there was no threat, no Ammon Vincent, no Cabot Roan. There was just the two of them and the wholeness they'd created together. If only that could last. How peaceful that would be—not just for her, he thought, but for himself as well. One gave up peace when one became a Horseman.

A breeze blew and he raised his hand to catch the wind. 'Autumn is coming,' he said softly. 'The wind feels different at the end of summer. It's still warm but there's a cool current beneath it now.'

She sighed against him. 'It was the first of September yesterday.' He supposed it had been. He'd been too busy squiring her around the city and escaping Roan to take note.

'The first of September is my mother's birthday,' Celeste explained. 'She would have been forty-seven.'

Only eleven years older than he was now. Forty-seven didn't seem terribly old, after all. 'What happened to her?' he asked quietly so as not to disturb their peace.

'What happens to many women. She died from complications of childbirth.' He felt her give a rueful smile against his chest. 'For a week, I had a baby brother. He was so small, and cute. Mother would let me climb on the bed beside her and hold him. I'd stay there for hours, all three of us snuggled together.'

She turned her green eyes up to his face. 'It might have been the happiest week of my life. Of course, I don't remember exactly, but I remember how that week felt. Father would come and read aloud when he was done with work. We were a real family. And then it was over. She went fast, in the night, before a doctor could come. Without her, my brother didn't thrive. Father said he didn't take to the wet nurse. He died the following week.'

Kieran thought of his own mother and the luck and ease she'd had bringing five healthy children into the world. He thought of his sister, Guenevere, who was expecting her first child in December, and his heart cracked a bit for the woman in his arms. 'I am sorry,' he murmured into the dark halo of her hair. 'Do you want children?'

'Wanting a child and the practicality of raising a child

are vastly different things. I would not bring a child into Roan's world,' she said solemnly.

'Nor would I bring a child into the Horsemen's world.' He held her a little tighter, feeling as if he'd found a kindred spirit who understood the dilemma between wanting and the reality of having. Satisfying that want was the height of selfishness. They stood a while longer, silent and still beneath the oak. He was conscious of the deep peace of the moment. He would not disrupt this until he had to or until they disrupted themselves.

But he could not let this last for ever. The day was advancing. 'We should go back,' he suggested quietly. 'It's time to get on the road. Bert will be waking up and the horses will be ready to stretch their legs.' He reached to pull a leaf from her hair. 'The weather's good today. Perhaps you'd like to ride with me? Tambor can carry two.'

'I would love nothing better.' She smiled and, as they strolled back to camp, he felt her fingers lace through his. This was progress and it was both comforting and complicated.

Chapter Eleven

In the span of a few hours everything had changed and yet nothing had changed. The thought chased itself around Celeste's mind as she lounged against the strength of Kieran's chest, her body far more relaxed sitting before him on his horse today than it had been a few days ago. It no longer felt strange or invasive to sit in the vee of his thighs, to feel the muscles of those thighs press about her. His body was known to her now, as hers was to him, and deliciously so.

What did their walk by the stream mean? Anything? Nothing?

And so, the thought came full circle again: everything had changed; nothing had changed. The latter was the implicit promise they'd made to each other. They were people of the world, experienced in the body's pleasure. Passion had many explanations; it was a natural outgrowth of having faced great danger and survived. It needn't mean anything more than that. It didn't change their circumstances.

No matter what they'd done beneath the oak or why they'd done it, it didn't erase the reality that Roan and Vincent were tracking them. There were only two outcomes. Either Roan or Vincent would eventually find them, or Kieran would find them. She was existing within the endgame, after which her fate would be decided. The point was there would be an 'after'.

These days on the road and the days that would follow in Wrexham would end, just as her days at various boarding schools had all ended. Like so much in her life, this interlude would be temporary. She could only allow herself to fall for Kieran Parkhurst with that single understanding firmly entrenched in her psyche: *this* was not permanent; it *would* end, and with it her association with him. She would go on from him and from Wrexham. Holding that understanding close would lessen the pain of parting.

Already, she didn't want to think about leaving him. Already, she liked him far too much on far too short of an acquaintance for the simple reason that, beyond the jaw-dropping body that possessed the ferocity and power of a warrior, and the dark eyes that promised a girl he could and would make all her dreams come true, Kieran Parkhurst was *nice*. And nice was hard to find in her world. He was nice to everyone, from the water-trough boy to someone like her.

It was that last piece that she found compelling. He could have strategically chosen to feign niceness to her in exchange for whatever it might woo from her— information or sex—but he'd had nothing to gain from being nice to the water-trough boy at St Luke's. He'd likely never see the boy again, and yet he'd done what he could in that moment to ease the boy's needs. She'd learned under Roan's tutelage that men were always willing to appear nice to a beautiful woman; pretending was easy. A person could always tell a man's true character by how he treated animals and the downtrodden. Kieran saw people, all people. He saw their worth and their pride. When he could have shown her pity, he'd shown her admiration instead.

'Penny for your thoughts.' His voice was low at her ear as they rode beside the coach. 'I'm only asking because I can almost hear you thinking, but not quite,' he teased.

She settled more firmly against him. 'I was thinking about you.'

'Did you reach a verdict?' He steered around a low spot in the road to spare Tambor the change in terrain— further proof she was right about him.

'I did.' She tilted her head up to see his face and smiled. 'You are nice.'

He laughed down at her and she liked too much how the corners of his eyes crinkled and his face broke into an infectious smile. 'I am nice. When I can be.'

She returned her gaze to the road. 'It must be difficult to have to always make that determination.'

'If I didn't, I'd be riding dead.' It was not a particularly funny joke, because he was right. A Horseman could not always be nice, could not always believe those who came forward with information or asked for help.

'What does it say about the world that we cannot simply be nice all the time? It's a sad commentary. You are right: one must mete out niceness as if it were the most precious of jewels.' She'd been nice to the wrong man once and thrown her proverbial pearls before swine. She'd paid for it, and she'd never forgotten the lesson.

'I'm sorry,' Kieran offered quietly.

'Why?' The words caught her off guard.

'If you understand the need to protect your niceness, then it means you've learned that lesson the hard way. So, I am sorry for that. It's not a pleasant lesson to learn, but it is one that stays with us.'

Ah, so the Horseman had some experience with that too. What a very *human* thing to have in common. She leaned back against him. His arm came about her in silent accord and for a little while she felt closer to him than she'd felt to anyone for long time. It felt good—dangerously good—to share such a connection. Old fantasies, old girlhood hopes and naïve dreams once locked tightly away began to rattle their cages. She let them, knowing full well it would make it more difficult to put them away when the time came—and the time always came.

Kieran didn't call a halt until the sun was setting. He told himself it was because they'd not set a gruelling pace this afternoon on account of the heat and the long night prior, but if he was being honest he might also have been reluctant to see the ride come to an end. It would mean relinquishing Celeste in exchange for the chores of establishing camp—a poor trade in his estimation. He'd enjoyed her presence today, the feel of her body against his and the way she tipped her head up to look at him when she teased.

She'd been completely herself this afternoon. There'd been no coyness, no guardedness. Her real self was delightful—fresh, fun and straightforward. But he positively hated that Roan had had access to that; had taken that wonderful freshness and polluted it. She'd said he was nice, but Kieran wanted to do violence to whomever had made her pay for her own niceness. He'd not pressed for her story, although his curiosity had been rampant. That she *had* a story told him all that was needed. He recognised the rest was only necessary for his own gratification—gratification that had been stoked further as a result of their interlude in the woods. It was an unlooked-for consequence—proof that, no matter what arguments he'd made in his mind about limits, intimacy was seeping in past boundaries he'd set despite his best efforts. This journey, this task, was quickly becoming about him and her and less about the Horsemen and Roan.

And he did not resent it; he did not necessarily want to change that trajectory. That was the real danger. Offering her pleasure today against the oak tree had been exquisite; watching her claim her passion, her long neck arched, pleasure purling up her throat, had been pure masculine delight. That alone would have been enough for him, but she'd taken it a step further and offered him pleasure in turn. The echoes of her hand on him still reverberated in his blood. She'd answered his body's needs instinctively, her hand sensing the pulse of him, the rhythm of him, and matching it in an intimate dance of cock and hand. In those moments he'd been met, answered and fulfilled most unexpectedly. It had not been mere physical release.

He was honest enough to admit that the interlude had rendered far more in terms of feeling and emotion than he'd anticipated. Having had a taste of the potential between them made him hungry for more but also cautious of such passionate gluttony. Forewarned was forearmed, as his grandfather liked to say. If they knew now how explosive it could be between them, then they knew empirically not to stoke the fire, even as the temptation to do just that still lay banked between them.

He and his men were efficient, and it didn't take long for their simple camp to be established. He made a trip to a nearby river for washing water. When he returned, he discovered Celeste had been busy too. While the men had been caring for the horses, she'd been caring for them. She looked up from a makeshift table where she was laying out an evening meal and smiled at him. She was slicing bread and the sight stirred something so dangerous, so strong, within him that he had to stop and gather himself. The table was nothing more than the storage trunk that had been strapped to the back of the coach, the meal was simple and was not even hot—he'd not wanted to risk a fire attracting attention—but somehow she'd transformed it into a feast. His mother had always said the fastest way to tame a wild man was to find him a cultivated woman. His mother may have been right. She usually was.

'Wash up, men, and let's eat. We can't come to this meal with dirty hands.' Kieran set the bucket down next to the basin and she flashed him a smile of appreciation for the support. But the appreciation, he thought, was all his. It took a special kind of person to put themselves forward; to make themselves part of a team that pre-dated their membership. What woman had he met this spring in London who would have done as much? Which of his dance partners, in their fine silks and jewels, would have joined in, laid out a meal or thought about others before themselves? He was fairly sure Lady Elizabeth Cleeves would have sat by the coach and expected to be waited on.

The five of them ate together, telling stories of past missions. Bert, Eric and Matt tried to outdo one another in an attempt to impress Celeste, whose efforts and comportment in difficult circumstances had won their approval. Overhead, the stars came out, a twinkle at a time in a lavender sky trending to deepest indigo. One by one, the men drifted off into the darkness to take care of evening needs and chores. Celeste rose and busied herself packing away the food in the storage trunk.

Kieran reluctantly went through the motions of converting the coach seats into a bed, privately acknowledging to himself that was the last place he wanted her to sleep tonight. He'd spent the meal in a state of semi-arousal, watching the evening light limning her profile, living for the moments when she looked across the circle of people and smiled at him while she laughed at something one of his men said. Here was a woman who might come alongside a Horseman, who, in her own way, had some experience living in a Horseman's grey world between good and evil and who understood the dangers inherent in that life. She was living those dangers right now and yet she was capable of conquering her fears.

Some might say his imagination was running rampant, his reason dragged away by a beautiful woman like a coach drawn by wild horses incapable of self-control. Logic taunted him: how could he know so much in so few days? He'd been wrong once before. But the rebuttal came swift and fast: it was his job to know and to draw accurate, fast conclusions. He'd learned his lesson with Sofia. He and his brothers had lived and died on those insights, on the ability to read the details and nuances. He had to trust himself that he would not be wrong again. And yet doubt niggled: *what if he was?*

Celeste came to the coach as he finished setting up the bed. 'The food is all packed away. I prepared enough for breakfast tomorrow. All we have to do is unpack it again,' she explained, poking her head inside the coach, but not before he caught a glimpse in her eyes of the reluctance he felt.

'Thank you for setting this up,' she began, fanning herself a bit. 'It was warm today. The coach is a little stuffy. I thought I might sit up a little while and let the night air do its job before I retire, if that's all right? I don't want to keep you up.'

Kieran laughed, his voice low, his words just for her. 'Too late. You've been keeping me up all evening.' A knowing light flickered in her eyes and he pressed his momentary advantage. 'Come lie with me. It's a beautiful night and we can keep each other company.'

Want and warning flashed in her eyes. 'I will, but just company, Kieran. Anything else might be too much too soon.'

He nodded and brought her hand to his lips for a courtly kiss. 'Come and keep company with me, my lady.' This afternoon had got to her too, it seemed. It had been moving, pleasurable, but it had not ended there; it had not been a shallow, purely physical interlude for either of them. It had opened deep places within them and now those places, those ideas, had to be contemplated before anything further could happen—or perhaps, like him, she might decide anything further would be too much.

They settled on his blankets far enough from the others to have their privacy and he drew her against him as they looked up at the sky. That she'd come to him spoke of the growing trust between them. She trusted him enough to expect he'd keep his word—company only tonight, no lovemaking beneath the stars. She liked him enough to want to keep this intimate company where they might lie together, their bodies taking comfort from the closeness of one another. There were many reasons for seeking such comfort and he was no stranger to them. They'd faced death yesterday. It was entirely natural to want to counter such an experience with seeking proof of life through physical closeness with another.

He would give her that comfort because she needed it, even if she didn't realise the deep-seated reason for it, and because it was all he could give her. He stroked her arm in a gentle caress, matching his breathing to hers as their bodies settled to one another. 'My brothers and I used to camp out in the summers, at Willow Park or at Sandmore—my grandfather's estate. There was a lake at Sandmore and Grandfather would set up tents for us. But we hardly ever slept in them. So, Grandfather would send our tutor out with us and make sure we learned the stars while we were at it.'

'Your grandfather sounds like a very astute man,' she murmured.

'He is. He's eighty-eight and I wonder how long we'll have him. He doesn't leave Sandmore anymore. He's turned the Horsemen over to Caine entirely, although he'll stay on to advise for a couple years—his words.' Kieran laughed. 'Grandfather's been in the game too long to ever really leave it. He can't quite let go.' He was silent for a moment, pushing back against the emotion that rose in his throat unexpectedly. 'I am not looking forward to the day when he's not here.'

'He'll never leave you. He'll be with you. You'll carry him with you in ways you don't expect and, when you need him, he'll be there.' She traced a soft circle around his heart with her fingertip. 'Perhaps it's silly, but I feel closer to my father now that he's gone. I'll be playing the piano and I'll hear him in my head saying, "that's a pretty tune…you play so well". Or I'll be reading a line from a book and think about how much he'd like a certain turn of phrase, or an author's new novel, and it's like sharing it with him as if he were really there.'

Kieran closed a hand over hers where it lay on his chest. 'I like the thought of that.' He played with her fingers, lacing his through them. 'You play the piano?'

'Yes!' She laughed. 'That wasn't the point of the story, though.'

He raised his head up far enough to kiss her fingertips. 'I know. But I like learning about you.'

She sighed against him and he thought this was what real contentment was, to lie here with someone and simply *be*; not to worry about 'the game'.

'I like learning about you too. Tell me more about your camps. Was your tutor successful in imparting any knowledge?'

'That sounds very much like a challenge. The late summer sky is one of my favourite times to look at the stars. The night air has a briskness to it, and the sky is bright. A lot of constellations are visible.' Kieran raised an arm, his finger tracing the sky. 'In the south, you have Cygnus, the swan. That bright star there, Deneb, is its tail.' He moved his finger from star to star, outlining the form for her. 'Cygnus has a long neck, like you—a beautiful, elegant neck.'

'You are a shameless flatterer.' But he noticed she snuggled closer. 'What else is up there?'

'Sagittarius in the southwest, just a bit to the left of Cygnus. Scorpio should be up there, too, but I can't find all of it tonight.' He moved his hand east. 'Pegasus is out tonight.' He reached for her hand and together they drew the shape. 'I think I have a star next to me,' he murmured. 'It has occurred to me that your name, Celeste, comes from "celestial". I believe the Latin for it is *caelestia*: heavenly.'

'You're very good with your Latin, Kieran Parkhurst.' She gave a throaty laugh that had him rousing.

'I'm good at other things too,' he murmured huskily.

'Yes, you are.'

He might have kissed her then, but he heard the drowsiness in her tone, felt the lethargy of encroaching sleep in her body, and he'd given his word. Tonight was for comfort. He let her slip away beside him, watching the details of sleep: her green eyes closing, her breathing slowing, her body sagging against him. There was pleasure in that, too—pride that he could give her the gift of safe, deep sleep.

He played with the soft skeins of her hair, drawing his fingers through them. What a woman she was. How unfortunate that their circumstances would allow for only further physical exploration of the potential between them. And that could only be allowed if they didn't let the fire consume them. There was no chance of exploring anything truly personal between them. That would require long-term association and they'd pledged themselves only in the short term. She would leave, and his circumstances did not permit him to offer a reason to stay.

Even when the threat of Roan had been exorcised and she was free of that bastard, he would not be free. He would still be a Horseman. He could not give her the fantasies that played in her mind, the fantasies she couldn't disguise—fantasies of family and home, of security and permanence. It was not wrong of her to want those things or to hunger for them. But it was wrong for him to pretend he could give them to her.

Horsemen were not marrying men. He and his brothers had decided that a long time ago. Caine had decided that when a society miss had jilted him for lack of a title when he'd been younger. Kieran had decided that when he'd lay close to death from a knife wound delivered by a woman he'd thought he could trust. Yet Caine *had* married. His grandfather had married, fathered three sons and managed to preside for decades as the patriarch of a large homegrown familial network. Horsemen *could* marry. If…and there were a lot of ifs…a wife was willing to live with danger, disruption and the possibility of being widowed or of being left behind to raise children on her own.

Thank goodness Stepan had not married. It seemed an unfair compromise to ask of a woman. Yet, Lady Mary had loved Caine enough to make the compromise. In the case of Mary and Caine, love had triumphed over worries and 'what ifs.' He laughed to himself. What an interesting, illogical exercise this was to lie here contemplating marriage to a woman he'd known less than a week.

Overhead, a shooting star crossed the sky and he tracked the trajectory with his eyes. That was all this was—he and Celeste were shooting stars, a moment of startling brilliance as their paths crossed. They would move on because that was how their lives worked and because the circumstance that had brought them together would be resolved. What did they have between them outside of Cabot Roan? A few days' adventure on the road? That was hardly enough to build a life on.

The road built a false sense of intimacy, and he ought to know better. This wasn't the first time he'd been with a woman on the road, surrounded by danger. He knew the nuances of these situations. This wasn't love. This was what happened when a woman in danger sought solace from her bodyguard. It was what happened when that woman's protector did his job. It was up to him to provide comfort in whatever form it might take. Yes, sometimes it felt more real than others. But then, when all was safe again, both parties quickly discovered there was nothing of substance between them. Nothing that would last.

He'd once escorted an ambassador's wife to Vienna. It had been a harrowing journey, fraught with the hazards of cross-country travel, including an incident with highwaymen. She'd been rather grateful for his protection on the road. But when he'd encountered her two months later in Vienna, at a ball, she'd given him only the briefest of nods.

Would he see Celeste after this? Where would she go? Would she want to see him again? Or would she, like the ambassador's wife, prefer to put him and all of this out her mind? He couldn't blame her. These were trying times full of things one did not expect to encounter. He'd killed two men in front of her. Women didn't mind it in the moment, but later they didn't care for the reminder of the violence. Or perhaps it was the reminder of their own reaction they didn't enjoy facing—that they'd slept with a man who'd killed and they'd revelled it; they'd cried his name to the skies and screamed their pleasure into the wild. They had to accept that, deep down, they were just as much an animal as he was. It was not something well-bred women were raised to do.

Celeste's chestnut hair spilled over his chest and he allowed himself the purely theoretical thought: maybe this time would be different. What would he actually do if that was the case? Maybe it would be easier if it wasn't.

Chapter Twelve

Being on the road in good weather made it easy to forget there was a world outside this journey. For Celeste, the days took on a pleasant rhythm all of their own. They fell into a routine of stopping, setting up camp, washing off the dust of the day, and preparing and eating an evening meal. All this amid stories of other journeys and other roads these men had travelled together and falling asleep beside Kieran while he told her tales of growing up at Willow Park, the stars keeping watch.

They'd not repeated the intimacy of the forest, which was both a comfort and a concern. They knew better now just how consuming their passion would be if unleashed. But that did not mean desire had subsided. It was still there, pushing hard against their defences, unwilling to be ignored or denied. It crept in, crawling closer with each story like an incoming tide, with each look, each touch, until it became a permanent presence between them with every day spent on the road.

They were not racing to their destination, but they were being deliberate and discreet in their route, staying off the main thoroughfares and choosing country roads instead, eschewing inns and villages. There'd been no sign of Roan or Vincent, or much of anyone. Cheshire, Kieran informed her, was a rural area devoted to cattle, cheese, salt and, most interestingly to her, silk.

'The best way to understand a place is to get off the beaten path,' he murmured in her ear late in the afternoon as they rode through the quiet countryside.

She thought the same could be said of people as well—get them out of their ballrooms and social cages, get them out into the country where there was nothing to do but talk to pass the time, and who knew what might be revealed? Talk built its own kind of intimacy, and its own kind of risk. It created a sense of knowing someone perhaps better than one truly did—a caution she'd best keep in mind.

'It's the lull before the storm,' Kieran commented as they passed a field of wheat, ripe and ready. 'The harvest is not far off. It's good we're passing through now. Next week, these fields will be full of workers, roads full of threshing crews. We would have been noted.'

'I like it the way it is now. It's as if we're the only people in the world, and that there's nothing to do but simply exist, eat, sleep and enjoy being in company with one another. It's a reminder that perhaps we complicate our lives unnecessarily. We need so little when we're on the road.' That had been true even when she'd fled Roan. It was amazing how portable her life had become in the last month.

Kieran laughed. She felt his chest rumble against her back, the chest she slept against each night. 'You may be disappointed to know that we should be in Wrexham tomorrow night.' Wrexham—the end of this journey and the beginning of another. The beginning of the end.

They'd not talked about Wrexham. Perhaps it was a tacit rule of the Horsemen not to plan too far into the future out of a need to focus on the moment at hand. 'You'll have hot water, a bed to sleep in and a warm meal,' he cajoled her when she remained silent.

'I have those things now.' She had so much more. She had this man beside her, and while they were out here she could pretend he was hers; that they were partners and equals. She could ignore the contradiction of wanting him while also wanting her freedom.

In Wrexham, she'd start to lose her power. She'd have to surrender the first half of the list. She'd have to remember that men stole a woman's freedom, that marriage stole a woman's freedom; that the things she treasured—home and family—could only be had at great personal sacrifice. Those things had killed her mother. In the long term, it would be best to let Kieran go before she gave him too much power.

'Let': that was a ridiculous word to use with Kieran. He was not a man who 'let' people decide anything for him. Letting him go was as much a fantasy as it was to assume he wanted her to stay or that he sought anything permanent. He didn't. Which made her own thoughts all the more ridiculous, too, and all this unnecessary worry that she'd have to decide to go or stay, to choose Kieran or her freedom. He'd not even asked that of her. He'd not spoken of a future that involved them together.

Wasn't that one of the reasons she felt safe enough with him to allow the intimacy—because he expected nothing in return, only the moment? No, her freedom was securely intact. Wrexham would end the journey but it would not end her bid for freedom. She ought to feel relief at the knowledge that she'd been arming herself for a battle she'd not have to fight, but there was only emptiness when she thought of leaving Kieran and that he'd let her go when the time came. It was not the reaction she'd expected.

'I see that life on the road has you in its thrall.' Kieran shifted in the saddle behind her, perhaps picking up on her unsettled mood. 'The road has a certain magic, but it's only been a few days. It does get old.'

'Out here, we can be whoever and whatever we choose.' She could lie beside this man, could walk into the woods and seek pleasure with him beneath an oak tree, sit beside him for the evening meal and lean against his knee. No one condemned her. 'But the moment we step back into civilisation, into even the most meagre village, our actions will be called into question.'

Unless she belonged to that man. Beneath the pomp and pageantry of courtships and weddings, that was what marriage was—the transfer of a woman's ownership from one man to another. She hated that. Ownership and guardianship were just polite words for enslavement. She'd had a large enough taste of that with Roan to last her a lifetime. Perhaps that reminder would make it easier to leave Wrexham and Kieran when the time came.

She could feel Kieran smiling. 'Who are *you* out here, Celeste?'

'A woman who can claim her passion. Who doesn't need society's permission to claim it, or censure her if she does.' She gave a toss of her head. 'Who are *you* out here, Kieran?' It was a fanciful question to ask. He was who he always was. A man could do and be whatever he wanted whenever and wherever he wanted.

'Don't you know?' His mouth was close to her ear. She would miss that little intimacy—the way his voice lowered, the way he might press the tiniest of kisses behind her ear as he spoke. 'Out here, I am yours. Yours to command.'

The words sent a jolt of awareness through her—awareness of him; awareness of her own power. He did indeed allow her to set the tone between them. He'd not pressed her for more since the oak tree. He'd been content to sleep beside her and to offer her the comfort of his body without requiring sex in exchange unless she desired it. She did desire it, but not yet, not when the boundaries between them were still unformed and still shifting; the relationship was still too new. They were still learning about one another. She'd rushed in too soon with David and she'd suffered for it. Yet each night when she'd lain down beside Kieran, the temptation had whispered that she could trust him with her body, that he would be different, and each night she'd got closer to giving in.

'Eric's back.' Kieran gestured to a growing speck in the distance. She'd hardly noticed it. Eric had left after lunch to ride ahead. Now, he came galloping back to give a report.

'There's a village up ahead.' Eric drew his horse alongside Tambor and the two animals touched noses. 'They're having a fair. There's games and booths, food, ale and lots of people,' he hinted broadly. 'We would hardly be noticed, and we're only a few miles from the border.'

'We *are* running low on food,' Celeste mused out loud. 'There's only enough left for either supper tonight or breakfast in the morning.' Although, it wasn't much of a worry. They'd be in Wrexham by supper tomorrow. They weren't going to starve. Still, the idea of a fair to celebrate their last night held some appeal. 'I think we've earned a bit of pleasure.'

'You heard the lady, Eric.' Kieran laughed. 'She wants to go to the fair. Tell the others.'

'Thank you,' she whispered as Eric galloped off.

'As I said, I am yours to command.'

An hour later, the horses had been put up at a livery, rooms arranged at an inn and she was strolling the booths on the common with Kieran beside her, excitement buoying her step.

'One would think you'd never been to a fair,' Kieran laughed as they passed a leather worker's stall showing exquisite sheathes and bridles.

She turned her green gaze on him, her smile wide. 'I haven't,' she said, and laughed at the look of surprise he gave her.

'Not *ever*?' he asked in disbelief.

'No. There were fairs near some of the schools I attended. There was a frost fair on the Neva River in St Petersburg. We could see it from the school windows, but fairs were deemed too dangerous for boarding-school girls.'

'I'll be sure to keep you close,' he teased, but she felt him tuck her arm more securely through his. 'The headmistress wasn't entirely wrong to worry. Pickpockets do abound at such events, and there are some charlatans among the legitimate vendors.'

'That sounds exciting. Who do you think is a charlatan?' She looked around the grounds, eyeing each booth, and he laughed.

Kieran discreetly nodded towards a booth selling 'Dr Graham's Medicinal Tonic'. 'There's one—that tonic likely doesn't lessen anything but one's purse.'

She tugged at him. 'I want to go and see him.'

They stood a little distance from the booth, listening to the respectably dressed, middle-aged man behind the counter in a dark suit profess the magical properties of the tonic. 'It'll cure female complaints, it'll soothe a teething baby, relieve headaches, muscle aches and so much more for just five shillings for the small bottle and eight shillings for the large. Then there's my special liver rejuvenator, made from the purest ingredients, only found high in the Alps...'

She watched, enrapt, caught up in the story. She turned towards Kieran for a moment. 'The gentleman is quite good. I like the part about the Swiss milk thistle.'

'A good story is central to selling the product,' Kieran murmured, his tone suggesting that, while she enjoyed watching Dr Graham, he was enjoying watching her, a thought that set something hot and wild loose within her.

'What do you suppose is really in it?' she whispered as the doctor's talk concluded and people surged forward, pressing coins into Dr Graham's hand.

'Alcohol, mostly—probably opium, so that it's addictive. It creates return customers.'

'That's a bit dark.' She frowned. 'And they'll give that to their children? Suddenly, I find this less entertaining. I feel like I should stop them. Five shillings is a lot; it's half a week's work in some places.' She glanced at him, frustrated. 'Can't we do something?'

'What would you have me do?' Kieran steered her away towards other booths. 'It's not our choice to make. But if it makes you feel better, it angers me too to see hard-working people swindled out of their money. Still, no one's forcing them. Dr Graham is just presenting them with a choice.'

They stopped in front of a booth selling various blades and he flashed her a smile. 'Just as I am presenting you with a choice. I think you should have a dagger. Fairs *are* good places to purchase daggers, unlike elixirs.' He grinned and directed her attention to a few of the blades on display. 'Try this one. It's pretty and well-made.'

He held it up for her, moving behind her and wrapping his arms around her as he put it in her hand. 'The handle is polished camel bone; the pommel is brass. Do you feel the balance? You could throw it if you had to. Try it.' He stepped back, giving her room to take few experimental strokes. 'Dagger work is close work, but you don't have to reload it.'

'It's beautiful, and light—much lighter than your pistols.' And it made her feel…powerful; more in control than she'd felt with a pistol.

'Then you should have it.' Kieran handed over the coins. 'I think a dagger is more portable than a pistol, especially for a woman. You can easily carry it on your person.'

She worried her lip. The dagger was beautiful but it was also deadly. 'You are preparing me for danger,' she said as the craftsman wrapped the blade.

'I want you to be safe, to be able to protect yourself.' Because he might not be there to do it; because their choices would take them in different directions and those decisions would be made soon.

'Protection through empowerment.' She flashed him a grateful smile. 'Thank you, Kieran. I will cherish this blade. Hopefully, I will never have to use it.'

'At least, not tonight.' He took her hand. 'Look, there's French milled soap made with lavender from Provence. We should stock up. We don't know what supplies will be like at the Hall.' He was diverting her and she let him. Tonight was not for gloomy thoughts, it was for living, and perhaps even for loving.

She reached for a bar of soap and inhaled, letting the lavender soothe away the dark thoughts. 'That smell is divine.'

'We'll take six bars.' Kieran flashed her a wink. 'Don't say a word, Celeste. It's your first fair and I mean to make it memorable.'

The woman working on the booth gave a knowing laugh. 'When your man wants to spoil you, never say no.' She leaned close to Celeste. 'Especially when your man is as handsome as this one. He could spoil me any time he wanted, but anyone can see he only has eyes for you.'

Her man… Celeste blushed at the woman's frankness but she liked the idea of that very much. It was a fantasy she could let herself indulge at least for the night, even if she could not for the long term. Fantasies didn't work that way. That was why they were fantasies.

The spoiling continued in earnest after that: a fistful of hair ribbons in a rainbow of colours because Kieran couldn't decide which colour he liked best in her hair; a pretty necklace of sea-glass, the colour of her eyes, strung on a sterling-silver chain, and silver ear-bobs to match, all expertly etched with Celtic runes. Then full darkness fell and lanterns were lit, giving the fair a festive atmosphere. They ate hot meat pasties and drank cold ale at a plank table, where Kieran laughingly licked a droplet from her lips with his tongue and turned it into a lingering kiss that fired her blood and had those around them clapping. She ought to have been shocked, she ought to have reprimanded him for such liberties, but what did it matter? No one cared and this was *fun*. There'd been too little of that in her life.

'How are we doing? Is the fair living up to your expectations?' he asked afterwards.

'Exceeding them,' she answered honestly as they left the plank table and began to stroll again. 'The fair is just as I imagined it. Boarding-school girls are guarded quite closely, sheltered intensely. Our childhoods are not at all like the one you describe at Willow Park with your brothers, all of you running wild. We saw little of the outside and nothing of the real world.'

She stopped to finger some fine lace, picturing it trimming a linen shift. Such delicacies didn't belong on the road or on the run. She turned from it and continued. 'We were told it was for our protection, but I know better now. We were valuable commodities. We couldn't be risked at fairs or market-day shopping excursions. We were being raised for one purpose: to advance our families in marriage. We were to be beautiful, well-comported, talented and intelligent when needed so that we might appeal to a powerful man. If we should be allowed beyond the school grounds, who knows who we might meet? We might meet the wrong sort of person and, heaven forbid, fall in love with them, or rethink our purpose in life.'

'Were the schools Roan's idea or your father's?' Kieran asked.

'I've come to believe they were Roan's. If I'd lived at home, I would have been a distraction to my father. I would have kept him from doing Roan's work. I think, too, that when I was at school I became leverage for Roan to ensure my father continued to do his bidding. It was not something I understood until after my father's death.'

Like her father, she had not understood the depth of Roan's control over those who were in his orbit until it had been too late to free herself.

'It sounds like a very restrictive way to grow up.' Kieran squeezed her hand, running his thumb over her knuckles in that soothing caress she'd come to associate with him, the one he'd used the very first day. She leaned her head against his shoulder as they walked, their pace slower now, their attention more on each other than the booths.

'It was, but tonight I got to have a dream come to life, so perhaps it was worth it.'

She was getting drowsy. It felt good to be held against him, to have his arm about her waist. 'I would look out of the school windows and see couples at the frost fair. I remember seeing a woman in a red scarf, and the man with her wearing a fur *ushanka*—you know, the hats with the ear flaps? They were ice-skating and there was this moment when she threw back her head and laughed and he swept her into his arms and spun her around. He was laughing too, and I thought to myself: I want that.

I want a day where I have no cares and where there is someone who delights in me. Tonight, I got to have that.'

'The night's not over. Are you ready to eat again? There's chocolate over there.' Kieran adjusted their trajectory and they made their way to the brightly lit booth with its cases of chocolates from all over Europe. 'What shall we get?'

'A little of everything. Not all chocolate is the same. Trust me, I've been all over Europe; I know.'

Kieran slanted her a playful look. 'I think I might put that to the test.'

They took their bag of chocolate and found a space just outside the lights where there might be privacy. He settled her on his lap. 'Close your eyes.' He held a piece of chocolate to her lips, his voice a seductive whisper at her ear. 'All right, take a bite and tell me where it's from.'

'Mmm. This is Dutch chocolate, without a doubt. It's smoother than other chocolate, and it's also less bitter.'

'And this?' He held up a second piece, his fingers lingering at her lips this time.

'Swiss. And, by the way, this is not fair—you're trying to distract me.' Although, she didn't mind the distraction and wouldn't mind if the distraction went a bit further than fingers on lips. Tonight was a night out of time, a night of make-believe where a fantasy had come true. Where one fantasy came to life, perhaps others might follow.

'That's amazing!' Kieran laughed after she'd correctly identified a fourth piece. His eyes rested on her face and she thought, of all the chocolate in the world, she loved the chocolate of his eyes best. '*You're* amazing,' he murmured, stealing a kiss, the chocolate game forgotten in the wake of another, more interesting game. 'You taste good,' he teased against her mouth. 'Germany, Austria, Switzerland and Holland all rolled into one delicious kiss.'

Her arms were about his neck. 'You taste delicious too,' she whispered, letting her tongue flirt with his. She loved kissing him; loved the way his dark lashes lay against his cheek bones when his eyes closed; loved the way he didn't rush, as if the kiss was important in and of itself, as though, if kissing was all they did, it would be enough. But kissing wouldn't be enough for her, not tonight. Tomorrow would be too late. The fantasy would be gone.

The kiss deepened and she gave a little moan. 'Take me to our rooms, Kieran. Take me there and be my man.'

'Absolutely, my lady. I am yours to command.' He lifted her in his arms, the obvious show of strength igniting something hot and primal within her. Her feminine core began to burn, a fire unfurling inch by slow inch.

'Do you mean to carry me all the way there?' She'd thought she was beyond the fairy-tale effects of such gestures. Apparently, not tonight; the flame within her only grew hotter.

'I mean to do better than that. I mean to carry you to *bed.*' Desire flared in his eyes, a naked flame of his own. Proof that what she saw in the dark depths of his eyes was desire uniquely for *her*, roused *by* her. The knowledge of it sparked something hot and wild, something untamed and unnamed within her that was potent and powerful; something that could not be stopped, only sated. Tonight, she wasn't just going to burn. She was going to incinerate.

Chapter Thirteen

He was Prometheus tonight, playing with fire, basking in its warmth and luxuriating in the power of its possibility as he carried Celeste upstairs. His body was rampant with desire even as he schooled himself to nuance. This was not to be an act of possession, but an act of partnership. He would not fall on her like a stag in rut, no matter how much his body clamoured for that. She had not asked for that—not with her body, nor with her words. She was not a thing to be taken. Although, if their previous encounters and kisses served as indicators, she was not opposed to doing some taking of her own.

Kieran was not wrong. He'd no sooner kicked the door to their room shut and set her down before she was tugging at his neck cloth and yanking shirttails from his breeches, her hands running up beneath the fabric and over his skin even as her mouth sought his in a fierce, greedy communion. 'Thank goodness I dress simply on the road.' He laughed against her mouth. 'Shirt buttons wouldn't stand a chance against you.'

'Against...yes, perfect.' The words were part instruction, part feminine growl, and he had only the merest of warnings before he found himself with his back to the wall. Her hands returned to the waistband of his breeches and he pulled his shirt over his head, balling it up and tossing it aside. He knew where this was going and it wasn't to bed, at least not yet.

Her mouth was hot on his—by all the saints, this woman could kiss! He reached for the bodice of her gown, giving a silent and perhaps inappropriate thanks to those same saints that a front-fastening bodice was also front-unfastening. He was good with laces and hooks but tonight he hadn't the patience for them. Neither did she. Deferred passion and desire were riding them both too hard. 'Did you bring another chemise?' he mumbled in her ear.

She drew back for a moment, eyes clouding in confusion, her voice a breathless wisp. 'Yes, why?'

'Because you'll need it tomorrow.' He took the thin linen in both hands and rent it.

She gave a surprised gasp and her eyes gleamed. 'You wicked man.' She laughed.

'You wanton woman.' He gave a husky chuckle. 'You beautiful, wanton woman.' He spun her around then in a hard turn, reversing their position. Her back was to the wall and her eyes were bright with anticipation. 'Are you sure you wouldn't rather use the bed?'

'I cannot wait for bed.' As if in proof, her bared breasts pressed against his chest, skin to delicious skin, flush with the heat of passion. Her hand dropped to the straining length of him jutting under his breeches. 'And you can't either.'

He lifted her then, her legs wrapping around his hips, her core meeting his. His blood ran hot and hard and his phallus throbbed and strained, a stallion waiting to be let loose of his reins. Good God, this woman drove him to the brink of madness…and pushed him over with a single, simple gesture. She raised a hand to her hair and with one pull of a pin sent it falling over her shoulders in a chestnut cascade while her eyes locked on his until he was an inferno of want.

She wrapped her arms around his shoulders, her body moving against his in invitation, a reminder to his fevered self that water slaked fire, that wetness solved heat. *She* would be wet…*she* would assuage his fire. He went into the wet channel of her, deep, hard and thirsty, the way a man on fire might jump into a lake. She arched against the wall, moaning in appreciation, the joining bringing initial relief. 'More…again,' she coached, moving her hips against him.

Yes, more. The simple command resonated with the instinct of his body. Once more, twice more, thrice more he drove into the welcoming wetness of her, fire banked, while desire roared until his body shuddered with it. He felt her nails dig into his shoulders and felt her body gather, preparing to claim her release even as he did the same. He felt her legs tighten as if she could hold him within her for ever—*something he absolutely must not let her do.*

In the recesses of his mind, caution awoke. Appealing as the thought was to spend deep inside her, he could not. The Horseman in him roused at the last moment: *protect, protect, protect…* What he could not do for himself, he could do for her. He felt climax claim her, felt her body gather and release, and then he was gone from her, groaning and shuddering with the power of his own completion as she held him to her and he spent.

They came back to earth very slowly after that, her legs eventually letting go of his waist, their bodies able to function at last without the support of the other, although they clung together long beyond what was necessary. He could feel the rise and fall of her breathing against his chest and could feel her breath slow. He could smell the scent of hyacinth on her skin mixed with sweat and the musk of sex—details to file away; details by which to remember this night when, for a while, he'd held perfection in his arms.

Kieran took a half-step back from her and kicked his breeches off the rest of the way before returning to her and gently removing her gown and the halves of her chemise. 'We are naked now,' he murmured against her cheek, his eyes half-closed as he breathed her in.

'Yes, we are. Wholly, completely, naked,' she replied with soft seriousness. She understood what he'd meant: this nakedness was more than the physical; they also stood before one another emotionally stripped to the skin and vulnerable. She wrapped her arms around his neck. He lifted her once more and at last carried her to the bed.

They were good at this, lying together in the dark. They'd had a few nights' practice, perhaps intuitively knowing they would lead to these moments, these revelations. A smart man could tell a lot about a woman by the way she made love. He'd not been wrong that she'd been looking for partnership, not possession. But now, he better understood why. The obvious answer was because she controlled her passion and she valued her freedom.

One might leave it there and feel satisfied. He'd known other women who'd valued their right to choose and to control their lives in and out of the bedroom.

But it was the reasons behind valuing her freedom that gave her away and set her apart. He was coming to learn that, for Celeste, freedom was a defence: she used it for control but also as a means to protect herself. Freedom was her shield.

'May I ask you a question?' he ventured in the dark.

Her hand lingered at his hip. 'If I can ask you one.' Her fingers idly traced the scar and he could guess the trajectory of her thoughts. 'How did you get this?'

'By being young and careless.' It had happened twelve years ago, and it was still hard to talk about, but it would be the price for the question he would ask her. If he did not share confidences with her, he could not expect her to share any with him.

She snuggled closer. 'It is hard to imagine you being reckless. What happened?'

'I was in Leipzig on an errand for my grandfather, delivering dispatches to the Allies. It was during the War of the Sixth Coalition that ultimately led to the liberation of Paris, so I suppose my sacrifice was not in vain.' He tried to make light of it. 'Caine was with me or I might not have made it out alive. It was just the two of us back then. Stepan and Luce had not yet joined us.'

She stopped her idle stroking of his hip and raised herself up on an arm. 'You're deflecting. Do you even realise you do it? Whenever something personal comes up, you immediately turn the conversation to your brothers.'

'I do not!' Kieran protested.

'Yes, you do. For instance, when I ask about summers at Willow Park, you talk about things you all did together. When we were gazing at the stars, you talked about camping.'

'Well, yes. Is there something wrong with that?' Kieran was intrigued now. Apparently, the insights tonight were not all going to be his.

'No, I liked those stories. But I also want to know about you too—just you, what *you* think, what *you* feel, *your* experiences. Yes, you are a Horseman, a member of a group. But you are also Kieran Parkhurst, a single individual.'

Her finger went back to tracing his scar in a long, deliberate stroke. 'Perhaps it's been a long time since you've thought of yourself that way. Perhaps this scar is the reason for that,' she prompted gently. 'Tell me what happened and don't gloss over the part that really matters—the part that changed you, the part that still haunts you.'

Good God, he'd never felt more naked than he did now, or more seen. When had someone actually looked that deeply into him? How he felt about that was rather confusing, awkward, perhaps because it happened so rarely. The tables had been completely turned on him. *She* should be a Horseman. With those insights, she'd be lethal at interrogation. A man's secrets wouldn't stand a chance. He had no excuse to put her off other than his pride. He settled back against the pillows and drew her close. 'It was on account of a woman.'

'Of course it was.' Celeste smiled up at him, hoping to ease his apparent lingering embarrassment. 'Go on.' If she didn't encourage him, she suspected he'd find a way to make the story disappear into a different conversation.

'I met her at an officers' reception in Leipzig. She was charming, cultivated and intelligent—a lot like you,' he teased, and she sensed he joked to make light of something that was not light at all. This vulnerability was an intriguing side to the all-confident Kieran Parkhurst and she rather liked it.

'We danced a few times and went out on the veranda for a stroll. She made sure I was aware of her interest in me—a touch here, a provocative remark there. I was twenty-four and perhaps too easily impressed with a slightly older woman's experienced attentions. We went back to my rooms, which was my first mistake. I'd nowhere to go after...well...afterwards. That made me careless. A Horseman never stays the night or never falls asleep. I usually left my lovers' chambers after we had our fun.

'But that night I dozed off. I awoke to find her rifling through my messenger bag. She found the dispatches I was to deliver the next day. I was groggy and I thought she was just looking for money. When I confronted her, she drew a blade on me and I was too far from my own knife. That was when I realised she'd known all along who I was and that she was not merely a guest at the party. I was her mark. She'd been sent by the French to intercept the dispatches.

'I charged her even though she was armed and I was not. I knew my duty and I knew those dispatches contained information about troops and munitions—information that, in the wrong hands, would lead to the deaths of Englishmen. I was betting that she was bluffing and that she wouldn't use the knife.'

'And you bet wrong,' Celeste whispered softly. 'What happened to the dispatches?'

'I saved them, at great expense to myself.' He was

becoming tight-lipped again. But she didn't need the details when she had the scar. She could imagine all too well the blood and the pain.

'And the woman—what happened to her?' Celeste asked quietly. It was perhaps a question that could only be asked in the dark and only discussed once.

'She died. Caine found us both on the floor,' he said quietly. Celeste made the translation in her head: the woman had not simply died, he'd killed her. He'd been forced to for his own survival and for England's. She kept the automatic words of sympathy to herself. He would not want her to be sorry any more than she'd wanted his pity. But she did want him to know she understood the import of his story and how that episode had shaped who he was. His disclosure had not been in vain.

'And since then, you don't mix business with pleasure,' she murmured. More particularly, since then he hadn't trusted women who were in the game. Or, perhaps it was that he didn't trust himself with women who were in the game. She traced his scar. No wonder he'd originally thought she was working for Roan, trying to draw him into a trap. He'd been trapped before by a pretty face. How hard it must be for him now, to let go of that narrative of deceit and embrace a narrative of trust with her, and her heart went out to him. She understood; they were alike in that regard. As much as she wanted to earn his trust, she was reluctant to give him her own. They had that in common.

'The aftermath was the worst part. It took a long time for me to recover. I'd lost a lot of blood. When I was well, I was hailed by those who knew as a hero for saving English lives, for helping to secure an Allied victory by protecting the plans. Parties were held for me. Not one person mentioned why I'd been knifed in the first place. No one talked about my mistake. No one would listen when I tried to explain what had really happened. That's the guilt I live with. For being careless, I was lauded as a hero.'

He was silent for a long moment and she wondered if he was thinking about other guilt—perhaps guilt over his missing or dead brother. Was there something he could have done? He blinked once, a long, slow sweep of his dark lashes as if he was putting the memory behind him.

'My turn,' Kieran said, and something in his tone made her brace. 'You know who hurt me. Now, tell me who hurt you. And, before you try to throw me off the scent, don't tell me Cabot Roan or Ammon Vincent. That's not the hurt I'm talking about.'

'What makes you think there's any other hurt?' She prevaricated with as much persuasive calm as she could manage. He was just guessing. How could he know? She kept it buried deep.

'Because you use freedom as shield. Just like you're doing now. Stay here beside me, Celeste. Don't move away.' She hadn't even realised she'd tried to move away until his arm tightened around her. 'You're protecting yourself, keeping yourself from getting too close or from giving up too much of yourself. You call it choosing, controlling your own destiny. But really, you worry about giving yourself up to the wrong person. One only worries about such things when one has already done it. Who was he?'

'You already know; you've said as much. Someone I thought I could trust; someone whom I thought cared for me.' She shrugged and fought the urge to break free or slink off to the far side of the bed and hide in all ways. 'There's nothing left to tell.'

He laughed against her hair. 'That tactic did not work for me. I am certainly not going to let it work for you. Celeste, you *can* tell me. I thought you'd decided that you were safe with me,' he scolded.

It wasn't him knowing that bothered her. It was what it might reveal about her—that she wasn't strong like him, that she'd been selfish. But she drew a breath and took the chance.

'He was a new client of Cabot Roan's when I first came to live at the house. He was handsome and dashing. He always made time for me. After he'd conducted business with Roan, he made a point of seeking me out. I was young and flattered.'

It hurt to talk about this. Had it felt this way for Kieran? She regretted making him tell her about the scar…almost. Perhaps she'd treasure what she'd learned all the more for the price it cost.

'He was my first kiss, and my first love. He seduced me most thoroughly. I thought he might even marry me.' She'd believed that so wholeheartedly, she'd gone to bed with him and made a habit of what she'd thought were lazy, decadent, stolen afternoons with him when Roan was out. 'But, as in your story, not all was as it seemed. He wasn't a client at all. He was a test of my loyalty to Roan and I failed. Roan told me that he was going to take David's—'

She swallowed. It was still hard to say his name years later. Kieran was patient with her, saying nothing and running his hand in a gentle motion down her arm, steadying her.

'Roan told me he was going to overcharge David for an order of weapons by making it appear that there was another buyer. At that point, I had become aware of Roan's deceits and of what he did to amass his wealth. I told David. I thought I could trust him with that information. I could not. He'd been working for Roan all along. David turned on me without any remorse and then Roan knew how much I despised him and what I was willing to do to spite him, to rebel. Things became infinitely more difficult for me after that.'

Roan had punished her.

'In what ways?' Kieran prompted gently.

'Do not make me say, Kieran. Please.' Roan had humiliated her in front of his men and it hadn't stopped there. She reached for him beneath the covers, thinking to distract him, but he was too fast.

'Keep your secrets.' Kieran covered her hand and set it aside. 'Sex can be a tool, a weapon even, but *we* will not use it between us as such. Isn't that why you wanted it to be tonight—because tomorrow it's back to the real world?' Because tomorrow they'd be at Wrexham. Tomorrow she'd need to surrender part of the list. Drat him for seeing too much. 'Circumstances may shift tomorrow, but not us. We can choose to be honest with each other. We can choose who we get to be.'

'And tonight?' she queried softly. 'Are you still my man?' Or had her disclosure changed his mind about that? Their stories had striking similarities but there was one key difference: she'd shown herself to be untrustworthy, even if it was on Roan's behalf, whereas he'd shown himself to be eminently reliable. In the face of danger and death, he'd not failed.

He rolled her beneath him, looking down at her, his dark curls tousled and his eyes once more dark with desire. 'I am always your man and this time we're going to take it slow.'

Chapter Fourteen

Wrexham Hall came slowly into view as the over-grown trees of the lime alley gradually gave way to a wider, open space set before the red-bricked Tudor home Kieran had inherited with his title. Just a little further, and they'd be able to see it in full.

'The trees have been neglected,' Kieran groused, eye-ing the lime alley with disappointment. The branches had grown overhead until the two sides had joined, form-ing a full, dense canopy.

'They're good trees,' Celeste commented. 'Look how thick those trunks are, and how sturdy the branches. A boy would love to climb up them.'

They'd been doing this all morning since they'd left the inn—commenting on their new surroundings for conversation. They'd crossed over the border into Wales amid a mist that had them discussing how the air felt as if autumn had arrived overnight. They'd made the short journey to Wrexham, noting how its unique topography contributed to the thriving town, set as it was between the Dee Valley and the Welsh mountains. The town itself had offered endless conversational openings as they'd passed St Giles church and the storefronts on the main street that promised an enjoyable shopping trip in the near future. What they didn't talk about, however, was what lay between them or last night.

Kieran understood the reason for it. Last night had been a moment out of time. Their lovemaking had reflected that in its fierceness, its tenderness and in the disclosures it had engendered. He was still reeling from it this morning. Never had he shared so much with another or *wanted* to. But Celeste had a way of pulling one's secrets out with her quiet questions, her calm demeanour and her empathy.

Now that the journey was nearly done, the carriage grew quiet, their stream of trivial conversation sputtering. He'd chosen to ride inside with her, wanting to keep their presence as anonymous as possible until decisions could be made about next steps. That was the other reason they'd tacitly opted to bury the morning in small talk—there were decisions to make, and difficult discussions to have. What *did* come next? Would she stay here with him at the Hall? If she stayed, how would that work? Or would he find a way to help her disappear safely into the mist, where Roan couldn't find her?

He knew what he'd prefer—that she stayed—and he knew why. In part it was because he'd be able to better protect her if she was with him. But that wasn't the entire reason. He simply wasn't ready to let her go. He wanted more nights like last night. He wanted more time with her. It was selfish, given that even more time with her would come to an end. He could not keep her. The concept sounded immature and childish: one did not 'keep' another person. One especially did not keep

Celeste, who'd already endured life as Roan's very kept ward. She would not appreciate the tenor of his thoughts.

Kieran slid a glance in her direction while she was busy peering out of the window at the lime alley. She would want to go; he was certain of it.

'The trees will be spectacular in October, decked out in their autumn foliage.' She flashed him a nervous smile from the window as the coach left the lime alley behind. 'I wonder what the house will be like inside.'

'Hopefully better than the lime alley.' Although it likely wouldn't be *much* better. The earldom of Wrexham had reverted to the Crown three years ago, and since then the estate had lain in unattended repose. He'd sent Matt and Eric on ahead to warn the staff they were coming. The staff was skeletal at best, according to his grandfather's information. They'd be scrambling at present. He did regret springing himself on them, but he hadn't known he would be coming.

The coach made a half-circle in the drive and pulled to a halt. Kieran was surprised to see that the minimal staff had taken pains to turn out for him. He'd not expected anyone to pay much attention to their arrival. They stood straight and ready on the steps, which was more than he could say for the lime alley.

'The staff awaits,' he said in quiet tones to Celeste. 'We'd better be on our best behaviour and wait for Bert to set the step.' Otherwise, he would simply have hopped out.

Celeste's hand flew to her hair, worried. 'How do I look?' She'd put her hair up in a loose twist this morning, having little success at retrieving her pins from last night's revels. She gave her travelling ensemble a futile brush with her hand and grimaced. It was the same ensemble she'd worn the day he'd taken her around London—the day they'd fled. That seemed a lifetime ago and the dress showed it.

He leaned forward and squeezed her hand. 'They'll understand that travel comes with its rigours.'

Her eyes went wide, questions flying as Bert's boots crunched on the gravel drive outside. 'We have no luggage. They'll think it's strange. Do they know who you are?'

'They know. Grandfather has been in contact with them.'

'You're the Earl, but who am I?'

Yes, how the hell would he explain *her*? She couldn't be a sister. A cousin, maybe? No; someone he met on the road? No; that wouldn't work unless she was leaving.

Bert opened the door and Kieran stepped out, turning back to hand down Celeste. A tall, thin man came forward and bowed.

'I am Trafton. My lord, my lady, welcome to Wrexham Hall. We are privileged to have you in residence—'

'I am not Lady Wrexham.' Celeste's words interrupted the butler's obviously rehearsed speech. He'd probably been working on it since Eric and Matt had arrived and thrown his household into chaos.

'My pardon, I misunderstood.' He looked to Kieran for direction. 'When I heard there was a lady travelling with you, I assumed you had married...' He was faltering and Kieran came to his aid.

'My brother was the one who married. Perhaps you've confused us; it is easy to do.' But that still did not explain Celeste's presence. Kieran improvised hastily with the first thing that came to mind. 'This is my fiancée, Miss Celeste Sharpton.' It was a good explanation for Celeste's presence. It would be less scandalous for a fiancée to have travelled with her intended and, even if someone did protest its appropriateness, the promise of impending nuptials forgave any transgressions.

Trafton was instantly relieved. 'Congratulations, Miss Sharpton; my lord.' Trafton beamed. 'When is the wedding to be, if it is not too bold to ask?'

'It is not too bold, but no date has been set. We needed to see the condition of the estate first,' Kieran said smoothly, aware that, while his answer had impressed and pleased his new butler, Celeste was quietly bristling behind a pasted-on smile. A sixth sense told him there was going to be hell to pay for this. He wished that sixth sense also would tell him when.

She was going to make him pay and she would, just as soon as she could find him. Not only had he involved her in the fiancée ruse in front of his staff *without* her permission, he'd *left* her in the care of the housekeeper—a very voluble Mrs Hanson—while he'd gone off with the steward to look over the estate. She had not seen hide nor delicious, dark hair of Kieran for hours now. If he thought he could avoid a reckoning through absence, or that she would cool down if given enough time, he would find himself in error. And if he thought she was going to preside over his household for him as a result of her sudden promotion to fiancée, he would be wrong there too.

Celeste paced the length of her newly aired chamber, her anger simmering. Not surprisingly, Mrs Hanson had put her in the countess's suite, which conveniently adjoined the earl's—just one of the many consequences of Kieran's hastily constructed ruse. At least now she could listen for telltale sounds next door that heralded the return of her errant supposed fiancé. *Aha! Voices...* She strode towards the connecting door, prepared to give him a rather large piece of her mind, and halted. He wasn't alone. *Drat.* She could not scold him for this in front of the servants. The canny man was probably counting on that, too.

Mrs Hanson bustled in; gowns draped over her arms. 'Good news, miss, I've found a trunk of the former Countess's things. They're a few years out of date, and perhaps a bit loose around the waist, but Enid is an excellent hand with a needle and we can take them in until your own wardrobe can be settled.' Apparently, confronting Kieran would have to wait. The housekeeper meant well, and Celeste would not vent her spleen on the undeserving.

At last, Mrs Hanson departed, taking a gown they'd decided on for supper to Enid, the maid. Celeste dusted her hands on her skirt. Time to deal with Kieran. This time, she was in luck. His room was quiet.

She burst into the room, armed with her indignation, ready for battle. 'What in Hades were you...?' She stopped mid-sentence, her eyes mesmerised by the sight before her: Kieran in the tub, his head thrown back, the cords of his neck exposed. His hand moved beneath the water and she felt her cheeks heat with curiosity and embarrassment—not embarrassment for him, but for herself. She was invading his privacy. The universe was not on her side today. Perhaps she ought to retreat. No.

This was too important. She had to stand her ground. She cleared her throat.

'Excuse me, I've interrupted.'

Kieran opened his eyes and sat up, unfazed by the intrusion. In fact, if she had to guess, he welcomed it. 'You're only interrupting memories of last night.' *Damn him.* Damn him for looking so good in the tub and damn him for putting her in this position and for being unbothered by it. That last restored some of her righteous indignation.

'No, you don't get to brush this off. I've been angry with you all day.' She knelt by the tub, her voice low and terse. 'What were you thinking to declare I am your fiancée? Do you know what you've done?'

'It was all I could come up with that was plausible. I couldn't say you were my sister.' He reached for a washcloth and soap, lathering up one muscled arm.

'Plausible? *Impossible* is more like it!' She fumed. 'You've made it so that I can never leave, not without causing a scandal.'

Kieran's washing stilled. 'Were you going to—leave? Nothing had been discussed.'

They'd wasted their time this morning, hiding behind small talk, running away from the remnants of the night. They should have been discussing what would happen at Wrexham.

'Eventually. My leaving is inevitable and I thought it was *assumed* between us. Now, in the matter of two sentences, you have Trafton and Mrs Hanson thinking a wedding is in the offing as soon as the estate can be repaired. I *can't* leave. You took that away from me without my permission.'

His wet fingers laced through hers, his dark eyes solemn. 'I see. It's not the ruse you mind, it's the lack of permission.' It wasn't a question and it stole the intensity of her anger—a very effective strategy for defusing a situation. She wasn't sure how she felt about that when she was the one being defused.

'Yes,' she admitted with a sigh. If she couldn't be angry at him...

He ran his thumb over her knuckles. 'We should have discussed it. I do apologise for that. Do you think you can live with it?'

She probably could, all too well. That frightened her. It would make it that much harder to leave him when the time came. He could not fully appreciate the fantasy he was asking her to step into or the kind of dreams it fed—old dreams, impossible dreams, from a girlhood before she'd realised the nightmare she lived in.

'How long do you think we have before Roan comes?' She reached for his washcloth. It was hard to stay angry at him. 'Here, lean forward and let me do your back.'

He bent, giving her access to the smooth muscles of his back. 'It's hard to say. Being out here means we're safe, but it also means we're blind. Based on what you've told me, I think four or five weeks, *if* Roan comes himself. Sooner if only his men come. They'll be back in London now, waiting for Roan's instruction and resupplying. I've sent Eric with a letter to Caine. He left this afternoon.'

She smiled. 'Eric has had no rest. We just got here.'

'He's hardy and he's used to it.' Kieran flexed his shoulders.

'You're tight.' She began to massage his neck. 'Mrs

Hanson asked about the menus for the week. I helped her with them. I hope you like braised mutton, fresh green beans and baby potatoes. I also counselled her to open a red wine so it could breathe.'

'That sounds delicious. Oh, that feels good...'

He gave a moan of appreciation and she moved on to his shoulders, a little wave of domestic pride sweeping through her. This was what it would be like to be his wife, his lady in truth. She would sit beside him as he bathed, talking about their days. She had to remind herself this was purely fantasy, not just for her but for him. A Horseman's days were not always like this. Kieran Parkhurst was no more a country gentleman who spent his days riding his acres than she was a countess planning menus.

Kieran rose in the tub, giving her an unadulterated full-frontal look at him as he sluiced himself off. Her mouth went dry and her eyes suddenly found themselves unable to look away from the muscles of his thighs and the phallus between them, ruddy, long and still in an interrupted state of semi-arousal. Her mind froze on one thought: magnificent; he was absolutely magnificent. There were certainly worse fates than pretending to be this Earl's fiancée, far worse fates indeed. But there were also potent fantasies, and that was what worried her. Potent fantasies were the hardest of all to leave.

Chapter Fifteen

The list was her antidote against the fantasy, the anchor that kept her from slipping entirely away from reality. Celeste smoothed the slip of paper flat on her dressing table and made a fold down the middle, dividing it in two. Tonight, she had to make good on her promise to deliver the first half of the list. She made a neat crease and then a neat tear before folding one half and tucking it into the bodice of the altered gown. She returned the other half to its hiding place until it was needed.

When might that be? Kieran believed they'd have a month before they needed to worry about Roan. When Roan was resolved, she would be free to go her own way and Kieran would be free to hunt down the men responsible for his brother. The thought should have filled her with expectation. She ought to be looking forward to the time when this interruption was behind her. That was really how she should be looking at these weeks with Kieran—as an interruption. She should not be looking at these weeks as an interlude, an idyll, a welcome stretch of time.

These weeks would end. Once Roan was dealt with, and once Kieran had the list, they would have no reason to need each other. There'd be no foe to fight and nothing to unite against. There'd be nothing she needed him for. The only reasons left to them would be their own and that would mean admitting to certain things—feelings that transcended their circumstances. She would not be able to hide behind her need for a bodyguard any more than he could hide behind his desire for the list and exacting justice for his brother. They would have to decide how much they meant to each other. They might decide they didn't mean anything at all; that it was their circumstances that had heightened their need to connect with another human being.

Until then, though, there was the fantasy. Already, this room looked like home. It bore her trappings, meagre as they were: her mother's pearls in a lacquered trifle box sitting beside her prized miniature on the dressing table; dresses meant for her hanging in the wardrobe. It was the details that made a fantasy real, that sucked a person in and allowed them to play out their dreams. She lifted the lid of the trifle box and traded her seaglass pendant for the pearls. She struggled for a moment with the clasp, a vivid image flashing through her mind of Kieran standing behind her, dressed in his evening clothes, smelling of spice, his hands at her neck as he solved the clasp for her like a considerate lover, like a doting husband.

She pushed the image away with a reminder that she didn't even want a husband. Men possessed; it was their nature. Given enough time, men betrayed. The only real freedom was the freedom she could give herself and that could only be maintained by being alone. To take a husband would be to trade power for protection. She thought of the dagger residing in her dressing-table drawer, the one Kieran had bought for her last night at the fair. He understood she would need to protect herself.

Celeste took a final glance at herself in the mirror and gave a little smile. She touched the pearls at the base of her neck. They looked well above the square-cut neckline of the dark-blue silk gown, shown to advantage by the maid's efforts with her hair, which had been swept to one side and fastened with a simple gold clip. Tonight, she looked like a countess. She pressed the paper inside her bodice with her fingertips, her touchstone with reality. She might look like a countess but she was only Celeste Sharpton, who had nothing but her wits to keep herself safe.

He nearly lost his wits when he saw her enter the drawing room. All that burnished chestnut hair was swept to one side, revealing the slim length of her neck, and that gown…oh, that gown. Dark blue was usually a matron's colour, but on her it was sophisticated— subdued elegance at its finest. Kieran crossed the room and took her hand, raising it to his lips.

'Civilisation agrees with you.' Then he added in a husky whisper, 'But I thought the road agreed with you as well.' He tucked her arm through his and began a slow stroll around the room. 'Would you like a sherry? Trafton tells me it will be twenty minutes before dinner is ready.'

She gave a throaty laugh and slid him a coy look. 'You clean up well, too, although I rather liked your look earlier.'

He had, too. There was something quietly potent

about the intimacy of a bath, of warm water and her hands on him, ministering to him and caring for him. It was an intimacy that transcended sex. He could have taken her on the bed afterwards and he had thought about it. He'd seen in her eyes when he'd risen from the tub that she was thinking about it too. But he'd not wanted to ruin the moment. Not everything had to lead to sex in order to be intimate. It was something he knew intuitively but seldom practised. That he was practising it now, experiencing it now, carried its own level of alarm and warning.

They stopped at the sideboard and he poured her a glass of sherry. 'Cheers; here's to a safe arrival and looking good in our second-hand clothes.'

She sipped her sherry, her sea-glass eyes intent on him over the rim of the tiny glass. 'I see we're playing by all the rules tonight: the clothes, the etiquette… You are a compelling lord of the manor.' She paused. 'But of course, you really are lord of the manor, Lord Wrexham.'

He could not tell if she meant that critically. 'You are playing your part admirably too, future Lady Wrexham.'

'All the world's a stage.' She offered the Shakespeare line with a little toast of her own.

Too true. While they were here at Wrexham, they would be on stage every minute of every day. The house and its staff, the vicar, and the townspeople would all require it of them.

'Did Mrs Hanson find the pearls for you?' he asked.

'No, they're mine, from my mother. My father gave them to me for my sixteenth birthday.' She smiled a little as she said it.

'When is your birthday? It seems like something a

fiancé ought to know.' A small detail to add to his growing horde of facts and observations about this fascinating woman.

'February.' She gave him a meaningful look, willing him to put the pieces together without comment. He could do that now. In some ways, it was a testament to how much he knew of her. February—three months before her father's death. They would have spent the birthday dreaming of their new home and their new life.

Trafton called them to dinner and Kieran leaned close to her ear. 'Are you ready for Act Two?' Perhaps it hadn't been fair of him to require such a large commitment from her. He was only now beginning to see the extent of the ruse. They could not let their guard down, even in their own home.

Dinner was delicious, but it was public. He'd not realised how public a gentleman's meal was until he was desperate for some privacy. Footmen stood nearby waiting to fill glasses, remove covers and hear every word. Everything he and Celeste said would be reported downstairs, so they filled their dinner conversation with a discussion of their day. While the steward had shown him the stables and the grounds, Mrs Hanson had toured her through the house, discussed linens and silvers and the need for more staff.

'I'll send enquiries to the town tomorrow and start the hiring process. I'll want to see the stables as well, so I can choose a horse for riding,' Celeste said from the other end of the table. The distance was ridiculous. He wanted her beside him, close enough to breathe her in.

'It would be much appreciated.' He felt caught in a limbo that was part reality and part make-believe. This was his home now; that part was very much real. But this taste of domestication, of discussing his day and handling the business of running a home with Celeste, was no less powerful for its pretence. They were pretending they were setting up house; that they would build a future here. That she would always be here. For better or for worse, this pretence would be finished within a month. And, when it was done, she would have stamped her mark all over it. He would sit in this room and imagine her in her blue silk. He would smell her scent in the countess's suite. He would awake at night, reaching for her. He would spend his days wondering where she was and if she was safe.

By the end of the meal, he'd had enough of being on display, and perhaps she had too. Her hand kept drifting to her necklace, her fingers worrying a pearl.

Kieran turned to the butler. 'Trafton, my compliments to Cook and to everyone who scrambled to make the meal possible. We'll have help for you as soon as we can. For now, consider yourselves dismissed until morning. Miss Sharpton and I can finish in here on our own. Close the door behind you.'

When they were alone, Kieran offered a smile. 'I am sorry I could not dismiss them sooner. It would have disappointed them not to serve on our first night.' His staff saw this visit quite differently from the way they did. For the staff, this was the beginning of a new lord to serve and the chance to be active once more after a three-year hiatus. This visit was about hope and new possibilities.

Celeste straightened her shoulders and set aside her napkin as if she were setting aside her role as Miss Sharpton, the Earl's fiancée. When she looked at him from the other end of the table, she was Celeste Sharpton, the keen-minded woman he'd met at St Luke's who'd been desperate to protect herself and was intent on trusting no one. 'I understand. You are playing a role and yet you're not playing a role. You are beginning relationships that will last throughout your lifetime. You must establish yourself.' Him. But not her. These were things that he, and only he, must do.

Kieran did not like the sound of that—how exclusionary it was, as if she'd already cut herself out of that future because she didn't belong here and she was not part of that world. Unless...came the unbidden thought...he invited her in... Unless he made a space for her in this world. Would she accept a space even if he could find a way to make one? It would require breaking promises he'd made to himself.

Her statement struck him as accusatory too, as if he was changing; as if Lord Wrexham and Kieran Parkhurst were two different men. 'I am still a Horseman.' He defended himself.

'Yes, and to that end we have business to conduct.' She rose from her chair and came towards him, hips swaying beneath the blue silk, conjuring hot images of what he'd like that business to be. He'd like to sit her on the edge of this table, spread her legs wide, bury his face beneath her skirts and pleasure her until she moaned his name, his own mind devoid of any thought but delivering that pleasure. She reached him and her hand went to the bodice of her gown. His cock hardened.

'The first half of the list.' She pulled out a slip of paper and his thoughts tumbled like the shards in a kaleidoscope, forming and reforming until the shape of them made sense. She was not seducing him; more was the pity. 'I promised payment upon safe passage to Wrexham. I always pay my debts.'

The list—the damn list. Something angry and hot flared within him. The anger was for himself. He'd not been thinking of the list but perhaps he should have been. That list was the key to avenging Stepan. Vengeance might be the only recourse they had. But he'd been too carried away with imagining his life at Wrexham, imagining her here and then imagining her gone, and thinking about what the future might look like when he should have been thinking about the present—about his brother. Goodness knew, there was plenty in the here and now that demanded his attention. He'd thought he was beyond such distractions, that he'd learned his lesson from Sofia, and that he had his attraction under control. Apparently, not as well as he thought.

'Put the list away.' He reached for her hips and drew her to him. Celeste was not Sofia and tonight was not for reviewing lessons or lists. Remorse could wait for the morning.

'I *always* pay my debts,' she repeated, putting the list on the table beside his plate, her tone challenging his command and her eyes like sharp shards. Her walls were going up. She, too, was aware of the magic this place was capable of. She, too, understood the lines between business and pleasure had been crossed in some irrevocable way. She was trying to hold back, trying not to take the next step over that line. He wouldn't allow it. He would break them down before they had time to set. He wanted her with him in this madness completely.

'Is that all this is to you—a balancing of the scales?

Is that all *I* am to you?' He would have the truth from her, and he would pleasure it out of her if needed. Her mouth might speak of business, but her body said she'd spent the meal struggling with the same dilemma that plagued him: how to balance personal want with worldly needs? And what happened when the thing, the *person*, you wanted required you to go against all that you thought you believed in?

'Don't ask those questions, Kieran. I cannot answer them any better than you can.'

She reproached him but her eyes were soft now, the shards gone. She reached a hand out to his hair, running her fingers through the tangle of his curls. He turned into her caress, letting himself luxuriate in her touch. Usually, he was the one doing the touching, perhaps because he knew how good it felt to be touched, how much he loved being touched and how powerful touch could be to heal, console and arouse. Here and now, her touch was all three. He wanted her with a fierceness unrivalled.

He rose, desire riding him hard. 'Close your eyes and make a wish.'

She did, a smile playing at her lips that said she guessed the direction of his thoughts and that she approved. 'I wish we were on the road again...' She breathed the words into reality. He wished that too. On the road, the world was simple. The road was not so much a place as it was a mindset. On the road, one could live in the moment.

'Your wish is my command,' he whispered against her ear. He lifted her to the table and knelt before her, pushing back her silken skirts.

This was his wish too—to lose himself in her pleasure

and to forget for a while as he placed slow kisses up the length of her leg, listened to her gasp when he tongued a sensitive spot behind her knee and heard the passion unfurling in the moan that purled up her throat when his mouth found the epicentre of her pleasure.

He felt the ripple of languid waves move through her and felt them grow to quakes until her body shuddered and shook with them until each lick of his tongue turned her moans into uncontrolled gasps and her breath became ragged...until her body arched and something on the table above him crashed. Her legs clamped around him, holding him to her as her pleasure fully loosened, his thoughts of lists, payments and revenge forgotten and set aside.

For a short while, all was right with their world. If only they could hold on to it. But that was an impossible wish. These moments, this time here at Wrexham, would have to be given up. Their lives would demand it, vengeance for Stepan would demand it, even if their hearts might request it be otherwise.

Chapter Sixteen

Celeste held on to the days that followed with both hands, despite the knowledge they would inevitably slip through her grasp. She'd never be able to hold on tight enough. They were happy, heady days. The proof was everywhere. One just had to ask Mrs Hanson, who insisted all was right at Wrexham for the first time in years. One just had to see the contentment on her face, or walk around the Hall to note the happy signs of progress: the polished banisters, the dust-free tabletops; the vases full of fresh seasonal flora decorating those tabletops; the beaten carpets, the swept floors and the polished silver that decorated the supper table each night for meals that featured farm-grown produce and locally raised meats.

'All thanks to you, miss,' Mrs Hanson would say. 'You've brought us all back to life.'

It was not just the staff, which now boasted several newly hired and rehired faces, or the dusty, neglected house, but Celeste had brought herself back to life as well for a short time. She was like the leaves turning in the autumn in a last brilliant sweep of colour before they dried up and were blown away. Deep down, she had to face the truth: these days at Wrexham would be her last with Kieran.

Despite the engagement ruse, she would have to leave, although it was easy to set that aside in the moment of the day. The key to any good fantasy was complete immersion and she'd mastered that, throwing herself into the role of lady of the house. She had a routine: hacking out each morning with Kieran before breakfast, then breakfast and meeting with Mrs Hanson. There were various projects to oversee in the mornings and then calls in the afternoon before dinner. She was good at running a large home; her boarding school education had seen to that. She enjoyed the challenges and planning that came with it. And it pleased her to please Kieran, to make this house a gift to him—a parting gift.

She regretted none of it except knowing that this time with him was not sustainable. Perhaps that was why she held on to the days so tightly and threw herself into her role so thoroughly. The perfection of these days was precious, but it wouldn't last. Therein, she thought, lay the reason for their perfection, for their preciousness: they were rare and short-lived, like the vibrant colours of leaves on the newly trimmed trees of the lime alley.

Today, she and Kieran were celebrating that foliage with a picnic on Wrexham land, and the day could not have been more perfect for such an outing. There was a coolness on the air as she and Kieran lay staring up at a crisp blue sky, the remnants of their impromptu picnic packed away in their saddlebags. The day was too nice to be indoors, Kieran had argued, and she'd needed little persuasion. Riding round the land at the Hall was becoming a delight, each bridleway a little more curated each day thanks to the newly hired stable staff. While she'd been busy in the house, Kieran had been equally busy with the grounds and the stables.

'Landownership suits you,' she said as she snuggled against him. It was just cool enough to appreciate the warmth of another body.

'It's a thankless task and a never-ending one.' Kieran brushed off the compliment but she heard the pride in his voice and how pleased he was with her words. He stretched and wrapped an arm about her. 'I did not think I'd like running an estate. More to the point, I did not think I'd like running this one.'

Her fingers played idly on his chest. 'Because you felt the title and the estate were recompense for Stepan?'

He nodded. 'I didn't want to like Wrexham but I do. There is work to be done here and there is a lot of potential that has not yet been tapped. This property could be a real legacy.' He was thinking of a family, a son or two to leave it all for. She loved listening to him talk like this, letting his thoughts and dreams play out. Through his words, she could see Wrexham Hall come alive. Those dreams danced in his eyes as he looked up at the sky and she had to look away. Those were dreams she could not be part of.

'The community would benefit,' he went on. 'There's coal here. If I rented out coal fields, we could bring more business to the area and create more jobs, more trade. Coal is going to be in high demand over the next few years.'

'You'll do it. You will do it all,' she encouraged, the familiar reminder flaring to life that she would not be here to see it. She tried not to think about that and most days she was successful.

'I suppose that's a rather long response to whether or not I've enjoyed being a landowner these past weeks.' He gave a chuckle, laughing at himself.

'What of you?' He raised himself up on an elbow, his gaze lingering on her face as if searching for something. 'Have you enjoyed these weeks running the house? I admit that I had not planned to put such responsibility on your shoulders. It was not intentional when I blurted out our ruse. I want you to know that.'

'I know,' she replied carefully, sensing that the question led to something more. 'I have enjoyed it.'

She paused, debating her next words. This was a chance to assure him she'd not been put out, and also a chance to remind him that nothing had changed between them or could change. Even if he might have forgotten it for the moment, she had not.

'When I ran Roan's household, there was no joy in it once I understood his intentions. It was all strategy. I felt like a general commanding troops for corrupt purposes. I'd plan meals for men who were in the business of killing, of harming their fellow man. I'd organise entertainments for men who deliberately made war. That made me complicit in Roan's evil. But here, my efforts are put to good. That pleases me. I like having a purpose.'

'It suits you. Mrs Hanson swears you're a marvel.' Kieran grinned. 'I think you're a marvel too. Likely for different reasons, though.'

He gave a wicked laugh that had her thinking of the nights spent in his big bed. She would miss those nights. She needed to be careful here; the look in his eyes was worrisome. He was contemplating diverging from their predetermined path. Being at home, *his* home, was affecting him. No doubt, he was reconsidering his stance on avoiding marriage now that he'd lived at Wrexham and seen its potential. He needed a wife. It was natural to look in her direction—she was close at hand. But it could not be her. She would need to maintain objective detachment for them both before this went too far.

'I am glad you're pleased. I want things in good order before I go so that you'll have something to build on.' She smiled to soften the introduction of a difficult topic. She did not want him to guess how much it cost her to say the words, how much it hurt to think of him moving on with his life without her, or to think of him bringing another here and having that other take over the work she'd begun. If he suspected how hard it was, he would use that to persuade her.

He met the mention of her leaving with equanimity. She'd not expected that. She'd expected an outburst, an angry protest. Instead, he kissed her fingers, each one in slow consideration, and posed the question that haunted her whenever she thought about going. 'What if you stayed?'

'What ifs' were dangerous ground, full of make-believe and things that simply couldn't come true. She pulled her hand away. 'Don't do that, Kieran. Don't play at such possibilities. You and I both know what we're doing here. We're playing house. We've created an incredible game of make-believe and we are falling for our own fantasies.'

'Make-believe?' He sat up, offended at her words.

Now she had a rise out of him. 'Do you really think that when we make love it's all pretend?'

She sat up too. She didn't want to quarrel with him. Their time together was too fleeting to waste it sparring over the inevitable. But the inevitable *must* be discussed and they'd been putting it off since the night she'd given him the first half of the list. 'Playing house doesn't put off Roan riding down the road towards us.' That was the most obvious reason they had to discuss.

There was a light in his eyes, a slow smile curling on his mouth. She wondered what trap she had sprung. 'What if Roan never comes? It's possible. I have made connections with people who caught him the first time—Preston Worth, who manages the coastguard, and Sir Liam Casek. If Worth can catch Roan before he even lands, or Casek can stop him in London, he will never come down our road. What do you say to that? Surely, that changes everything?'

It was a large assumption, though. 'Even if it were true, it wouldn't be enough,' she said softly, hating to play the devil's advocate, but such an advocate was desperately needed when one stayed in a fantasy world too long. 'It doesn't change the fact that you're a Horseman. There is the list. You have a brother to avenge and there will be missions after that. You can never solely be the lord of the manor.'

'Can you not live with that duality?' Kieran questioned. 'It did not seem to be a concern on the road or up until now.'

'It didn't *matter* up until now. On the road, what we had between us was only an affair, two people taking comfort with one another during a crisis. Even here at

Wrexham, this was to be a ruse with an end. There was no need to contemplate the future. The future comes with different expectations than the present does.' Life with a Horseman, life with a man who would always keep her safe while constantly putting himself in danger, would mean never completely getting away from the world she'd run from. She'd merely be on the other side of it.

'Don't you think it could end another way?' Kieran prompted.

'Do *you*? Really, Kieran? I think you're caught in the fantasy of playing house. A few weeks ago, you were determined not to wed, as I was. Have you forgotten that neither of us are the marrying type? Now we're trying to convince ourselves otherwise simply because what we have at present is...nice.'

'Nice?' He snorted at that. 'We have something better than *nice* between us, Celeste.'

'But there is more than that to us, more between us that must be sorted. We have our own needs. Marriage requires the surrender of my freedom. I do not want to be owned by a man, Kieran. I've already travelled that route. As my guardian, Roan possessed me. I promised myself when I fled I would not put myself in that position again.'

'I would not ask it of you. You would not be my slave, Celeste. Surely, in the time we've been together, you know that? Surely I've shown you I would not treat you like that?' He paused, another thought crossing his dark eyes. 'Is that what you think of me—that marriage to me would be akin to being Roan's ward?' Kieran was either aghast at her thoughts or the dark direction of their conversation.

'Yes and no. Legally, the ownership would always be there. Marriage is easy for men, Kieran. Men give up nothing. Even so, I wonder if you're truly free. You are owned by your grief. You will spend the next year hunting the men on the list because you can find them, whereas you cannot your brother. You've not dealt with the loss of your brother. I... I am not sure there's room for another in your life until you can accept that he is gone.'

'He *is* gone,' Kieran said forcefully. 'But I refuse to forget him. I do not want to erase him.'

She grabbed his hands in her earnestness. 'No, of course not. I'm not saying to forget him. I am saying I'm concerned about what this list will do to you. I regret offering it to you. It's a tool for revenge. It would be easy to think that you owe your brother that revenge. It would also be easy to think that, by avenging him, you will fill the space his loss has left. It won't. Violence solves nothing but it does beget more violence.' She'd lived through it. She did not think she could live with herself if he died pursuing that vengeance.

His dark eyes were obsidian-hard. 'Am I to ignore the list, then?'

She would make this demand and force him to see that she asked too much of him; that his fantasy of playing house asked too much of him and that it existed in contradiction to the life of the Horsemen. 'I think you must if you want to keep a family safe. I do recall that was originally your biggest opposition to marrying when we first met. You cannot seek out violent men and expect them not to retaliate. You would be deliberately bringing that violence home.'

Kieran was quiet for a long while. Her argument had hit a target. 'My brother has chosen marriage. Grandfather chose marriage and kept his family safe for decades.'

'But what if you can't? What if the worst did happen? If you're going to play with "what ifs", Kieran, you have to play with all of the possibilities. Could you live with yourself if anything happened to them?' He already had one scar and she suspected that was merely the visible one. 'You still carry Leipzig with you, in your mind. The blame, the guilt for letting down your guard just the once, has left you with doubt.'

She relented for a moment, lying back down on the blanket before launching her last salvo, a gentle arrow aimed at his heart. God, how it would hurt to give this man up. He was certainly too good for her. She had to help him see that. 'Even if all of your "what ifs" were right, I would not be a credit to you.'

He followed her down and propped himself up on an elbow. 'How can you say that, when I look at the progress you made in the house, when I hear Mrs Hanson sing your praises? I see what you've done for me, and for others, even though your role is only part of a ruse. But you haven't treated it as such. You've made these last few weeks *real*. I don't believe they are all pretence for you. You don't want to walk away from this or from me.'

So, he *had* seen the truth despite her best efforts. He was too perceptive by half. 'As you said that first night, our being here is different for the staff, for the town, than it is for us. They're counting on me. They need more from me than a façade.' She tried to rationalise why she'd thrown herself into her role wholeheartedly.

He reached a hand out to stroke her cheek and push back a russet strand of hair, and her resolve trembled. 'What about what I need from you? Maybe *I* need you to stay, Celeste.'

He needed her. It was a wonderful, warming thought. His eyes lingered on her mouth, dark and burning. It would be easy to let the conversation go, to let sex replace words, but it wouldn't solve anything, and she didn't want him to think he'd won this argument.

'I am not countess material. Yes, I went to boarding schools with the same girls who were raised to marry titles and run noble homes. But their reputations were spotless. There was no blemish to their name, no scandal. I am none of those things, and you know that.' He was too smart not to, and he knew how Society worked.

'I am none of those things either. I've killed men, I've stolen secrets and I've spread false information to confuse enemy troops. I've had numerous affairs, some with married women.'

'And for that, Society calls you a rake and celebrates your behaviour. Women do not have that leniency. We are either Madonnas or whores. Neither are actually celebrated. Madonnas are too ethereal and whores are too earthy. We can't win.'

She could feel his gaze on her, considering, weighing her words, and feel the warmth of his hand on her hip. 'No decent girl would be caught on a picnic blanket like this.'

'Then we will be scandalous together and everyone will say how well we suit.' He was patently avoiding the arguments she'd made earlier, treating them as if they didn't exist or matter.

'That won't last. We'll be outcasts, and not because of you but because of me. I am the ward of free Europe's sworn enemy, and the personal enemy of the Horsemen.'

She lowered her voice even further. 'No one marries the ward of the man responsible for killing his brother. A man of your standing does not marry a woman who has nothing. I have no money, no title, no bloodline. You are an earl and the grandson of an earl. Your sister is married to a duke. I am beneath you in every way. You are a man of honour but I am a woman of dishonour— my father's and Roan's. I am dirty, Kieran.'

And there were all the ways in which she'd abetted Roan's perfidy. These were considerations that might be overlooked for an affair on the road, but must be weighed in the balance when one contemplated a future in which they were tied to one another.

He dismissed her arguments with three simple words. 'I don't care.'

How nice it would be to think that was true, that his words would be true today and on into the future. But there *would* come a time when he would care—for the sake of his family and for the sake of his children. He was being stubborn. He didn't like to lose. She had to make him see the impossibility. 'I care, though—for you and for me. Maybe you have talked yourself into the idea of making this fantasy real, but I have not.'

Perhaps he, too, sensed they were at impasse. He shifted on the blanket and changed his tack. 'Instead of a life together, you will seek a life of loneliness when you leave here? You would trade what we have and could have for that?' It was cannily done. He knew very well her plans for the future were unformed, contingent on the outcome with Roan.

'I object to the word "loneliness". I will seek a life of freedom and independence,' she corrected. 'Why is it so hard for men to see that?' Probably because they'd never been without those things and didn't understand their worth. His eyes were dark with thought. She'd disappointed him. No doubt he was seldom disappointed by women. But he would appreciate it later.

'I can give you more than that. I can give you a home. I see how you crave this place. I saw how your eyes lit up from the first day. I can give you a family. You envy me mine—in the best of ways.'

'At the expense of my freedom and your happiness?' She shook her head. 'Kieran, it's not that I don't care for you. It's that I care too much for you. I can't make you happy. Your misery would become my misery.'

He gave a dry laugh. 'Is this the part where I am supposed to say, let me be the judge of that? We don't have to decide anything today. I did not mean for our picnic to turn into this and I don't think you did either. But, if you're thinking about leaving, promise me you will also think about what I said. Think about staying…because I want you to.'

'I will.' She could give him the words. It wouldn't change anything; it couldn't. But heaven help her when he looked at her with those eyes and stroked her hip with his hand. He wasn't making it easy. She was going to have to fight a two-fronted resistance—one against him and one against herself. History was not kind to such battles. They were seldom victorious strategies.

Chapter Seventeen

He was losing her. It was not something Kieran was used to. He wasn't in the habit of women telling him it was over—quite the opposite—and now he didn't know what to do, only that he must do something. He ran a hand down the oak surface of the banister on his way to the study. His fingertips trailed over the smooth, polished sheen of the wood in idle acknowledgement that even the banister bore her stamp. In the time they'd been here, Celeste had managed to put her mark on this space, and on him as well. Just as he'd predicted.

When had it happened that he found himself thinking beyond the weeks here, thinking into a future that he'd not thought of or dared to dream of for years since becoming a Horseman? Yet, her presence had called those dreams of home and family to life. He didn't quite understand it. He'd been with women, beautiful women; women he'd met under varying circumstances, both tame and risk-laden. It had never been a problem to leave them when the time had come. There'd been women he'd missed more than others, but there'd never been a woman he'd wished had stayed. Until her: until Celeste Sharpton. How like fate to play such a cruel trick. The one woman he wanted to stay was the only one who wouldn't.

In the office, he went to the big desk that already felt like his—also thanks to her. Celeste had gone to the stationer's in Wrexham and ordered stationery with a majestic, curlicued 'W' embossed on thick, cream paper. Kieran smiled to himself, remembering how she'd come home from that particular visit to town, laden with packages. He'd thought she'd gone dress shopping. Wasn't that what women usually did? He'd been surprised to discover all the packages were for him: stationery, calling cards and a beautiful round brass ink-well supported at its base by four bent-backed Atlases at the cardinal directions.

'Because that's what you do, Kieran.' She'd sat on his desk and wrapped her arms around him. 'You hold up the sky for all of us, whether you are Wrexham or Parkhurst.' She'd kissed him, long and hard, whispering, 'I missed you today…' And he'd not been able to resist giving the desk a proper baptism.

Kieran scraped a hand over his face. Would he think about that *every* time he sat here? It would be hard to get work done, or hard to concentrate. He needed to be able to do both today. Perhaps this was a reminder as to why he made a habit of never engaging his feelings in relationships. Sex did not require it, his women did not require it and the dark edge of diplomacy certainly did not require it—preferred the opposite, in fact.

Celeste had engaged his feelings whether he'd willed it or not and now he was back to the question he'd started with: how had that happened? How had she slipped beneath his guard? Why was he so ready to throw away his standards, or the code of conduct that had kept him safe all these years? Why was he ready to forget the lesson from Leipzig for a woman who didn't want to stay, and who would choose to give *him* up? She'd said as much yesterday on the picnic blanket even as she'd touched him, roused him, her eyes telling a different story than her words.

Kieran took out the precious list of names with its rough edge where she'd torn it. He looked at the list with new eyes today after their heated discussion on the picnic blanket. It *was* a tool for revenge, something that could eat him alive under the guise of seeking justice. Was she right? He couldn't deny that the names on the list *were* meant to be tracked down, if not by him, then by others in his grandfather's network. He'd sent Bert with a copy of the names to his grandfather in the hope that Grandfather would recognise them or have some insight into who they were. He'd also sent the list for safekeeping in case...Roan made it to Wrexham and the worst happened so that he couldn't deliver the list to his grandfather in person.

From a desk drawer, he took out an exquisite leather-bound appointment book with his name etched in smart, tiny gold letters on the lower right-hand corner of the cover, another thoughtful present from Celeste. He opened to the front, which contained a full calendar for each month, and made another mark. September had come and gone. October was underway. He closed his eyes. His five weeks were up. The time had flown. A reckoning was closer than ever.

He flipped through the book, coming to the pages where he might record his appointments and notes for each day and re-read them. He'd been tracking Roan as best he could, estimating when the man would land in England and how long it would take him to journey from the coast to London. London would slow him down but it would be a necessary stop. It was the last place Celeste had been seen. Roan would retrace Celeste's steps, perhaps stopping at the boarding house. Kieran did not expect the landlord and his wife to be loyal. Roan was too persuasive for that, but he did hope the landlord and his wife were safe.

It would be difficult for Roan to gather information about the Horsemen. London was empty and Roan couldn't move around in the open. Any whiff of his presence in the city would bring the law. It would take him a little time to learn the Horsemen had been given titles and estates. Then, he'd have to decide—would this be a divide and conquer action? Had Celeste and her Horseman gone to Barrow, to Cheshire or to the estate in Sussex? He may well come to Cheshire. The question was how many men would he bring and when?

He tapped a finger on the diary page. Soon…any day…today…tomorrow… Unless…what a powerful word that was. Hope sprang eternal. He did have some hope in Casek and Worth, as he'd told Celeste. They'd captured Roan the first time a few years ago and put him on trial. But Roan had powerful friends in the Duke of Amesbury's family and justice had not prevailed. Roan had escaped to Brussels and continued to operate as usual. If anyone could stop Roan, it would be them. He'd have no way of knowing immediately, though, if Worth or Casek had any success, just as he had no way of knowing if Roan was on the road right now, coming for him and the woman he cared for, or if he'd already been caught. It was a damned helpless feeling to be so blind, not knowing if help or hell was riding down the road.

He was missing his brothers keenly, not only for help with Roan but for advice regarding Celeste. He did not want to lose her but how did he convince her to stay when there were so many reasons for her to go? All of her arguments were valid. If they were to let logic dictate their decisions, he ought to let her go. What he wanted from her and for them was beyond logic. Ironically, it would require a leap of faith from two people who did not operate from a position of faith and trust, and who had in fact been betrayed by those very things in the past. In order to be together, they both had to break the cycle.

There was a knock and Celeste peered around the edge of the door. 'May I come in? I need your opinion.' She was all smiles as she twirled in front of his desk, the skirts of her gown belling out in a feminine swirl of deep russet silk. Matching slippers with tiny black bows peeped from beneath. 'Do you like it?' She flashed him an expectant smile.

Did he like it? Dear Lord, he was rock-hard at the sight of her. The *modiste* in town had outdone herself. The bodice was tight and streamlined to show off her slim torso in contrast to the billowing fullness of the skirts—on which fabric had not been spared to make deep, luxurious folds. He pretended to give the gown serious contemplation, letting his gaze drift over the tiny sleeves, the scoop of the neckline and the way her breasts pushed upward, making no secret of their fullness and their firmness. He knew how those breasts felt.

Even now, his hands itched to fit themselves to her and to fill themselves. He gestured for her to give another spin. Lord, he loved that skirt, never mind that such full skirts were not quite the fashion.

'Well,' he drawled, teasing. 'After giving the dress full consideration, my only concern is the bodice.'

'What's wrong with it?' Her hands went protectively to her midsection, her eyes showing genuine concern, and he regretted teasing her.

He came round the desk and put his hands on her hips, luxuriating in the feel of her beneath the smooth folds of silk. 'Can you breathe in it? I can nearly span your waist with two hands.'

'You have very large hands,' she flirted, her worry starting to fade.

'I do. I have other large parts as well, which leads me to my second concern,' He gave a wicked grin. 'That gown fastens down the back. It will take for ever to get you out of this.'

Her green eyes sparkled. 'You're not meant to get me out of this. You're meant to dance with me in it.' She gave him a smile and a twirl and he thought it had never felt so good to please someone, to spoil someone, as it did her. 'The gown is for the harvest ball.'

She held out the skirts and bit her lip in that characteristic way she had when she was unsure. 'You *do* like it? The bill should arrive later today. The dress was a bit dear, but I wanted to be certain we made a good impression. It's your first official formal outing as Earl of Wrexham.'

She smiled up at him and he drew her close. In that moment, he didn't care what the gown had cost. 'I can always sell my ink stand if needs must.' He gave a husky laugh. 'I am holding autumn come to life in my arms. I can hardly put a price on that.'

He bent his mouth, capturing hers in a lingering kiss, the forbidden wish springing to mind—that she was his wife, that this was for ever and that Roan would not be riding down the road to wreck this. *Let him try*, the Horseman in him roared with fierce protectiveness. A Horseman protected what was his, and fought for what was his, and this chestnut-haired, russet-gowned beauty *was* his whether she liked it or not. Heaven help Roan if he laid a hand on anyone under his protection.

Kieran's hands tightened at her waist and she stepped back. 'Careful, you'll crush the fabric and then I will look like a smashed pumpkin,' she scolded with a coy smile. 'Give me half an hour to get out of it and then come upstairs. I'll have something more…practical on.' She tapped him on the arm. 'That should give you enough time to finish whatever I've interrupted. Back to work with you.'

She was off in a silken swish of russet skirts, leaving a trail of hyacinth promise in her wake. How would he be expected to work after *that*? Coupled with the fact that she expected him to sit back down at the desk they'd vigorously christened not so long ago.

To his credit, Kieran did try. He *did* sit down at the desk. He *did* stare at the list before putting it away. He was starting to resent it and how it stood between him and happiness. He started a letter to his grandfather but his mind wandered to other more important consider-ations: was this what it had been like for Caine when he'd fallen for Mary? Had it been impossible to keep his mind on work? Had he been desperate to keep her, fearful she would leave? And even more fearful that she would have to leave; that the relationship was impossible? Had he wondered if this, at last, was *love* and what to do about it? Had he wondered how to fight it and then realised he didn't *want* to fight it but that he wanted to join it?

Kieran rose from the desk and checked his pocket watch. He had just enough time to visit the family vault. If Celeste wanted them to make a good impression, the future Countess of Wrexham, ruse or not, needed something more than a pretty sea-glass pendant from a village fair or her mother's pearls. People would expect it and, if it happened to compel her to revisit her thoughts about staying, and about making their situation more reality than ruse, so be it. He was not opposed to fighting with all the weapons in his arsenal to convince her to stay.

'You do *not* fight fair,' Celeste murmured, her hand trailing over the topaz necklace at her throat, the bed-sheet riding low on her hip. This afternoon had been decadent—lovemaking, jewels and Kieran lying un-abashedly naked beside her in the aftermath.

'Who said anything about fighting? Are we fight-ing?' Kieran protested with false innocence. 'You were the one who insisted we make a good impression, that's all. People will expect us to put the Wrexham vault on display. They will think I am miserly if you show up in anything less.' He grinned.

She felt her resistance start to slip. She ought not let him spoil her like this—like a husband spoiling a wife—especially after yesterday's discussion. It might give him the wrong impression—that her resolve was wavering and that she was indeed reconsidering. She might give herself the wrong impression too—that the future he laid out was possible and that her reasons for resistance could be overcome. She must remain resolute; it was for the best.

'I feel positively wanton wearing jewellery while I lie abed naked in the middle of the afternoon, like someone's wicked mistress.' She laughed softly.

'Good.' Kieran reached for the box. 'Try the bracelet.' He helped her with the clasp, his fingers skimming her skin in tiny strokes that set the want loose within her yet again. 'The set is quite the heirloom. It's part of the original estate, dating back to the fifteen-hundreds.'

He adjusted the bracelet and held up her wrist to the light, letting the stones dance and change from red to russet in their gold settings. They would look dazzling with her gown. 'It's made from Imperial Topaz, found in Brazil and acquired during some early exploration efforts. The first Earl of Wrexham had the stones cut into shapes of leaves as a wedding gift. He and his wife were married in the autumn, so it seemed appropriate.'

'Sold.' Celeste leaned back against her pillows with a laugh, studying the bracelet. 'Have you ever thought of selling jewellery if dark diplomacy doesn't work out? I'm sure Rundell's would hire you. All you'd have to do is put a bracelet on a woman's wrist, run your fingers over her skin and tell her a story. Husbands would hate you.'

He leaned close, gently screwing an earring onto each ear. They were long, slim dangling affairs and he turned her chin this way and that, smiling in satisfaction. 'I wanted to see how they'd catch the light. Stunning...' He breathed.

'You should definitely not sell earrings.' Every husband in London would call him out.

'Well, I'd keep my clothes on, of course.' He nuzzled her neck. 'I only take them off for my special clients.'

'I don't think clothes would change your sales.' She laughed. 'You're just as charming with them on.'

'Is this your way of saying you like the set, or your way of saying you like *me*?' He drew her close, kissing her neck. Very soon, conversation would be *de trop*—again—not that she minded. There were worse ways to pass an afternoon and she did not want a repeat of yesterday.

She wrapped her arms around his neck and looked up into his face, at those beautiful dark eyes and that thick, wavy hair that was always in disarray. 'You're shameless, fishing for compliments, Kieran Parkhurst. You know very well that I like you.' She more than liked him. He'd shaken her world, forced her to test her assumptions about her future. If she wasn't careful, he'd upend that world.

Enough to stay...?

The words lingered unspoken between them. She didn't want them to come to life and wreck the peace of the afternoon. Celeste draped a leg over his hip and levered herself upright, catching him by surprise.

'We've already done you on top this afternoon. This time, I'm on top.' She lifted her hands to her hair and let it fall through her fingers, watching his eyes go wide, watching all thought recede until she had his full attention here and now. The afternoon was safe again, she was safe again, her priorities still intact. There would be no more talk of leaving or staying, or of the future that was quickly becoming the present.

Celeste moved over him, letting her breasts brush his chest, the topaz teardrop of the necklace dangling between them. 'You will have to tell me,' she whispered, 'how the jewels look when I do this…' She sat up and moved back, lowering herself onto him. She moved her hips with a coy smile, sensing she was in control for the moment. 'Well?'

His Adam's apple worked as he looked up at her. 'They look good.' His hands bracketed her hips as he caught on to her game. 'Try moving up and down.' He sucked in his breath as she moved on him. 'Oh, yes, now they look even better.' He levered himself up to steal a kiss, his abdomen muscles flexing. 'Now, how about we make those jewels bounce?'

'You are a wicked man.' She laughed, fully enjoying herself as he became an active participant in the seduction.

He grabbed her around the waist and flipped her beneath him. 'I am, and I am all yours.'

Her one thought as climax claimed her was: if only this could be true; if only this could be for ever, maybe then a compromise would be worth it. Or maybe, he was right—no compromise would be needed between true partners. Maybe, with Kieran, things could be different, but only if she could be different. Nothing would change unless she did, and he did. They would have to change together for it to work. That would take a leap of faith.

Chapter Eighteen

Dangerous thoughts grew, fed by the mind's willingness to rationalise away opposition until there was nothing left to keep her from staying. The longer she was with Kieran, the less reason there was to cling to her arguments for leaving and the more powerful the 'what if' became. By the evening of the harvest assembly, her optimism was riding high as she sat before her dressing table, letting Enid do her hair.

Perhaps it *was* possible to stay and have this home, have this life—a life free from Roan, where everything she touched or did would not be tainted by corruption. Surely Roan would have come by now? The five weeks Kieran had theorised as a timeline had passed—albeit only by a few days. If Roan never came, no one need ever know who she really was. She need not be anyone but the Earl of Wrexham's fiancée, and subsequently his countess.

If she was willing to belong to him. Her hand stilled on the leaf necklace at her throat. She'd been so excited about wearing it and about tonight, so caught up in the possibilities of her new thoughts, she'd not listened to the words in her own head: to be *Wrexham's* fiancée, to be *his* countess. To be those things meant allowing her identity to be defined by the man at her side, which was the very thing she'd wanted to protect herself against, the very thing that threatened her freedom.

Do those things threaten your freedom, or is it Roan? Would Kieran Parkhurst be the same?

That was the new challenge: her thoughts had conjured support for the idea that perhaps Kieran would be different and that she could justify having what she wanted—Kieran and her freedom—when the law was clear that these two items were diametrically opposed.

'Miss, are you all right? You've gone a bit pale,' Enid observed. 'Have I laced you too tight?'

Celeste put a steadying hand on her stomach and took a breath. 'Just nerves about tonight.' She smiled in the mirror to cover the half-truth.

'It's a big night, to be sure,' Enid empathised. 'You and the handsome Earl making your debut. You're a wonderful couple, so beautiful together and so dedicated to this house.' Enid squeezed her shoulder. 'You will both do fine. Everyone is so glad the house is occupied again. It's good for all of us. We'll be even happier when you and the Earl set a date for the wedding.'

She gave a shy smile. 'A Christmas wedding at the Hall would be lovely. Can you imagine yourself walking down the chapel aisle in a gown of winter velvet, the pews draped in evergreens with white ribbon and silver bows?' Enid's eyes lit up as her idea came to life. 'The baker in town could do the cake.'

'It sounds lovely, Enid, like a dream.' It did, and in that moment, Celeste wanted that dream—the velvet, the silver bows and Kieran waiting for her at the altar to step into 'for ever' with her. Her eyes smarted with the sudden sting of tears.

'Miss, I didn't mean to make you cry. We can't ruin your face.' Enid hurried to find a handkerchief.

'I was just thinking about my parents missing the wedding, how much I'd want them there.' Celeste improvised. As far as anyone at the Hall or in Wrexham knew, her parents were both dead, which was the truth. There'd been no need to elaborate.

Enid passed her a handkerchief and tried to make repairs. 'You and the Earl will make a new family to love. Wrexham Hall was made for big families.'

If only she could have that and keep her freedom intact. If she could trust in that, then all the world would be possible.

Kieran knocked on the connecting door. 'May I come in?'

She appreciated how he didn't barge in and how he asked a question instead of saying, 'you must hurry, we're late'.

'I'm nearly ready.' She reached for the dangling leaf earrings and screwed them on while Enid fetched her black velvet wrap.

'There is no rush.' Kieran took the wrap from Enid and settled it around Celeste's shoulders. 'You look beautiful, my darling.' He placed a kiss on her neck despite Enid being in the room and Celeste felt herself blush.

'You are looking fine, yourself. The new clothes fit well.' A little too well to the eyes of someone trying to keep her wits about her. She'd seen him in dark evening clothes before—he'd worn the former Earl's the first night here—but those had not been made for *his* shoulders. There was something undeniably elegant about the way a man wore bespoke clothing.

Kieran tugged at his cuffs, showing off onyx cuff-links that matched the cravat pin. 'The tailor did well; I am glad you approve.' There was a twinkle in his eye as he offered his arm. 'Our carriage awaits. Shall we be off to the ball?'

In truth, to call it a ball would be an overstatement. It was an assembly, held in the rooms above the largest inn in town in honour of the harvest and the autumn. It was an annual affair and everyone turned out for it, from the merchants who lived in town to the farmers who lived in the countryside. There was a festive air about the streets as the coach pulled up to the door and they joined the stream of arriving guests.

Inside, the inn was decorated for autumn with arrangements of corn sheaves and pumpkins filling corners, and garlands of dried leaves in bright golds and oranges looped about the banister leading up the stairs to the assembly rooms. Downstairs was set up for refreshments and there were tables where people might visit away from the music. There was laughter and loud chatter as friends called out to each other. Women met, exclaiming over each other's dresses. Men shook hands and greeted each other as if they hadn't seen one another earlier in the day.

A wave of emotion swept Celeste at the sense of community the event fostered. Kieran caught her eye. 'It's not fancy,' he began, perhaps misreading the expression on her face.

She turned to look up at him. 'It's better than fancy.

This feels *right*.' No supper or ball she'd ever hosted for Roan had felt like this—the simple pleasure of friends and family celebrating together. Crystal chandeliers and cool champagne were no substitute for joy.

Kieran covered her hand where it lay on his arm, his voice quiet as he read her thoughts. 'Don't think of him, and don't think of the past tonight.' He flashed her a smile, dispelling her ghosts. 'I want to dance with the loveliest woman here—will you do me the honour?'

'And I want to dance with the handsomest man,' she flirted as he led her upstairs. It took them a while to reach the dance floor. People were eager to meet them and they were eager to oblige. Some of the people they encountered on the stairs were people they'd already met and some were newly introduced. Celeste savoured it all.

'I'm sorry, that took longer than expected,' Kieran apologised as they joined a set for a quadrille.

'I don't mind. I liked meeting everyone.' Those moments on the stairs, talking with people, had been a glimpse into a future—a future she could choose if she was brave enough. A future full of more nights like this one, in which she would be part of a community and in which she would be more than a man's tool, something to be used to manipulate other men.

More than that, she thought as the dance began and she and Kieran bowed to the others in the set, she'd liked watching him greet everyone. He was affable, friendly and interested in what people had to say, even though their small talk afforded him nothing. There was no great intrigue to ferret out here. Kieran took her hands and they sashayed about their set, his gaze smiling at her. She smiled back, remembering the night she'd told him he was nice. She'd not been wrong. Roan gave the appearance of being nice when it got him something. Kieran was nice even when nothing was at stake.

The dance ended and she and Kieran moved off to the sidelines to talk more informally to the group with whom they'd danced. This was further proof of Kieran's niceness. There was no requirement for him to spend time with anyone and yet he was willing to do it.

'You will make a fine earl,' she said once the group had finally broken up. 'You are patient and giving of your time. You listen to people. You make them feel valued. That's a great gift.'

He'd been that way with her from the start. She'd just been too wary to appreciate it. She'd seen it as a strategy only, a way to get beyond her defences. This was further proof that he was different from the men she'd known. The hopeful conclusion leapt forward once more—if he was different, then it followed that together they could be different, too. Being with him need not mean committing herself to a social prison. For the first time since she'd promised herself to seek and protect her own freedom, she saw that promise not as a shield for her happiness but as a limitation to it.

The little orchestra struck up a waltz and they took to the floor once more.

'Get ready to fly.' Kieran grinned, and fly they did. It was the most wonderful sensation, to feel his hand at her waist, to feel her skirts bell out and to know that, no matter how fast they danced, she would not fall. He would catch her. Kieran Parkhurst would always catch her if she would just let go. Maybe she could, after all.

They were one of the last couples to leave the assembly shortly after midnight. She had a small hole in the bottom of her right slipper and her feet would be sore tomorrow but she didn't care. After the waltz, she'd danced with the doctor, then with the squire, the vicar and then Kieran again. It had been a wondrous evening full of high spirits, perhaps due in part to her own realisation: Kieran Parkhurst was not Cabot Roan; he never had been. He was a man who deserved to be judged on his own merits. She didn't have to give him up. She could stay. They could build a life in Wrexham, a good life as the Earl and the Countess. In the euphoria of the evening, her mind was willing to overlook some of the details that went with wanting to claim that life. In the happy moment, those loose ends didn't seem to matter.

'Everyone adored you, but none as much as me.' In the carriage, Kieran put his arm around her and she snuggled against him, flexing her right foot and celebrating the hole in her slipper. Celebrating, too, that she was finally able to put the past behind her. She was not Roan's ward, not his hostess and no longer his conspirator in crime planning his parties and escorting his guests. She had a new life here if she was brave enough to take it. It was not the life she'd thought she could have. Tonight had shown her otherwise. Perhaps all these weeks had been building towards it and tonight was just the pinnacle. Perhaps not every man would treat her as a partner but, as long as this one did, that was all that mattered.

'You belong here, Celeste. You belong with me,' he murmured against her hair.

Yes, she did. For the first time, she believed it. She sighed against Kieran's shoulder, drowsy from the dancing. Perhaps she would stay after all. Perhaps, the next time he asked her into his future, she would say yes.

Lights still glowed in the windows when they arrived home at Wrexham Hall: four lamps, one in every window on either side of the door.

'What a lovely sight to come home to.' Celeste thought they looked warm and inviting, flooding the crisp autumn night with their light.

But Kieran instantly tensed. 'Those are the Horsemen's lights—our signal. Something's happened.'

He was out of the carriage before it stopped, hastily helping her down. His tension was contagious and she felt a knot take up residence in her stomach. *The Horsemen's signal.* The euphoria of the evening leeched away.

The front door opened. Trafton had been watching out for them. Two other men were with him, tall, dark-haired, dark-eyed and dressed in clothes that showed signs of hard travel: his brothers; the other two Horsemen. Fear and panic rose.

'Caine, Luce...' Kieran strode forward, his welcome confirming it. He embraced them. 'Has there been news?'

News that had sent his brothers all the way to Wales...

Caine spoke, low and serious. 'There's been word from Casek and Worth. Roan has slipped through our watch on the coast and we lost him in London.'

She watched his eyes close, his throat work as he drew a deep breath, digesting the news and what it meant: for her, for his brothers, his family, for England and for Europe...never just himself alone. Knowing Kieran, he was planning his next moves even now. When his eyes opened and he looked at her, the dancing, laughing Earl that had spun her across the floor for the closing Roger de Coverley less than an hour ago was gone, replaced by the man she'd met in St Luke's. Perhaps when he looked at her she was no longer the possibly future Countess of Wrexham, but Celeste Sharpton, Cabot Roan's ward once again. They'd come a long way in the past weeks but they'd not come far enough.

'He is coming.' She said the words for him, holding his gaze, taking strength from his eyes, careful to match his even tones with hers even as she fought back her rising fear. He needed her to be strong. The euphoria of the evening vanished, taking with it her newly burgeoning hopes. Tonight, she'd felt like the Countess of Wrexham. For a while, she'd lived a bucolic life, a safe life, and it had felt as if she'd truly put the days of living in Roan's world behind her. She'd fooled herself into believing the impossible. She'd told herself a lie and nearly made dangerous choices based on that lie.

She would never only be just the Countess of Wrexham any more than Kieran would be just the Earl. He was also a Horseman, and this was a Horseman's life— one moment a country earl, the next moment danger and intrigue landing on his front step that would take him from home with no guarantee of return. She had not escaped that life after all. But she knew what to do, and she knew what Kieran needed from her.

'Trafton, please wake the servants. We'll need tea and food with some substance to it. These men have ridden hard and have a long night ahead of them.' As did she. Decisions had to be made.

Chapter Nineteen

'Roan has crossed the Rubicon. There's no turning back for him. In truth, I think we've got him in a good spot.' Caine built another sandwich from the tray. 'Essentially, Casek and Worth's men are driving him towards us. He cannot turn back now without being captured by them.' Caine gave a smug smile. 'He'll run straight to the end of his line, which is us, and we'll be waiting. He has to be wondering at this point who is hunting whom.'

Kieran nodded. He'd thought the same a few weeks ago when he and Celeste had first taken to the road. 'Still, it's a dangerous game. Celeste must be protected.'

She'd sat beside him through the conversation, listening silently. But he could feel her mind racing with a thousand questions, a thousand debates she was holding with herself. He desperately wanted time alone with her. A chance to peel off her russet silk gown and assure her that this changed nothing, that they'd always known they would have to face down Roan in order to move forward. He wanted to assure her she would be safe, that he would protect her. Roan and his minions could not harm her any more. But the Horseman in him knew that, for those assurances to have value, he had to set his personal desires aside. For the moment, conversations with her had to take second place to conversations with his brothers.

Luce nodded and addressed his response to Celeste, even though it was Kieran who had spoken. 'Do not worry, Miss Sharpton. If you keep to the house, you will be safe. We'll set pickets about the estate so that we're aware of anyone coming onto the grounds, and by morning we'll have people in the village who can alert us to any new arrivals.'

Kieran managed a laugh. 'I see Grandfather has taught you well.' Their grandfather excelled at networks. Even in his home village at Sandmore, he still had local messengers in place who could ride to Sandmore ahead of any new arrivals. Between them, the brothers joked that their grandfather had news before it actually happened.

Luce grinned at the compliment. 'I think a network is the most crucial part of an operation. You've done well too, making connections in such a short time in this part of the world. I can't set up a network if there's no one willing to participate, but everyone here likes you. They'll want to help. You're part of that too, Miss Sharpton. The staff is loyal to you. You've inspired their confidence. I must say, it's easy to see why. You look stunning tonight.'

Oh, that was too bold, even for Luce. Kieran felt more than a twinge of jealousy. He flashed Luce a strong, brotherly look—*stop flirting with her, she's mine*—but it only served to encourage Luce.

'I am sorry, Miss Sharpton, that the evening has not ended on a high note,' Luce consoled her. Damn it, but it should be him consoling her, not his brother.

'Roan is coming for us, and for her.' Caine shot both of them a withering look that brought them back to business. 'But the reality is that he is really coming for her. We are merely a bonus for him. Men like us are a constant in his world. He can deal with us whenever he chooses. There is no immediate need. The battle between us and Roan is continuous.' Caine levelled his piercing gaze at Celeste. 'But he is keen to get to you. I'd like to know why.'

Kieran felt her tense and watched her hands quietly fist in her silken skirts. He fought the urge to answer for her but she would not appreciate the action even if she understood his motive for it—to protect her. If he were to prove to her that her freedom would not be compromised in a relationship with him, he had to start with things like this.

'I have a list of names, all of whom are valuable connections to Roan and who were involved in the effort at Wapping. He will not like that information being put into your hands. If you went after those men, it would destabilise his whole network and quite possibly bring down his empire, man by man, without you ever having to destroy Roan himself.'

Without having to kill anyone either, but just take their money and their schemes, Kieran thought. Economic death—a brilliant idea and also a subtle attempt to steer him away from violence as per their conversation yesterday. She was bold to think to manipulate Caine on such short acquaintance. A bolt of admiration shot through him. There were a lot of ways to die besides physically dying—socially, politically or economically—and sometimes those other deaths were worse because one had to live in the aftermath.

Caine was not satisfied with the answer. 'Roan has to know that information has already been transmitted. He cannot prevent that now. So, why risk coming to England where he could be arrested, tried and found guilty for a variety of crimes, and hung for them?' Caine crossed a booted leg over one knee, looking large and imposing. 'I think he is here for *you* quite specifically. He does not want to let *you* go. What are you to him? I think there is more that you aren't telling us.'

That was more than enough. Kieran was not going to sit here and listen to Caine interrogate Celeste about such intimate details. 'What does it matter why he wants her back? The reasons don't change the fact that he is coming and this is our chance to put an end to him,' Kieran retorted sharply. Caine's gaze drifted between the two of them, landing on him last, considering and fierce. Kieran met the gaze with a challenge in his own. Celeste was his to protect, even if it meant protecting her from his brothers.

Celeste rose and they rose with her. She stifled a yawn that Kieran thought might be feigned. She'd picked up on the tension. 'It grows early, gentlemen, and you still have much to discuss. Unless my presence is needed, I think I would like to go and sleep while I may.' She flashed him a final look and he kissed her goodnight with his eyes.

'I imagine you had a different ending in mind for this evening,' Caine drawled to Kieran once the door had shut behind her.

'I did,' Kieran answered tersely.

One that had involved him and Celeste naked in bed together and her saying the words he sensed she was close to saying: *I will stay.* He'd exerted considerable persuasive influence to hear those words, a testimony to how much he wanted her to say them. Recent events, however, had likely undone much of that work.

'She's a smart girl. She knows when to leave a room,' Caine persisted.

'Or when she's being chased from one. You were interrogating her,' Kieran accused. 'And you—' he pointed a finger at Luce '—were flirting with her. One should expect better from his brothers.'

Luce held up his hands in a gesture of surrender. 'I didn't realise she was out of bounds. I assumed the fiancée thing was a ruse when your butler mentioned that Lord Wrexham and his fiancée were out for the evening.'

Caine's sharp eyes were on him. 'Is that how it is, Kieran? Is she your woman, your fiancée? You clearly have feelings for her and she for you. Has this gone further than an affair on the road?'

So, this was how it would be. If Caine couldn't interrogate Celeste, he would interrogate him. 'I would like to make the ruse a reality.' To confess those words out loud made his hopes all the more real. It was what he hoped for—to live here with Celeste and to build a life at Wrexham—but tonight had shown him the compromises that would come with that dream. What they'd lived these past weeks was a fantasy. Real life would look somewhat different, even if they could come to compromise.

Caine gave his answer thoughtful consideration. 'You are deciding this on the acquaintance of a few weeks and under the circumstances of a crisis. Do you think that wise?'

'You knew Lady Mary for less time.' Kieran dismissed the concern.

'Yes, but Lady Mary was not the ward of our fiercest enemy. Her father was merely a bad judge of character and invested poorly. I could also argue that I'd at least known *of* Lady Mary for years, given that she moved in our milieu.'

'I think marriage and a title have made you a snob, Caine.'

Caine shrugged. 'That's a non-responsive argument. I have concerns, Kieran, about *her*—about where she comes from, why she's here now. Where does she fit into all of this?'

'She is a scared young woman fleeing an untenable situation.' Kieran would share that much. 'Roan forced her to act as his…hostess.'

'She's quite beautiful. I couldn't take my eyes off her,' Luce put in.

'I noticed,' Kieran snapped with censure.

Luce leaned forward. 'Before you get prickly, all I am saying is that she's the kind of woman a man falls for, fast and hard. She would have been an extremely valuable asset to Roan, sitting at his table, providing a cultivated presence for men who live hard lives. She probably acted on those men like a tonic.'

The reference had Kieran's thoughts flashing back to Dr Graham's magical elixir at the fair—a tonic that was designed to be addictive and to bring a client back for more. Celeste had acted as Roan's tonic in that regard.

Luce continued, 'She'd smile at them, perhaps touch

them on the sleeve, take a walk around the room with them and they'd be spilling their secrets before they knew it.'

Celeste had told him as much, although not in such detail, perhaps to spare her pride or his. It had been difficult for her to talk about her years in Roan's household.

Caine drummed his fingertips on the arms of the sofa. 'Have you thought that perhaps she's still doing that? That she's Roan's mole here? That he is letting her lead him to you—to us?'

Kieran felt his temper prick at the suggestion, although he'd thought as much in the earliest days of their association, right up until Ammon Vincent had chased them through the alleys of Soho. That night had changed everything for him.

'Roan has threatened her, terrified her with the prospect of being turned over to one of his most vile henchmen for the man's pleasure. If you knew what she'd endured, you would not dare to think such things.'

'So she says.' Caine braved the rebuttal.

'She would not lie to me,' Kieran snarled, locking eyes with Caine. 'I saw her freeze. I felt her fear the night Ammon Vincent nearly caught us in Soho. That was not a lie.' His body tensed for a fight. 'You can't have it both ways. A few minutes ago, you were suggesting Roan was hunting her, and now you're suggesting she's his tool in his hunt for us.'

'I am merely posing hypotheses, considering all angles. You've been on your own too long without input. You see the world as you are, as opposed to how it is. As a result, you've become too defensive to consider any of this objectively.'

Caine was on his feet and Kieran rose to meet him,

matching him in height. It had been a long time since he and Caine had gone toe-to-toe in a boxing ring to settle their differences, but he was not above it now.

'Gentlemen!' Luce stepped between them; arms stretched out at his sides. 'Stop this at once. What would Grandfather say if he could see you two squabbling over a woman in the midst of our opportunity to catch Roan? Have you stopped to think how this divisiveness serves Roan? Your quarrelling divides us at a time when we need to stand together. This is how it always happens in the old stories.' Luce looked between them and gave a sigh when they offered him blank stares. 'Helen of Troy, the face that launched a thousand ships...?' he explained patiently. 'Anne Boleyn starts a war between England and the Catholic Church... Shall I go on?'

Caine shook his head and stepped back. 'No, you've made your point. We'll play it innocent until proven guilty until she demonstrates otherwise.'

'Thank you,' Kieran said with severity.

Caine shot Kieran a strong gaze, naked with emotion. 'Damn it, I am trying to keep you alive.'

Kieran read the pain there and read the unspoken message: *because I've already lost one brother. I could not stand to lose another.* Perhaps Celeste was right. They were all still trying to come to grips with losing Stepan. The tension between them eased slightly. Caine pushed a hand through his hair. Kieran reminded himself his brother was tired, had ridden hard, likely without sleep, and had left his honeymoon and his new bride. All for him, to warn him and to be by his side so that he did not have to face Roan alone.

'I'm glad you've come,' Kieran offered. 'Although I

am surprised Mary allowed it. Aren't you supposed to be setting up house at Longstead?'

'You're my brother. I will always come as long as there is breath in my body. Mary understood that when we wed.' But Kieran wondered if perhaps Mary hadn't expected to have those words put to the test so soon.

'You're a good man, Caine. Remind me to thank her when I see her next,' Kieran said quietly and moved to embrace him. Luce was right: there was no greater treasure than a brother's love. 'If you will excuse me now, I am going to go up and make sure Celeste is all right. It is good to have you both here.' He meant that. He was going to need them in more ways than one to get through whatever came next.

Celeste was dreading that knock on her door as much as she was hoping, wanting, to see Kieran stride through the connecting door between their chambers. Tonight had been dreadful in its extremes. She'd gone from the euphoria of the ball, of almost convincing herself that she could embrace the new direction Kieran had outlined for them, to the crashing reality that she could not escape her fate and who she was. She didn't know exactly what that might entail or require, only that some way, somehow, they could do it. Then that had blown away as quickly as it had been built. That was what happened to all houses built of straw—quickly assembled, quickly destroyed. The Horsemen, their business and their suspicions were here in this house, the house that was to have been hers. One should be safe in one's own house. But Caine Parkhurst had been relentless in making her feel otherwise.

The handle of the door moved and she sat up straighter, steeling herself. 'Celeste?' came Kieran's whisper as he stepped into her room. 'Are you still up?'

'Did you think I could sleep with your brothers and their doubts downstairs?' she said sharply. He needed to know she'd not taken their conjecture lightly. 'Your youngest brother is a flirt, by the way.'

'I spoke to him about it. It won't happen again.' Kieran gave a soft laugh but she cut it off. There was nothing to laugh about at present.

'And your other brother—the Marquess? Did you speak with him about his suspicions?' She needed Kieran to see their arrival in the same dark light she did and to understand that tonight was not an anomaly.

'I did take him to task for it. He should not have—'

'Spoken his mind?' she interrupted. 'You cannot censor him. Nor should you.'

'I should when he speaks poorly of the woman I care for, the woman I intend to marry.' Kieran came towards her but she moved from the chair to the window, dodging him. 'I will always defend you, Celeste.'

She shook her head, looking out into the night. The moon was bright. It would be good for travelling. 'You should not have to defend your wife against your brothers. You love them. You should not have to choose between them and me. Defending me will only cause a rift that will grow over time. Do you think this is the only time you'll have to do that? It won't be. The echoes of Roan and the echoes of your brother, of that list, will ripple long after this situation is resolved. I will always be Roan's ward to them, always connected to a dark time in their lives.'

'Celeste, Caine was out of order. He was tired; he'd come from his honeymoon.'

She whirled from the window. 'Do not make excuses for him and what he thinks. This is exactly what I'm talking about.' She would tear him and his brothers apart and she would not be responsible for that. Such a rift would steal Kieran's happiness.

'What do you want me to do?' Kieran held out his hands in a gesture of bewildered helplessness but there was heat and anger in his voice.

'There is nothing you can do. You can't change who I am, what I've done, who I've been with or what they think. But you can accept that I won't fit here and that all the hopes and dreams we've been playing with are just that. It's time for them to end.'

She drew a shaky breath. 'I think it is best for all of us if I leave. The Horsemen will keep Roan busy. Roan will believe that I am still with you. It will be enough time for me to slip away to the coast and sail to Dublin and go on from there. I may need passage. I hate to ask—'

'Stop.' His tone was thunderous. 'You are going nowhere. I do not want you out there, alone.' He randomly flung an arm out towards the window. 'Knowing that Roan is out there, wanting his best weapon back. He doesn't care about the list; he cares about *you*. He needs you to sit at his table and charm his compatriots. I won't stand for that. You are not his tool.'

She gave him a smug smile. 'You won't control me? You won't act as if you possess me or make decisions for me? You're acting just like every other man I've known.'

His face clouded. That had got to him. 'The difference is that I love you.' He growled the words. 'I want to see you safe.'

Under other circumstances, hearing those three words, *I love you*, would have meant the earth. But to-night, she simply had to ignore them.

'Then let me go. I can take care of myself. You take care of Roan so that I can be safe,' she argued.

Kieran sighed, something in him seeming to stand down from the anger rising between them. 'It's late. The night has been full of emotions, both good and bad. We are not thinking plainly. Perhaps we should discuss this in the morning with cooler heads.'

She gave a nod of agreement. 'Perhaps we should.' He'd unwittingly given her what she wanted, what she needed—time and space to do what needed to be done. 'Goodnight, Kieran,' she said softly for the last time.

'Goodnight, Celeste. I'll see you in the morning,' he said, gently closing the connecting door behind him. A few moments later, she heard his footsteps in the hall, going to check on his brothers no doubt. She was glad they were here for him. He would need them. The morning would break his heart…for now. This was going to end for her the way it had begun: on her own. There was nothing for it.

She pulled her valise out from under the bed and began to pack quickly. She told herself it was because time was of the essence. Kieran would come back up-stairs and she feared if she lingered, let the heat of anger cool, she'd change her mind. But leaving was the right choice, the best choice for her and Kieran. She wrapped her mother's pearls and the miniature in the cotton folds of a spare chemise to keep them safe and tucked them at the bottom of the bag.

She would not come between Kieran and his brothers. He loved them. His family meant everything to him. He'd told her endless stories about them because they were integral to his life, to who he was. He needed them more than he needed her. They would keep him safe and they would get him through whatever heartbreak he might imagine for himself afterwards. And then he'd move on. Just as she was moving on tonight.

She would do her part to keep him safe. Caine had not been wrong about Roan's incentive to come after her. It had occurred to her that Kieran was only in *immediate* danger because of her. If she left, she could protect them both. If she was gone, Roan would come after her; she could draw him away. She should have stuck to her original plan. She'd never meant to get involved with a Horseman, or perhaps the reverse was true—she'd never meant to involve a Horseman with her. She'd only meant to warn them and give them a tool in their quest to bring Roan down.

Celeste snapped the valise shut and began to struggle with the laces of her gown. It felt momentous to take it off, the last step in setting aside the life that had been hers for a short while. She changed into her travelling clothes. They were clean but they felt old and worn after a month of wearing fine garments. She lifted her skirt and felt at the hem for the last of the list. She would fulfil her end of the bargain and leave it for him.

Celeste flattened the crinkled paper with her palm and put it on her dressing table. The little vial of perfume beside it tempted her. He'd ordered it just for her, a token of how much he'd noticed about her—right down to her scent. But she resisted. She'd already justified taking the sea-glass necklace and the dagger since they'd been gifts. She would not leave with more than she'd come with. He could not say she'd played him false.

That wouldn't stop Kieran from being furious, though. She was counting on Caine and Luce to calm him down, to see reason and see that this was for the best; to help him remember that he wasn't really a marrying man. It was what she'd tell herself too, as many times as it took for her to believe it. She wasn't a marrying woman. She wanted her freedom. She didn't want any man to tell her what to do. Celeste took a final look at the room and slipped down the back stairs, into the night with its bright traveller's moon. If there was one thing she knew, it was how to run.

The moon was both a blessing and a curse. On the one hand, it offered a natural guide for her. But, in the unlikely event someone was out at this hour, they'd see her. Celeste stumbled over a root sticking up from the ground. Bright as the moon was, it was still hard to see, and hard to make significantly good time.

She stopped to rub her ankle. Especially when one had just spent the evening dancing. Her feet had already put in a good night's work. Wrexham was two miles away, and there was a small hamlet two miles beyond that. It was the hamlet she was making for. She would not be recognised there. Four miles by dawn…

The undergrowth and grass became too thick for her to navigate and she was forced closer to the road. She looked up into the sky, gauging the time by the position of the moon, but she was no expert. The stars were out tonight in a clear autumn sky. She ought not to have looked. She spotted Scorpio and recalled lying next to Kieran, his long arm pointing out the constellations. She did not need the memory at the moment. It was difficult enough to keep going.

In the dark, second guesses were coming hard and fast. Perhaps she should have waited for morning and discussed this privately with Kieran before leaving. Perhaps they would have found a way through together. Perhaps she should have trusted him to keep her safe. Perhaps she should have given up a little of her independence in exchange for something greater. She told herself that was just her fear talking and that she was doing the right thing. But it didn't feel right now that she'd set out. She stumbled again and cursed. Four miles felt like an eternity. She was tired, discouraged and footsore.

Close to dawn, the jangle of a horse harness caught her ear, followed by the rumble of coach wheels. Coaching lamps shed a welcome ray of light on the road. Celeste shielded her eyes and turned towards it, her heart leaping with her thoughts. Had Kieran already discovered her gone? Had he come after her? No, it wouldn't be Kieran. It was coming from the town. Perhaps this was a merchant and his wife on their way home from the assembly. People had stopped dancing at midnight, but many had lingered downstairs, eating a midnight supper and drinking autumn ale.

The coach rolled to a stop beside her and for a moment she felt the universe had given her a sign, some help in her escape. She'd caught rides when she'd run before. Then a man stepped out of the coach—tall, lean, with straight, dark hair. 'Ah, Celeste, it *is* you. How fortuitous,' he said in silken tones.

Roan. Fear spiked and paralysed her. He had found her, completely by chance. Doubt over her decision rocketed through her. She'd thought she had more time. She cast about, but there was nowhere to run to, not in the dark. An outrider had come to stand behind her. She was trapped.

'I was just on my way to Wrexham Hall. I fancied breakfast with the Horsemen.' Roan gave a cold laugh. 'But this will be so much better.' He held the coach door open. 'Come in and rest your feet, my dear. Ivan can help you up if you need it.' The man behind her stepped closer and she had little choice but to get in.

'Back to the village.' He called instructions to the driver. 'We'll delay our visit to the Hall for a bit. We have work to do.' Celeste fought back panic. The village wasn't so very far. Someone might recognise her. She had options but Roan was ruthless.

Roan resumed his one-sided conversation as if they were friends. 'I did not think to find you so quickly. But I am not surprised you're out here. You're good at running, you're just not very good at not getting caught.'

He gave her a slow perusal. 'How long do you think it will be before your Horseman notices you're gone? I suppose it depends,' he added off-handedly, 'if he's sleeping in your bed or not. What are you worth to him, Celeste? As much as you're worth to me? We'll find out soon enough.'

She let him talk as recriminations flooded. She was in the hands of the one man she'd sought to avoid, back where she'd started as if she'd never left Brussels. She'd misjudged the situation and now she was going to pay—and Kieran too. This would never have happened if she'd stayed at Wrexham Hall.

Chapter Twenty

Celeste was gone. Not just gone—she'd left *him*. Kieran stood, rooted in place in the centre of her room, his mind unable to accept the evidence of his eyes. She must have left soon after their quarrel. He'd not dissuaded her. Her bed had not been slept in. Her russet gown lay spread atop it, her dressing table devoid of her personal effects. The miniature and the pearls were gone, as was the seaglass necklace and the dagger. At least she had protection. There was some comfort in that. He wished she'd taken more. The Wrexham Imperial Topazes lay neatly in their velvet box. She could have lived a while on them.

Most telling of all was the scrap of paper atop her dressing table—the damn list. He knew what that list was to her—currency, her ability to pay her way. *I always pay my debts.* But now it was also symbolic of all she thought stood between them, the changes neither of them could make. She didn't mean to come back.

He'd thought they were beyond such score-keeping and scale-balancing. There was no note, nothing. How had she left? Had she taken a horse? She was heading for the coast; he could follow her. His brain started functioning; he'd check at the stables. Or had she sim-

ply packed a bag and walked down the lime alley into
the night? How far did she think she'd get in the dead
of night? If she was on foot, he'd easily overtake her.
There was hope in that.

He hoped she wasn't lying on the side of the road
with a twisted ankle or worse because she'd been foolish
enough to set off in the dark. There were other questions
too: why? Why had the woman he loved left him? But he
knew why. She wanted her freedom and she thought the
odds between them were insurmountable. There was no
pleasant answer to that. Was his love not enough? His
protection not enough? Was what he offered not enough?

Worse, he had to go downstairs and tell his brothers
and then he had to go after her, assure himself that she
was safe, get those answers and change her mind. She
belonged here. She belonged with him.

Kieran found his brothers in the breakfast room, helping themselves to huge plates of eggs, fresh baked rolls
and bracing mugs of steaming coffee after having been
up all night. Caine looked at him as he entered, instantly
concerned. 'What is it? What's happened?'

'Celeste is gone. She's taken her things,' Kieran managed in a steady voice. 'She must have left before we set
the sentries. I'm going out to look for her.' He expected
his brothers to say they'd come, too.

'No.' Caine shook his head fervently. 'You cannot go
out. Roan is likely out there somewhere. It is a miracle
that we arrived before he did. I think it is only because
he's travelling by coach and we had the luxury of riding
cross-country while he had to stick to roads. You cannot
be out there, riding willy-nilly. You'd be easy pickings,
especially distracted and distraught.'

Kieran balled his fists. That was not acceptable. 'Am I to sit here and do nothing while Celeste is out there? If Roan is a danger to me, he is most certainly a danger to her. What if he finds her?'

Roan, who'd set her up and betrayed her; Roan, who'd meted out a punishment to her so humiliating she'd not told him what it was. Roan, who'd used her in despicable ways without a second thought. Ammon Vincent was also out there, waiting to claim his prize. Her dagger wouldn't be enough if they found her.

Caine remained cool. 'If Roan has her, we'll know soon enough. He'll want to use her to bargain with.'

'And if she's out there alone?' Running into anonymity… The longer she had a head start, the harder it would be to find her. If she made the coast and found a ship, it would impossible.

'Then you have to let her go. If she doesn't want to be found, we have to honour that.' Caine gestured to a seat at the table. 'Sit down and eat. We've all had a long night full of unpleasantness. Hot food will help.'

The note came in the middle of Kieran's third cup of coffee. He read it with growing grimness. The confrontation he'd known was coming had arrived. The Horsemen would face Roan…but now with the complication that Roan had Celeste. Roan wanted to meet. The note had come in her handwriting.

'Why would he want to meet?' Luce asked as the note was passed around. 'You don't actually believe he'll give up Celeste, not when he's come all this way to retrieve her?'

Kieran hadn't quite worked that out for himself either,

but neither was he inclined to overlook an opportunity to see Celeste and try and rescue her. 'We can't simply ignore this. She must be terrified.' It was the things she'd left unsaid that haunted him now. Whether she wanted him or not, he would not leave her to that fate.

'If you were Roan, what would you want?' Kieran posed the question.

'Safe passage?' Caine offered. 'That's one thing he doesn't have and perhaps we are in a position to give it to him.'

'Revenge,' Luce answered simply. 'He wants revenge against her for selling his secrets, for running from him, making him look like a fool. If his ward can escape him, what does that say? He wants revenge against us for foiling his attempts at Wapping. He's shown himself to be vindictive over and over. This is just more of the same. And he wants it to be painful. We have taken his freedom from him and we've injured his business, forcing him to rely on others. He wants to pay that back. He wants to take something of value from her and from us.'

'Roan never gives anything up,' Kieran mused out loud. 'Perhaps he thinks he won't have to. He wants us and he wants her. He'll use her as lure to draw us out but will have no intentions of effecting any negotiation.' Roan would mean to shoot on sight.

Caine nodded thoughtfully. 'We'll be ready too. We'll go to his meeting, but only one of us will show themselves—the other two will stay out of sight. We'll quietly take out any hidden gunmen so that the surprise will be on Roan.'

'I'll show myself. It will play into his hand in regard to Celeste.' Kieran glanced at Luce. 'Unless you'd rather do that? It will be a deadly day.' Luce was the youngest, the one with the least experience of missions where letting one's enemy live to tell about it was not an option.

'This is for Stepan. I can do it,' Luce assured him.

'Then, if your horses are rested, we ride,' Kieran said. 'I know the place he means. It's on the north-west corner of the estate. There's an old gamekeeper's cottage there.' His blood was starting to hum with the anticipation of a mission, his unrest settling now that he had a sense of action.

Within twenty minutes, the horses were saddled: Tambor for him, Caine's Argonaut and Luce's Ulysses. Three black horses for three dark-haired brothers. He checked his pistol and slipped his knife into his boot before mounting. The brothers rode out, three abreast, all armed for war and blood.

At the north-west corner of the estate, Kieran gave the signal and the brothers split, Caine going left, Luce going right, to form a ring of surveillance and, if needed, a ring of death. Kieran rode to the hut.

'Roan! I'm here!' Kieran called out when he was a fair distance from the hut—close enough to be seen but not close enough to be shot at. He waited, Tambor stamping his feet impatiently and tossing his head. Even Tambor was ready for action.

There was no sound, no movement. Did Roan think he was going to fall for that and let curiosity get the better of him so that he'd dismount and approach the hut on foot? It was far easier to overpower a man on foot than a man on horseback. He would not give up the advantage so readily. He called out again—still no answer. He scanned the area around the hut, looking for signs that someone had been here or was still here. But there were none—no sign of horse droppings, no markings from a coach or wheels, no ash from a fire, no residue from a meal. No signs of life.

Kieran heard the shrill whistle of a starling—Caine's sound—counted to five and smiled when it was answered by the fast-paced cheep of a garden warbler— Luce's call. He'd taught him that when he was seven. A count of five later, Kieran added his own, the fluted sound of the song thrush. It was the call given to signal safety and that all was clear. Usually, it was a welcome sound. Today, it was a confusing one. This had not gone as expected. In fact, one might say it hadn't 'gone' at all.

Kieran wheeled Tambor round and rode back to the pre-arranged rendezvous, his brothers already there. 'No one?' he asked Caine.

Caine shook his head. 'No one and no sign of anyone having been there.'

Luce confirmed the same.

'There's been no one at the gamekeeper's hut either.' Kieran drew out a worried breath. 'This feels wrong. We've missed something.' More than that, he felt as if they'd played into Roan's hands. 'Why would he ask us to meet him here and then not show up?'

He exchanged a concerned glance with Caine, who said, 'Because he wants to be elsewhere, and he can't get *there* if we're not *here*.'

'Deflection. It's a chess gambit.' Luce spoke up. 'You bait a trap for your opponent with a piece they want to take—really want to take—and it will draw them away from their usual territory, leaving it undefended for you to move in and put them in check.'

Kieran's mind worked. Celeste was all he wanted, so what did Roan think he was drawing him away from?

Caine sniffed the air. 'Do you smell that? It smells like smoke. Is anyone burning leaves today?'

Kieran smelled it too. 'Not that I'm aware. We don't have any burning scheduled.'

Then the pieces clicked into place. What had they said earlier? That Roan wanted to take from them the things they'd taken from him: his freedom, the things he valued. Kieran lifted his gaze to the sky and found it—the wisp of grey smoke—and his heart pounded. That was what Roan wanted—to draw them out away from the Hall so that he could get *into* the Hall!

'Good God! The bastard is trying to burn my house down.' And Celeste was with him. This was punishment—revenge against both of them. His thoughts went rampant with fear. He wheeled Tambor around in a circle but Caine grabbed his reins.

'You cannot go tearing back there. He is calling you home with that smoke. He wants you to know he is there and he wants you to come charging in mad as hell. He's not negotiating, Kieran. He is looking to shoot first and last. We must make sure he doesn't get that chance. You have time. The house is brick and stone; it will burn slowly.'

'But does she?' Kieran breathed, exchanging a knowing look with his brother.

'We can't save her if we're dead,' Caine argued calmly. 'Same plan as before. We'll take out the snipers while you take out Roan.'

They rode hard then, Kieran in the lead, Tambor's hooves thundering across the countryside, a single

thought thundering through his head: *let me be in time*.
This was the great fear of the Horsemen—that their
weakness would be discovered and used against them.
The choice not to marry had been their solution to that
fear and it had worked, for a while. He would ride into
hell for Celeste and he knew Roan was counting on
that. He'd protect his home; Roan was counting on that
as well. He simply couldn't choose not to. It was not the
Horseman's way to let innocents suffer. A Horseman
protected those he cared for. But it made family and
home a vulnerability, one Kieran had not had to deal
with until now. He bent low over Tambor's neck, taking a country stile.

I am coming, Celeste.

'Do you think he'll come, Celeste? Were you charming enough?' Roan tested the bonds around her wrists
where they looped over a tall bed-post in one of Wrexham Hall's many bedrooms. This one overlooked the
front drive. 'There, nice and tight. I don't think you'll
be going anywhere soon. But you have a good view for
our little pageant,' Roan added conversationally.

'He'll recognise your handwriting, yes? I'd hate to go
to all this effort and not have him appear. How embar-
rassing for you, too, when you thought that he loved you.'

Kieran did love her. It was why she'd left him. It
would have made him weak, made him take chances.
She didn't want to be used against him and didn't want
to be the cause of his death. Love was scary. Freedom
was easier, lonelier, safer.

Ammon Vincent entered the room, carrying a musket, and she paled, bargaining quickly. 'I wrote the note;

I dismissed the staff just as you asked,' she reminded Roan through gritted teeth. She'd got them all to safety with her lies. They would not suffer for her. She'd not wanted to write that note. It would ensure Kieran walked into Roan's web of diabolical revenge. Dismissing the staff had ensured their safety but it had also taken away any chance of an ally for herself or for Kieran. He would have only his brothers—three against however many men Roan had with him.

But, if there was to be a chance for her, she had to think of herself in these moments. 'In exchange, you said—'

'I know what I said.' He gave a cold laugh and turned to Ammon. 'She doesn't want you to touch her. She'll do just about anything to keep that from happening.'

'Anything, boss?' Ammon gave her a cruel look. 'I bet I know one thing she won't do.'

'What's that?' Roan played along and her blood curdled.

'Die—she won't die. When it comes down to it, everyone has a price. Everyone wants to live.' He smirked. 'Isn't that right, princess?'

She said nothing and Ammon shrugged. 'Boss, let's make a bet between you and me. I win, I get her. If you win—well, then I was just wrong. I think, if she has to choose between living or dying, choosing herself or her Horseman, she'll choose living. She won't die for him. I'm going to tie this musket to her side.'

He jabbed the gun into place, lashing it tight, the barrel poking into her flesh. He moved her bound hand into position over the trigger, the horror of his sick riddle filling her with cold dread. 'It's an old dilemma, but still an interesting one, isn't it? She can see her Horseman ride up into our killing zone, where we will catch him and his brothers in a little cross-fire. She'll see him well in advance though, and she *could* warn him with this musket. He'll hear the shot soon enough to ride off and live to fight another day. I don't think she'll do it, though.'

Roan slapped his leg and laughed. 'I like it. Weren't you telling me just this morning, Celeste, you'd rather die than be Ammon's whore? I guess that has been arranged.' He tweaked her chin and pulled out his watch. 'Ammon, have you started the fire?'

'Yes, Parkhurst should be seeing the first signs of trouble about now.' Ammon gave a grin that revealed holes where teeth had once been before they'd been lost in a fight. 'I'll go to work on the rest of it.'

Roan gave her a ruthless look. 'Never say I don't give people choices, my dear. There are a lot of ways to die today: musket ball, fire, smoke, broken heart... Choose one that suits you. It's a shame to waste your beauty and your talents, but you've proven disloyal to me twice now, just like your father. He thought he could slip away to the Alps with you, so he had to die. Now I've come all this way to make you pay for your betrayal. Understand, it's purely business. I can't have people saying I've gone soft.'

She felt her gorge rise, emotions coming in waves: grief anew for her father, who had loved her and who had been trapped into a life of deceit by this man. Then the anger came. Roan had taken everything from her: her father, her freedom...and he'd take Kieran too, if she let him.

She tugged at her bonds, shaking the bed-post in her

rage. 'There is a special ring of hell for men like you.' If she were free, she'd plunge her dagger deep into his heart. But her bonds held. If there was any plunging of knives to be done, it would be up to Kieran now.

He smirked. 'I have no plans to find out today.' He left her then. A few moments later, from her vantage-point, she saw him take up his position on the front lawn.

Celeste drew a shaky breath. She'd been a fool and she would die today for her mistake; that was a certainty, the only one she had. She was tied to a bed-post, a gun strapped to her side, in a house that was slowly burning down around her—a house in which she'd lived the best month of her life with the best man she'd ever known. That man had shown her true partnership and true courage—not because he'd killed two men in an alley for her but because he'd had the fortitude to re-examine his preconceived notions about love and marriage. He, too, had once believed those were things he could not embrace. Yet he had been compelled to take the leap and had held out his hand, waiting to help her across that same chasm.

She had hesitated in both word and deed. She'd not leapt when he'd asked her and she'd not spoken the words in her heart when she could have: *I love you*; three simple words. Instead, she'd opted to give voice to doubt, to obstacles and to improbability when she should have chosen hope.

Now it was too late. There would be no more time for words, no more chances to say them. He would never know just how much he'd meant to her. What did her paltry sense of freedom mean beside the enormity of his love—*their* love? She would regret those hesitations for the short remains of her life.

If she was brave enough, she could save Kieran. If she was a coward, she'd see him shot down before her eyes on the lawn of the home he was making here and that would be her fault, because he *would* come for her, as undeserving as she was. There was no doubt in her mind about that. As long as the smoke didn't get to her first.

Chapter Twenty-One

The first detail Kieran noticed as he pounded down the lime alley on Tambor was the smoke: how much more of it there was, how dark it was as it filled up the sky. Time was slipping away. He and his brothers had spent much of it on the perimeter, quietly taking out one man at a time. Stealth had been their friend. They couldn't expect to safely or effectively overcome Roan's coterie of mercenaries all at once. They'd be outnumbered and, while numbers were not always the deciding factor when up against the Horsemen, it did increase the chance of not reaching their goal without sustaining injury, and injury would slow them down at the critical moment.

The perimeter had involved bloody knife-work and it had taken time—time Kieran was not certain he had, by the looks of the smoke-filled sky. The end of the lime alley neared. His brothers would be in position. Caine had gone round to the east of the house, Luce to the west. It had seemed from the position of his men that Roan had hoped to draw them to the front of the house and catch them in a cross-fire. It was a good plan, but one that they'd effectively reversed. The surprise would be all Roan's.

Kieran drew his pistol. There was no more need for silent killing when he faced Roan. He must be ready, but not reckless. A tall figure stood on the front steps of *his* home and rage began to boil. He pushed the rage away. Rage was what Roan wanted. Rage and heroic recklessness made a man an easy target. Roan liked to play games. If he was to win, he needed to think clearly and quickly. He had to choose his shot carefully. He could not shoot Roan before he knew where Celeste was.

'Good day,' Roan called from the steps. 'You took longer than expected. I was beginning to think none of this mattered to you—the house, the lovely Celeste. It's not every man who can ride away from such beautiful things.'

Kieran halted Tambor on the drive and held Roan's gaze as he went on the offensive. 'There was business to take care of first.' He was in the centre of the drive, a perfect target for Roan's men if they'd been at their positions. Soon, Roan would realise his men were gone.

'Have you come alone?' Roan's eyes looked left and right without his head moving.

'I'm sorry if that disappoints you.' It took all his patience not to shoot Roan where he stood and dash into the house. There were flickers of flame visible now at the far end of the east wing.

'I didn't think the Horsemen worked alone,' Roan drawled as if this were a leisurely conversation between gentlemen. Then again, Roan knew he had time on his side. This whole interaction had been designed to favour him. So, that was the first level of the game, Kieran thought—time against speed.

'Only when needs must,' Kieran replied tersely.

Roan made a show of reaching for a cigar and lighting it. Kieran slowly counted to five in his head, giving Roan time to realise his trap had not closed.

'Was the cigar supposed to be a signal?' Kieran took some satisfaction from Roan's paling face when the expected shots didn't come. 'I think you'll find your men have been relieved of duty. It was the reason for my delay.'

'It doesn't matter. There's still one gun in play.' Roan recovered from the news. 'Celeste controls it. I gave her the option of a single shot she could fire to warn you.' Roan nodded. 'She can probably see you from the window even now, and she's wondering if she has the courage to pull the trigger, the love to pull the trigger.'

He tapped ash from the end of his cigar while rage rocketed through Kieran. *The bastard.* Of all the cruelest tricks to put her through… What she must be feeling right now—grief, fear, self-recrimination because she couldn't pull the trigger or because she could. He didn't want to think of her doing the last. He couldn't afford to wallow in the morbid image of it.

Be patient, my love. I am coming. He willed his thoughts to her. *Yes, you are my love. Both of us walk out of here alive today, or neither of us will.*

It took all of Kieran's willpower not to look to the upper floor, to focus his attentions searching for a glimpse of her face.

'It's quite the Orpheus and Eurydice dilemma, isn't it?' Roan tapped more ash from the cigar. 'Do you dare risk looking for her? Or in that time will I pull a gun of my own? Or possibly even a glance from you will give her the courage she needs and you can watch her die for you.'

All true. All reasons why he fought the temptation to look up, desperate as he was for a sight of her. That was what Roan wanted—for him to break his concentration both physically and mentally. But Roan had given important information away: Celeste was currently alive. She was in the house. She was upstairs. Those details mattered when time was racing.

'Surely, the longer I stay here, the more obvious it will be to her that your plans have gone awry? And the less tempted she'll be to pull that trigger.' That was what Kieran hoped. He also hoped he sounded cool enough to be convincing with that argument. Inside, he was seething with a dozen different emotions that were waiting to boil over and he couldn't allow it. A berserker rage would not help him, or Celeste.

Roan gave a shrug of contemplation. 'There is merit to what you say but the longer you sit there on your horse, the longer my fire burns and the closer it gets to her. The smoke may already have reached her.' More information: that meant she was in the east wing. In his smug certainty that he held the upper hand, Roan was giving himself away. Roan could tell him little more that would keep him alive. Kieran could take the shot now.

'That's where you're wrong.' Roan laughed coldly, guessing his thoughts. 'I know who the Ottoman sympathiser is. I know where you can find him—the man responsible for organising Wapping and subsequently your brother's death.'

Did Roan think that would keep him alive? Kieran shrugged. 'I have the list. I will find the man eventually.'

'Maybe. These are men who are good at hiding, at changing their names and their entire identities. I think a name is not enough. You will need more than that. Celeste does not understand that a list is not as powerful as she thinks. A list is just words.' This was the second game: Roan wanted him to choose between his brother or the woman he loved. There was no time for this. Kieran raised his pistol.

I am sorry, Stepan. You are already dead, but I might still save her.

A clear, single crack sounded and Kieran went still, his own pistol unfired as Roan crumpled on the front step. Caine was running forward from the east side, pistol in hand, yelling instructions, but Kieran was already off Tambor and sprinting up the steps as Caine knelt beside Roan.

Inside, Kieran could smell smoke even on the lower level. Was it a second fire or had the smoke drifted this far already? He took the stairs two at a time, calling her name, letting Celeste know he was coming, that help was coming. She just had to hold on a little longer. Smoke, not Roan, was the enemy now. It was thick in the east wing and growing thicker the further down the corridor he went.

Kieran tore his cravat from his neck and fastened it around his nose and mouth. It was harder to call for her now, the smoke turning his voice hoarse. It would be hard, too, for her to answer. He'd been counting on her being able to make some sort of sound, so that he didn't have to waste time opening each door.

A hulking shape loomed in the middle of the hall. Kieran recognised Ammon Vincent. He carried a bulky mass over his shoulder and a gun in his other hand. Was the man pillaging already? Kieran squinted against the smoke, new dread filling him. That wasn't bulk, that was a person: Celeste. Ammon Vincent was risking much to come up and get her. Or perhaps Ammon Vincent had seen Roan fall, and knew the others were gone, that he was on his own. If he had Celeste, he could barter for his own freedom and his own life.

There was only one way for Vincent to go and that was to come towards him. The back staircases at the end of the hall were lost to him. Vincent would be near enough to see him soon. Kieran raised his pistol and stepped into the centre of the hall. 'Put her down.'

A moment's surprise flickered in Vincent's eyes, red and watery from smoke like his own. 'Or you'll what—shoot me? I don't think so. Not while I've got her. The risk is too great you'll hit her instead.'

Kieran blinked, trying to clear his vision. Celeste was so still where she lay over his shoulder. Another tremor of fear ran through him. Was she conscious? Was she alive? She must be. He didn't imagine Vincent would risk himself to haul out a body. He coughed, a reminder that time was running out. There was no time to think, only time to do; to take action and sort it out later. He would have to take Vincent in two stages. A lethal shot was not possible without risking Celeste but a disabling shot was. He gave himself over to the Horseman within and fired, taking Vincent in the leg.

Kieran was already running forward, slipping his knife from his boot as the big man went down, dropping Celeste and his weapon in his pain and in his need for self-preservation. Kieran was too fast; he didn't give the man time to draw a weapon. He slid his blade between the big man's ribs and thrust up. He knew he need not linger over Vincent; confident his blade would do its work.

His concern was all for Celeste. He lifted her in his arms and raced for the stairs, his breathing laboured, the air stinging his lungs. Someone was coming up the smoke-clogged stairs. *Luce!* Luce threw an arm around him, lending him strength as they made their way to the door, towards fresh air.

'Take her into the drive,' Luce instructed when he would have laid her down on the front step. 'We want her far enough from the fire if it should spread.' The extra steps seemed like miles. He wanted to lay her down and see her face, to assure himself she was breathing.

'I don't know if she's alive,' he gasped hoarsely, his thoughts jumbled, his fear giving him the power to make the last steps of the journey. He set her down at last, pressing a finger to the pulse that ought to beat at her neck, a pulse that had beaten fast and hard for him but now seemed non-existent. 'I can't find it, Luce, I can't...'

His voice broke, a thousand terrors racing through his mind. He'd been too late. He should have ridden faster; he should have killed the men on the perimeter faster; he should never have let her leave; he should not have put off urging her to stay and should have promised her whatever it took. He loved her and he needed her. Let the house go, he thought—he'd build another. But there wouldn't be another her, another love for him—never.

He gathered her in his arms and gave her body a shake. 'Celeste, wake up, my love. Come back to me. We have so much to do. I need you. I love you.'

* * *

He loved her. She must be dead. All her wishes were coming true. Wasn't that what happened when one died? There was peace and comfort; worries faded… If one's life had been good, one got one's rewards. Kieran was her reward—all she'd ever wanted, although she'd been too stubborn to see it, too set in the path she'd charted for herself. There was cool air here, too. That was nice. It soothed the burning in her throat. There'd been fire just before it had all ended. There'd been a gun and a man—a bad man. And a knife—her knife. A dagger…

The grey fog of her mind cleared. Her memories sharpened. She was back in the room at Wrexham, hideously bound with a hideous choice before her, the room filling with smoke. She was choking, suffocating on it. The door burst open and Ammon Vincent was there, cutting her bonds and grabbing her. There'd been a moment when she'd had a chance to reach for the dagger beneath her skirts and she'd seized it, attempting to stab him. She'd not been strong enough.

She'd fought him then, punching, kicking and struggling, knowing it was futile. He was twice her size and without remorse. Her head had slammed back hard into a wall—hard enough that she'd fallen and the room had spun. Her awareness had not lasted long after that. She recalled thinking perhaps it was better this way, as the smoke was bound to get her. It would be less painful when it did. She'd simply drift off and it would all be over. Only it wasn't over…

Someone was calling her. Kieran was calling her, his voice raspy with smoke and tears. Suddenly, she wanted nothing more than to wipe those tears away and ease his fears the way he eased hers—with comfort and strength. To do all of that, she had to open her eyes, which seemed at the moment to be a Herculean feat. But it was worth it when she looked up into dark eyes the colour of melted chocolate.

'Swiss.' She managed the single hoarse word, watching his expression change to perfect, pure, unadulterated joy, the way the wind chased away storm clouds from the sky. 'Your eyes look like Swiss chocolate.'

Then she was locked in his embrace as he rocked her back and forth, happiness and tears mixing with his laughter. 'Only you would think of chocolate at a time like this. You almost died. You almost died.'

'But I didn't.' She might have, for a little while, but she'd come back—for this man, for this chance. She reached a hand up to his cheek, soothing and stroking, afraid to look away from him for fear it was all a dream and he was right—she had died. She didn't want to be dead. She wanted this to be real.

'I was nearly too late.' Something dark lurked in his eyes.

'No, you were just in time.' She held his gaze. There would be time to tell the tale of this day to each other later when they had recovered. Not all wounds were visible and there would be some trauma to overcome, but they would do it together. For now, it was enough to be in his arms, to feel his comfort around her even as she offered comfort to him. This was true partnership.

Luce knelt beside them. 'I've brought water.' Kieran took the tin cup from him and held it to her lips.

'We're gaining on the fire.' Luce offered Kieran a report as she sipped.

'Is it bad?' She looked at Kieran, horror in her eyes. She'd forgotten about the house. She struggled for a moment. 'I should get up. People will need help.'

'Spoken like a true countess putting her people first.' Kieran kissed her forehead. 'But not today. You've had an ordeal and you need to rest.' Kieran smoothed back the tangle of her hair. 'The east wing has suffered. We'll need to close it off and rebuild.'

Tears smarted in her eyes. This was the final straw after so many. 'Your house, your beautiful house! I am so sorry.' He'd saved her today but he'd lost his home and she was to blame,

'*Our* house, Celeste. It's yours as much as it is mine. I've only had it for a few months. We will rebuild and I dare say the rest of the house is plenty large enough for the two of us until then.' He was smoothing away her tears with his thumbs. 'It's just the east wing. I could have lost much more than that today.'

'You saved me,' she whispered.

'But you saved everyone else. You saw the staff safe. Celeste, you are the most selfless person I know. You've lived amid corruption and coercion and you've never faltered in your convictions. It is just one of the reasons I love you.'

She smiled through her tears. 'And I love you, Kieran Parkhurst. It was all I could think of…up there.' Her voice choked over the words, the remembrance. 'I thought I was going to die and I wouldn't have told you the one thing that truly mattered: that I love you.' Now that she'd said the words once, she wanted to say them over and over again.

'Enough to marry me?'

'Yes.' Today had shown her much. There was freedom, and then there was the freedom that came from love. What Kieran offered her was the latter, although she'd nearly been too blind to see it. It had been a hard lesson to learn but she would not make the mistake again.

'When?' Kieran's eyes danced with teasing and with joy—joy that she'd put there.

She leaned up and whispered a single word in his ear. She'd set out to save the Horsemen, but instead a Horseman had saved her. She would grab on to life with him with both hands and she would not let go, come calamity or calm, come lull or storm.

Epilogue I

December, Wrexham Hall, 1826

Kieran stood at the front of the Wrexham Hall chapel, taking in every detail of the setting. Today was his wedding day and he wanted to remember all of it. The chapel was turned out in wintry glory. Evergreen boughs twined with white ribbon draped the pews held in place by bows of silver and gold. The exquisite sounds of a lone violin played discreetly. Everything was beautiful, simple and elegant, like the woman whom he would marry.

The heavy oak doors at the back opened and Kieran's breath caught as Celeste stepped through, head held high, eyes confident and glowing as she made the walk towards him, ready to continue life with him.

Kieran watched each step she took, wanting to memorise every moment: the chestnut sheen of her hair in its elegant braid; the way her pearl ear-drops swung delicately against the length of her neck; the exquisite simplicity of her gown, whose best adornment was the body within. There was no lace, no seed pearls and no bows. Just simple green velvet with tight sleeves, a straight-cut bodice that showed her mother's pearls to perfection against her skin and a skirt full enough to sway when she moved.

She reached him and he took her hand, kissed it and together they prepared to say the vows that would bind them for ever and always.

The vicar began the ceremony with the eternal words, 'Dearly beloved, we are gathered here today...'

They were indeed gathered, family and friends. Kieran looked out at the guests assembled. His parents were in the front row with his grandfather, who had insisted on making the journey from Sussex—no small ordeal for a man of eighty-eight now, though Kieran had it on good authority that his father had put every comfort into the journey, with frequent stops at fine inns. The trip had taken a week and a half instead of five days, but that was what family did for one another.

Luce and Caine sat behind them, Mary with them. Mary had arrived last month and she had become instant friends with Celeste, the two of them having more in common than he'd have guessed. Only his sister, Guenevere, was missing. She was due any day with her first child and was spending Christmas with her husband's family. She'd written a lengthy letter, though, instructing him on how to be a good husband, which had made him laugh even as he'd taken notes.

The vicar continued, 'Through the gift of marriage, a man and woman may grow together in love and in trust...'

Kieran had heard these words before, they were standard wedding fare, but today, when he looked at his bride, they took on extra meaning. Today might be the first day of their lives as husband and wife but their life together had started that first day at St Luke's, and it had been a journey of trust ever since. It was perhaps a journey that would never end for them. Trust would be pivotal. He had no illusions that life with a Horseman would be a normal life. He would require her trust in ways that transcended the usual marriage. And she would require his. Cabot Roan was recovering from his shoulder wound under strict guard in London, awaiting trial. But there would be other threats that would challenge them throughout their marriage.

'Marriage is the foundation of family life into which children are born...'

Yes, God willing, Kieran thought. But all in good time. Once the Hall was restored, once he and Celeste found their feet as the Earl and Countess and as husband and wife. Caine and Luce had been generous with their time. They'd stayed on after the fire to help get things underway with rebuilding. They would stay for Christmas, which was just a few days away, and then the brothers would part again—Caine and Mary to ring in the New Year at Longstead with his people, and Luce back to his library in Surrey—until the next time the Horsemen were called.

Kieran said his vows, his eyes locked on his bride, intent that she see and hear each word as a solemn pledge to her, to them.

Please, God, he prayed silently. *Give her no reason to doubt me. Let me serve her as she deserves to be served for the rest of her life.*

He kissed his bride and the celebrations began in earnest. Mrs Hanson had been more than equal to the task of a wedding breakfast to which many of their new acquaintances in town were invited. There were toasts and kisses until the crowd slowly ebbed away, leaving the family to end the celebrations on a private note.

The Parkhursts gathered in the library, Luce's eye already running over the collection of books, their grandfather in a big chair by the fire and commanding everyone's attention.

'There is a gift to give.' He tapped on his glass of port and reached inside his coat for an envelope. 'A few months ago, my grandson was named the Earl of Wrexham, the inheritor of an estate that was run down and going to seed. I did not know what to expect when I arrived. I was beyond proud to see what he and his fiancée—' everyone laughed at the word 'fiancée', because in hindsight it had always been true '—had accomplished in such a short time. There is still a lot of work to be done, but Wrexham Hall is on its way, despite the best efforts of a fire to waylay that progress.

'But progress takes funds and we all know the estates did not come with financial legacies.' Dowries had been expected to fill in that gap, another incentive for them to marry if they meant to keep the estates.

Grandfather handed the envelope to Kieran and Celeste. 'This contains a cheque that should cover the restoration expenses, and whatever you need to ensure the spring planting is handled in the best way possible.'

'Grandfather, I don't know what to say.' Kieran was at an unusual loss for words. This was unlooked for—a miracle, really.

Celeste pressed his hand. 'I do,' she said softly. 'Thank you, Grandfather. This relieves a great burden for us.' She kissed the old man's cheek.

His grandfather's eyes twinkled suspiciously with tears at her kind gesture. 'I know it does.' He rubbed his hands on his trousers to cover the emotion. 'Well, that's one burden solved.'

His eyes fell on Luce. 'Two grandsons down, one to go. Your turn next, young man. I can hardly wait to see what the New Year brings.'

'I can't wait either,' Kieran whispered to his bride. 'Why don't we go upstairs and finish this wedding by ourselves? I think my family can manage on their own for a while.' He flashed a quick glance at Caine, who interjected with a clearing of his throat.

'Ahem, speaking of the New Year, Mary and I have something we'd like to share. We are expecting a happy addition…'

It was exactly the cover Kieran needed. Amid the 'Ooh's and 'Aah's, the hugs and excited questions from his parents, Kieran slipped upstairs with his bride and started working on a life of their own. He didn't exactly believe in prayers but, if he had, he'd definitely have believed his had been answered.

Epilogue II

October, 1826

Ellen's prayers had been answered. She'd prayed for a man and she'd been given one. In a most circuitous way, and not in the straightforward form one might expect, but they'd been answered, giving credence to the oft-heard platitude that God worked in mysterious ways and by His own divine timeline, which had *not* neatly aligned with hers. Still, at the last moment, the water had delivered her a man, just as a river long ago had delivered baby Moses to the Pharoah's daughter.

Ellen set down her heavy market basket and raised a hand to shield her eyes from the brightness of the autumn afternoon. In the distance in the field, she could see him, her river man, scything the wheat, with his shirt off, his chest and back gleaming with the sweat of exertion. She told herself she stared for medical reasons. She wanted to be sure he wasn't overworking. Just a month ago, he'd been abed, weak and helpless.

But the honest part of her knew she stared because she was a woman and he was a man—a handsome man— who lived in close proximity with her and about whom she knew very little and because pleasant surprises were rare in her world. Quakers eschewed luxury of all kinds, and surprises were a type of luxury. Plainness was preferred: plainness of dress, plainness of life, routine over upset.

Her brothers worked alongside him: twelve-year-old Philip and thirteen-year-old Andrew. She could hear their laughter faint on the breeze. Her man from the water was good with them. He treated them as if they were men, his equals. He did not condescend to them even as he kept them in line. Her brothers did have a rambunctious streak. He must have brothers of his own.

She didn't know because he didn't know. He didn't know his family. He didn't know his name. Had no idea how he'd come to be in the water or in possession of a knife wound on his arm. From the looks of things today, that wound had healed well enough for him to swing the scythe and she was grateful for it. She'd been concerned about her ability to bring in the harvest. She and her siblings couldn't do it alone. She'd have lost the farm. The community would have asked her to relinquish it to a man who was more capable, or to take a husband—likely Francis Hartlett, a heavy-set, dour widower twice her age who'd been looking to join their lands since her father had died last year. She'd not been amenable to it, so she'd prayed for a man, someone to deliver her from that fate.

God had sent her the water man. Peter, they called him, because Jesus had fished Peter from the rocks and, whether this man knew it or not, he'd become their rock, their protection. For now... The Lord gaveth but inevitably the Lord also took away.

But not too soon, she hoped. Ellen picked up her market basket with a sigh and made her way towards her men in the field. There'd been a story in a London paper that had made its way to their isolated village which niggled at her. A story about an accident in Wapping... a dead man with a knife wound recovered and another man missing. There'd been no further details. The article had been careful not to speculate, or perhaps the author had been encouraged to keep the details out of the public eye.

She was just making trouble, letting her imagination run away with her because part of her refused to accept that things had worked out and that everything would be fine. She wasn't used to things working out. Her father had only had a cough. He was supposed to have got well. He hadn't. Still, there seemed a little chance that the man she'd found on the beach was in any way connected to the incident in Wapping.

Peter raised his hand when he saw her coming and reached for his shirt, motioning for her brothers to do the same. Such a gentleman, Peter was. She'd noted his manners immediately. Even lying abed recovering, he'd been full of 'please's and 'thank you's for her efforts.

'Let me take that.' He reached for her basket, lifting it from her arm with a smile.

'You're not overdoing it, are you?' she asked, looking him over. He glowed with ruddy health these days. It was hard to reconcile the man who'd walked beside her with the one Andrew and Philip had carried back to the house in a stretcher made of an old quilt.

'Not at all. We should have the wheat in by tomorrow.' At the little cottage, he held the door open for her and allowed her to precede him inside. Anne was in the kitchen, making preparations for supper. He set the basket on the table and peeked beneath its cover. 'Did you get a good price for your eggs?'

'Yes, enough to pay the miller to grind the wheat.' Which meant they could sell flour, and that meant income. She didn't dare hope it would go far enough but it would be a start.

'I'm glad.' He smiled and she felt herself melt with its warmth. She'd never seen a smile like his. Nor eyes like his—the colour of chocolate. 'The boys can finish up on their own. We were nearly done. Let me wash up first and then perhaps we can take a walk. I want to talk with you about something.'

That sounded ominous. Did he want to discuss leaving? Had he remembered something?

Please, Lord, don't take him from me yet, she prayed. *I still need him.*

When would *be a good time?* her conscience mocked.

After the harvest there would be winter preparations to make, the roof to see to. Winter would make the roads and sea hard to travel on. Perhaps she could convince him to stay until spring? But then there'd be the planting to do, and the cultivating all summer. By the time he had washed himself, her stomach was in knots.

You're being ridiculous, she scolded herself. *He has to leave at some point.*

Peter offered his arm to her and they headed down the lane towards the beach, not that they'd walk that far.

'I was thinking, the day after tomorrow, the boys and I would go over to the Pratts' and help bring their crop in. Daniel Pratt doesn't have any sons to help.' The Pratts were her neighbours two miles away on the other side from Francis Hartlett. 'But only if you can spare us. If there's nothing else that needs doing here?'

'No, not at all.' Relief flooded her. He wasn't going to leave. 'It's kind of you to think of them.' She smiled up at him and he smiled back, another melting smile that had her insides warming, her mind coming to life with a hundred dangerous fantasies.

What would it be like to be married to a man like him who was kind and considerate? Someone who consulted her; who enquired about her day and the things that were important to her, such as the eggs and mill money? That was not the sort of man Francis Hartlett was. But they were fantasies only. She could not marry a man with nothing, not even his own name. Someday his memories would return and then what? What if he remembered he had a wife and family somewhere else?

'How was the market other than good egg prices?' he asked. 'Any news of interest?'

Ellen worried her lip. Ought she tell him about the news story? What if it triggered his memories? He would leave then. What if she didn't and he heard the story first from someone else? He would know she'd withheld information from him. He would not respect that.

But, Lord, I need him, came her selfish prayer. *I don't want to marry Francis Hartlett. I don't want to lose my father's farm and be taken into someone else's home like a poor relation, to have my family split up. They're all I have left.*

What had she done in her life to deserve such suffering?

'What is it, Ellen? Is there bad news?' Her hesitation had alerted him and he was all concern, those soft brown eyes fixed on her. She could not lie, and omissions were a type of lie.

'There was a newspaper in town, quite an old one—you know we don't get a timely paper here. There was a story in it. It's probably nothing, I don't want to get your hopes up.' Or to set hers down, but she was nothing if not honest.

Peter felt her hand tighten on his arm and he knew—she thought the story had something to do with him. She was frightened to tell him, his brave Ellen who'd taken in a half-dead stranger from the sea because her conscience had demanded it, even when her pocketbook couldn't afford it. His eyes had missed nothing in the days of his recovery, when he'd been able to do nothing more than lie in bed and watch life in the cottage. He wasn't supposed to notice that she'd given up her bed for him in exchange for a pallet beside the fire so that he might rest, or that she'd often slipped her portion of supper to him so that he might have a faster recovery. But he had noticed.

'Whatever it is, Ellen, it doesn't mean I'll leave,' he promised. He owed her. She'd invested resources in saving his life, resources she could not easily spare. He knew enough from the boys' chatter in the field that she was being pressed to marry, an arrangement that was unsatisfactory to all of them...and to him. He wasn't staying simply to satisfy a return on her investment. He wanted to stay. He liked life in the little farmhouse: the simple, hearty meals at the wood plank table; the warmth of the worn handmade quilts at night; the close company of the four siblings. Had his old life contained such elements? Was that why he found comfort in them—because somewhere in his mind he'd known this life?

'There was an incident in Wapping. A man died. His body was found, dragged out of the river. But the other man was not found.'

Peter furrowed his brow. 'Do you think there's a chance I am the missing man? That seems…far-fetched. We're a long way from Wapping.'

'The dead man had a knife wound,' Ellen added quietly. 'His proved fatal, just as yours so easily could have. He was pulled from the water as you were, just different water. He was found but you were lost.'

He could see the picture she was piecing together in her head: there'd been a knife fight on a wharf in Wapping that had progressed to the water where he'd been successful in killing the other man. 'You think I am a killer?' he asked in quiet shock. Was he? Did that *feel* right?

'No!' she was quick to rejoin, regret flashing in her pretty blue eyes. From her horrified expression he could see that she'd not thought the scenario all the way through, to the conclusions and consequences of accepting the picture she was constructing.

Even with her quick abnegation, the picture she offered certainly didn't feel flattering. What would that make him—a criminal? Was he even now being hunted by the law in conjunction with the murder? A flash of panic took him at the thought. 'Do you want me to leave?'

The words were hard to say. He didn't want to leave. He liked it here. It felt right. In a world where he had no basis in fact for who he was or where he'd come from, he had only echoes in his bones, feelings of comfort, of what he might have known some part before. A large family, a cozy home, a certain familial rumbustiousness felt right, felt natural. In the months he'd been here, those things had become his tenuous anchor to this new reality. He did not want to let them go. They were all he had.

She shook her head, a strand of her wheaten hair falling loose. 'You do not need to go.' She paused, the conversation making her obviously miserable. 'It is rather mad, isn't it? Too far-fetched that you would be the man from Wapping.' She was looking for assurance.

'I cannot say. It all seems a bit dramatic.' It was the most he could give her by way of assurance. The dangerous nugget of 'what if' had burrowed quickly in his mind and had taken efficient root. He had the scar of a knife wound. Even if he wasn't the man from Wapping, he was a violent man. Violence had no place in a Quaker community. He stopped in the lane to face her. 'I do not want to bring you trouble.'

Panic streaked her gaze. 'I want you to stay.' The words came out in a rush.

He gently gripped her upper arms, suddenly desperate to make her understand. 'I know about Widower Hartlett. I wouldn't want him to make a scandal for you because of me, to have him use me against you to force your hand. A man of violence has no place here.'

How long could he last here before the community began to question his origins, his intentions? Time was passing. Any day, now that the harvest was nearly in, people would turn their attentions in his direction and he didn't think the gossip would go well for Ellen or him. The community would push for marriage or exile.

Neither was a palatable option. He could offer Ellen nothing as a husband, not even a name. And he was not ready to leave. She needed him here. In his own way, he needed to be here. He needed to be with her. He did not want to leave *her*.

Widower Hartlett was just the internal threat. Discovery was the external threat. 'What if I killed that man? What if the law comes looking for me?' He could not bring that sort of danger to her home.

Her blue eyes held his. 'We will hide you.'

He frowned. 'The village will not tolerate it. Someone in the village will give me away.' Especially if there was a reward. Widower Hartlett would certainly inform on him, even without a reward, if it cleared his path to Ellen. 'I would not want you to be seen to be deliberately aiding me.'

In the span of a short walk, he'd become dangerous to her. It was the last thing he'd intended after all her kindnesses to him. He really should go. He would take his new name with him and go and build a new life somewhere. The prospect did not excite him; it saddened him.

'Please don't go, not yet.' She whispered the words, her eyes pleading in desperation. 'Not until we know something more.'

'More' being the return of his memories, which would commit him to his life in the past. 'More' being further proof that connected him to the missing man in Wapping.

'Yes.' He breathed his promise. 'I will stay.' He would not abandon her. It was not what a gentleman did. It was not what a protector did. A man did not run at the first hint of potential trouble. A man did not seek his own self-preservation at the expense of others' needs. He put others he cared for ahead of self. *That* felt right.

Ellen's arms were around his neck and she pressed him close in a tight hug. 'Thank you…' She breathed; her relief palpable against his body—a body that had not forgotten how to rouse to a woman. Holding her in his arms felt right. And, for that, he would stay as long as the fates allowed.

* * * * *

If you enjoyed this story,
make sure to read the previous book in
Bronwyn Scott's
Wed Within a Year miniseries
How to Court a Rake

And while you're waiting for the final instalment
why not check out these other captivating reads
by Bronwyn Scott?
The Viscount's Christmas Bride
Cinderella at the Duke's Ball
The Captain Who Saved Christmas